THE RING OF FIVE

The RING OF FIVE

Eoin McNamee

WENDY
LAMB
BOOKS

Copyright © 2010 by Eoin McNamee

All rights reserved. Published in the United States by Wendy Lamb Books, an imprint of Random House Children's Books, a division of Random House, Inc., New York.

Wendy Lamb Books and the colophon are trademarks of Random House, Inc.

Visit us on the Web! www.randomhouse.com/kids

Educators and librarians, for a variety of teaching tools, visit us at www.randomhouse.com/teachers

Library of Congress Cataloging-in-Publication Data

McNamee, Eoin.
The Ring of Five / Eoin McNamee. — 1st ed.
p. cm.
Summary: Kidnapped on his way to boarding school, Danny Caulfield, who has one blue eye and one brown eye, ends up at a mysterious academy of spies, where he is to be trained in the art of espionage in an effort to keep the Upper and Lower worlds from colliding.
ISBN 978-0-385-73731-9 (trade) — ISBN 978-0-385-90658-6 (lib. bdg.) — ISBN 978-0-375-84635-9 (pbk.) — ISBN 978-0-375-89664-4 (e-book) [1. Fantasy. 2. Spies—Fiction. 3. Schools—Fiction.] I. Title.
PZ7.M4787933Ri 2010
[Fic]—dc22
2009033345

The text of this book is set in 12-point Horley Old Style.

Book design by Trish Parcell Watts

Printed in the United States of America
10 9 8 7 6 5 4 3 2 1

First Edition

For Vincent and Donna

A JOURNEY

Danny didn't want to go. He loved their house with its creaky floors and high windows with shutters you could close at night and attics you could explore. He liked living there, and the idea of far-off boarding school didn't appeal to him. He didn't even like the name of the school: Heston Oaks. He imagined it full of muscled goons who were good at sports and not much else.

Danny was too small to be good at sports, and got a hard time on the football pitch. When he thought about it, he got a hard time more or less all the time at school. His eyes and his general appearance were the targets of constant cruel jokes. Because of an accident during an operation when he was young, his eyes were different colors—one blue and one brown. And if that wasn't enough, his face was a kind of triangular shape, with a sharp chin, and he had pointy ears. Danny the Pixie was the mildest of his nicknames.

The abuse was one of the reasons, his parents said, that they had decided to send him to boarding school. He doubted that Heston Oaks was going to be any better—it would probably be worse. But his mother had visited the school, and said it was perfect for him.

It wasn't as if they were going to miss him, Danny thought bitterly. His father, a tall stooped man with a high forehead, was away at work most of the time. And even when he was home he would walk into a room and look at Danny for a moment before recognition dawned on him. He would flash a smile, grunt a hello and leave the room.

Friday had been Danny's last day at school. Friendlier classmates had said goodbye to him at the gate, and he had got on the bus, realizing with surprise that he was going to miss the shabby old building with its run-down classrooms and potholed playground. The other students had waved, even the pupils who had tormented him, and he'd waved back and tried to smile.

That night he had lain awake, listening to the familiar noises the house made: the hot water pipes groaning, the loose slate that always rattled in the wind, the leaky drainpipe outside his bedroom window. He knew that he would be back at the end of term, but it felt as if he was leaving forever. Late at night, his bedroom door opened and light from outside the room fell on his face, and he was vaguely aware of his mother looking down on him. Then he went back to sleep.

Like his father, his mother was always busy. She was

rarely home when he got back from school, and often went out at night, leaving him alone in the house. Danny was used to it. There was always cold meat in the fridge, or pizza in the oven. Besides, she always seemed to be present in some way. There was a hint of expensive perfume in the air, a silk shawl draped over a chair as if she had just left it there. It wasn't much as mother's love went, Danny thought, but it was what he was used to, and he couldn't imagine swapping it for a cold dormitory.

The weekend dragged. He woke on Sunday morning with a feeling of dread. His suitcase was packed and sat in the hallway. His father had left the night before. Danny's mother had had to remind him to say goodbye to Danny. He shook his son's hand, looked as if he was about to make a speech, then merely grinned at Danny, swept up his coat and bag and was gone. His mother spent most of the day on the phone, making plans, it seemed, for the week ahead, when she would be free. His father had arranged for a taxi to pick Danny up at the house at three. Danny waited in the hallway, sitting at the bottom of the stairs. Three o'clock came and went and there was no sign of the cab. Outside, the sky darkened and the wind tossed the trees in the garden.

An hour passed, and then two hours. His mother looked anxious.

"I really must . . ." She frowned and looked at her watch. She tried to phone Danny's father to check the arrangements, but he didn't answer. At six o'clock she came into the hallway. She was wearing her coat and gloves, and Danny's heart sank.

3

"Danny, I hate to leave you," she said, "but there is somewhere I absolutely have to be. You'll be able to wait for the cab on your own, won't you?"

He could feel hot tears prick his eyes, but he refused to cry in front of her, so he nodded dumbly. She crouched down in front of him and took his face in her hands.

"You're going to have a great time," she said gently. "It won't be easy at first—I know that—but you'll make friends and learn lots of things you wouldn't learn if you stayed here. Make sure and write every week if you can."

She leaned forward and kissed him on the forehead, and for a moment he felt enveloped by her soft hands and her perfume. She released him, stood up and walked to the door. She opened it. It was getting dark outside. The wind tugged at her coat, and behind her he could see the storm-tossed trees. She put her hand to her lips and blew him a kiss. For a moment he thought he saw her eyes shining a little too brightly in the hallway shadows. She put a gloved hand up to her face, then slipped through the doorway and was gone.

Danny heard the sound of her car starting and wheels crunching on the gravel driveway. He got up and went to the old gilt mirror on the wall and looked at his reflection, the different-colored eyes and the pointed chin, and wished that he was someone else.

It was dark when he saw the lights of a car coming up the drive. He went to the window. An old-fashioned black taxi pulled up at the curb. The trees were swaying wildly, and Danny could see rain and dead leaves being driven almost horizontally in the car's headlights.

The driver got out and came up the front steps. Danny went to the door and opened it, having to struggle to hold it against the wind. The taxi driver seemed to fill the doorway. He wore a black greatcoat and a black cap, like a sailor's cap. A large and bristling mustache hid his mouth, and large dark eyebrows almost concealed his deep-sunk eyes. It was hard to tell what color they were, but they gleamed from a great depth.

"Taxi," he said, his voice deep and graveled, then turned and walked back down the path and got into the cab.

Danny took a last unhappy look round the hallway. He touched the familiar chipped wood of the banisters one last time, looked up into the darkness of the stairs that led to his room, then lifted his suitcase and closed the door behind him.

Outside, the wind tugged at the suitcase so that he could barely carry it. He waited for the driver to get out and help him put the case in the cab, but he didn't move, so Danny heaved it into the backseat and slid in. The driver swung the taxi out into the road, sending Danny thudding back against the leather armrest. By the time he had straightened himself and looked back, the house was no longer to be seen.

They drove along the country road until they reached the main road. Ten minutes later they were on the motorway, but after half an hour they turned off, onto an unfamiliar road. Danny looked out the window for land-marks, but the rain was so heavy he could only see blurred lights, and then, after a while, nothing at all.

"Is this the right way?" he asked. "I thought Heston Oaks was further down the motorway."

"Diversion," the driver said, almost growling the word. Danny wanted to ask more, but something about the man intimidated him. In fact, the whole situation was so strange he didn't know what to say. It was bad enough going to boarding school without all this: The musty cab interior. The silent driver. Even the cab radio seemed strange, a voice coming through every so often, as happens in a taxi, but the voice hissed and crackled more than normal so that you couldn't make out what it was saying. Although, if he hadn't known better, Danny would have said that it wasn't speaking English, but a jagged and alien-sounding tongue.

They drove for a long time. At first there were the lights of passing cars, and then there were no lights at all. The cab was unheated, and Danny's feet were frozen.

"How much further?" he asked. In reply the cabdriver reached behind him and slammed the little window between the driver and the back closed. Danny reached up and tried to open it again, but he couldn't. He rapped sharply on it. The cab man turned to look at him. Despite the darkness, Danny could see his eyes. Or rather, he could see a gleam deep in the sockets, and knew that the man was much older than he appeared, and full of grim knowledge. The man held Danny's gaze for what seemed far too long. How was he keeping the speeding car on the road? He turned slowly back to the steering wheel. Danny fell back against the seat. His heart was pounding, and the palms of his hands were wet. The engine note of the car rose to a kind of howl. Although he couldn't see anything out the window, he knew that they were traveling at tremendous speed. On they went, the driver hunched unmoving over the wheel, Danny gripping the door handle, hardly able to believe what was happening.

"Checkpoint!" he heard the driver say.

And then suddenly the engine note started to fall, the cab decelerating quickly so that Danny was thrown forward. The glass partition shot back. The cab man's hand grabbed the front of Danny's shirt and hauled him up to the opening. Those eyes met his again, like chips of light in a dark tunnel.

"If you breathe a word, it'll be the last," the cab man said, almost in a whisper, his voice laden with menace. Danny was closer than he wanted to be to a face that was veined and wattled, with a big nose, and teeth that looked like tombstones. Danny nodded dumbly, and made a zipping motion across his lips.

"Not a word," he wheezed, half strangled, "promise." The cab man released him. Danny could see lights up ahead, as if someone was carrying a torch. The cab slowed to a halt. There was a sharp rapping on the driver's window, and the cab man slowly wound it down. A torch was shone into the driver's face. Danny found himself sliding across the seat to the far side of the cab.

"Good evening, Mr. Fairman," a clipped military-sounding voice said. The cab man grunted in reply. Danny could see the hand that held the torch, the jacket

7

cuff above it like that of a uniform. The torch swung toward Danny. He held one hand up to his face to ward off the dazzling light.

"A human cargo tonight, Mr. Fairman?" the voice said, an oily quality creeping into it. Once again the cab man didn't reply.

"And a suitcase? What is in the suitcase, Mr. Fairman? No breaches of the treaty, I hope?" Danny made to speak, then remembered what Fairman had said.

"None of your business, Sranzer," the cab man said gruffly.

"You will let me search the vehicle."

"You know that those given passage are outside your jurisdiction. You can't touch anything. Now get out of my way, I'm in a hurry."

"It's my job to make sure the treaty isn't broken."

"Be about your business, Sranzer, you know I'm the only one allowed to cross these days," the driver growled. The torch moved away, and the cab shot forward. Danny caught a glimpse of a cold, pale face at the window, and then it was gone.

"What was that?" he gasped. "Who was he?"

"Never mind who he is," Fairman said.

"I don't understand," Danny said. "What's going on?"

But instead of replying, Fairman floored the accelerator. If the cab had been moving quickly before, then the speed was blinding now. Danny was thrown from side to side, and the vibration was so great that he could hardly see. He didn't know how long this went on. It seemed like hours. He closed his eyes and wedged himself in the corner of the cab and tried to shut out the noise of the engine and the wind whistling past outside. Then, with a great shudder, the noise stopped.

Danny opened one eye, then cautiously stretched his cramped limbs. He looked out the window. They were on a long avenue that wound upward. To either side there were trees, their dark limbs covered in lichens. As the car went upward the trees began to give way, and the cab was driving through lawns. In the headlights he saw moss-covered urns standing on plinths. And then the drive turned to the left and the headlights swept across a large building five or six stories high, its weathered front punctuated with many diamond-paned windows. There were turrets spiraling up into the sky, and buttresses, and niches containing statues. Ancient ivies clung to the red-brick walls, hiding much of the building from view. The roof met the walls in many different shapes and at many angles, and great tangles of ivy hung from the guttering, obscuring the upper stories. Imposing stone steps led down from large oak doors in the middle of the building, and it was in front of these that the cab jolted to a halt.

"Where are we?" Danny asked. "This doesn't look like a school. . . ."

"This is as far as I'm paid to take you," Fairman replied, getting out of the cab. He opened the rear driver's-side door, grabbed Danny's case and threw it onto the steps.

"Out."

"But I don't even know if I'm in the right place. . . ."

"Out."

9

Danny scrambled toward the door. Anything was better than another minute in Fairman's cab. His feet hit the gravel in front of the building and he looked up at it. It could be a school, he supposed. And in fact, when he looked, he saw a weathered sign over the door saying RECEPTION.

"Is this where I'm supposed to go?" he asked.

"I don't know anything about that. I was paid to bring you over and I brought you," Fairman said. He leaned over Danny until his face was just inches away, his gleaming eyes the only spark of light in his dark bulk.

"I done what I was paid to do," he growled once more.

The taxi man swung away from him, and before Danny could do or say anything, Fairman had leapt into the driver's seat of the car and slammed the door. The black cab turned hard, sending gravel flying in all directions, and sped off the way it had come, leaving Danny staring after its taillights. A gust of wind struck him in the face and he realized how cold and hungry he was. There was nothing for it. He lifted the suitcase and marched up the steps.

There was no bell that he could see, so he put his weight against the great oak doors. They swung open, creaking in protest. He hesitated, until another gust of wind drove cold rain down the back of his neck.

The room he entered was large, with high ceilings and wood-paneled walls. There were portraits of sad aristocratic-looking people on the walls, and logs burned and crackled in a massive open fire. The lighting was dim, but he could see signs attached to the paneling in various

10

places. Some of them said things like BALLROOM and NIGHT PORTER, which he understood. But there were others saying things like GENERAL TRADECRAFT and INKS, which were strange to him. At the back of the room was a reception desk with a bell on it. He carried his case over to it and rang the bell.

Afterward he puzzled about where the man who appeared had come from. There didn't seem to be any doorway behind the desk, and yet the moment Danny's hand touched the bell, the man was there. He wore a dark suit and had gold glasses perched on a sharp nose. His gray hair was brushed neatly back. He peered at Danny over the top of his glasses with a disapproving look in his shrewd eyes. He glanced around as if there was a danger of them being overheard, then leaned over the counter and said in a low voice, "Were you followed?"

"Er, I don't really know."

"What do you mean you don't know?" The man's voice rose. "Don't you know how to spot a tail?"

"A tail . . . What do you mean?"

"Tails. Spotting them and losing them. It's a basic."

"I came in a cab. Fairman's cab," Danny said. "He went very fast. . . ."

"Ah, Fairman! Yes, of course." The man seemed satisfied. "Not many could keep a tail on Fairman. But you're not due until tomorrow morning."

"Like I said, he went very fast," Danny said, losing patience. "Maybe that's why I'm here early. I don't care. I'm tired and I wouldn't mind something to eat."

A large ledger appeared in the man's hands. He flicked rapidly through it.

"You are Daniel Caulfield." The man studied the page he had stopped at. "No known alias or nom de guerre?"

Danny shook his head dumbly. What was the man talking about?

"There's no one but you booked in, and since you are early, we'll have to put you in pre-enrollment."

"What's pre-enrollment? Where are the teachers? This is Heston Oaks, isn't it?"

The man gave him a long, grimly amused look.

"Heston Oaks? No, this is not Heston Oaks. You have been sent for instruction. My name is Mr. Valant."

"What? Sent? What do you mean?"

Valant came out from behind the counter. He was taller than he had looked behind the desk, and thin, and he glided rather than walked.

"Enough questions now," he said softly.

"What do you mean, enough questions!" Danny exploded. "I want to know what's going on!"

Valant grasped Danny's wrist gently with one hand and placed the other on top of Danny's hand. Without seeming to exert much force, he pressed Danny's hand downward. The pain was exquisite. Danny felt his knees buckle.

"Now, Daniel," Valant said soothingly. "Come along. Do you think you are the first reluctant recruit I've welcomed?"

*   *   *

Two stories above, in the library of the third landing, Master Devoy waited impatiently. The news from Sranzer was disturbing. Fairman had carried a passenger, a young man, across the border. The problem was the usual one. Could Sranzer's information be trusted, or was it a ruse put out for some other purpose? Devoy walked to the fireplace and threw on another log. The fire flared up, illuminating the great bookcases, the gleaming oak floors, the life-size portrait of Longford, who looked down with amusement in his eyes. The portrait had been left up there as a warning, and an admonishment.

Devoy straightened and caught sight of himself in the mirror above the fireplace. It was a Mirror of Limited Reflection, and showed only his long pale face as though it floated in a pool of darkness. He noted with satisfaction that the face was perfectly expressionless, despite his inner agitation. He had trained it to be so. It was said that even under torture, Devoy's calm mask would not crack. He turned his back to the fire and waited. Rain spattered against the windowpanes. The library on the third landing had one door and three secret entrances, one of which had never been discovered, and as he waited, Devoy saw a shadow move behind the statue of Diana the Huntress in the corner.

"You can never resist it, can you, Marcus? You can never just walk in through an open door," he said. A cloaked figure slipped out from behind the statue and threw back his hood. Marcus Brunholm had thick dark eyebrows over brown eyes, long black hair and a heavy, sensuous mouth almost hidden by a large drooping mustache. He crossed the floor to the fireplace and warmed his hands at it, his movements quick and furtive, his expression masked by shadows.

"What did you want to see me about, Devoy?" he asked.

"Don't act the innocent, Marcus," Devoy growled. "Fairman brought a boy across the frontier tonight."

"Who is at this minute receiving the tender ministrations of Mr. Valant," Brunholm said smoothly.

"I can't believe this, Marcus!" Devoy's voice exploded into the library, yet his face remained tranquil. "What about the treaty? You know the Ring are only waiting for an excuse. The Two Worlds are poised on the brink!"

"Have you seen him?" Brunholm said quietly.

"Cherbs are raiding every night as it is. Recruitment from the Upper World is expressly banned."

"He is perfect. He is the one."

"We must not let the frontier become open. The harm would be immeasurable."

"We can't last like this forever," Brunholm said, straightening suddenly. "We have to act, to take a risk. We grow weaker by the day. The boy is perfect. In every way."

As he looked up at Devoy, who was a few inches taller, Brunholm's brown eyes seemed to plead. The way a dog might look at you, Devoy thought, a dog that wags its tail when it is in front of you and bares its teeth when it is behind you.

"Perfect in every detail, you say?"

"Yes, Devoy." Brunholm could not keep the eagerness out of his voice.

"That cannot be taken for granted."

"Of course not."

"I will see the boy tonight."

"Thank you, Devoy."

"We shall see whether thanks are due."

Devoy's gaze fell on the Mirror of Limited Reflection. Brunholm's eyes followed. For a moment their faces floated side by side on an infinity of darkness.

THE BALLROOM

Danny was in a small comfortable room. There was a bed and a writing desk, and a fire flickered in the grate. There was a table in the window alcove, where Valant had placed a tray with a glass of milk and a cheese and pickle sandwich. The man had been kind enough, but Danny remembered the pain in his hand. He had been hustled swiftly along a corridor, but his hand had hurt so much that he had barely looked about. Once they'd reached the room, he'd thought of making a bolt for it, but Valant had stayed between him and the door. Besides, where would he have run? He had gone to the window and looked out, finding to his surprise that they were high above the ground, although he was sure they hadn't climbed any stairs. Far below he could see the graveled entrance to the building, then the lawns, and dimly, trees tossing in the wind, giving way to darkness, although on the horizon there was a glow of light on the underside of the clouds.

Valant had put logs on the fire, then gone out and returned with the food, careful to lock the door behind him. He had refused to answer Danny's questions, telling him each time that he would find out in the morning. Finally the man went out, and Danny heard him lock the door once again.

Danny carried the milk and sandwich to the fireplace and curled up in a shabby armchair. Although everything else about the day had been odd, there was nothing odd about the milk and the sandwich, and he devoured them. It couldn't be so bad, he thought sleepily. Anything was better than the back of the taxi, anyway. He would see the proper teachers in the morning and everything would be explained. The fire blazed merrily, and he stared into it, his eyelids growing heavy, until finally, he fell asleep.

At first he couldn't tell what had wakened him. A strong gust of wind against the windowpane, maybe, or the dying fire collapsing in on itself. It was a moment before he realized where he was. He was stiff and the room was chilly. He stood up, half asleep, stretched and yawned. Then he heard it again, the noise that he knew now had awakened him. It was the sound of feet outside the door, a quick shuffle, as if there was more than one person moving swiftly. He went to the door and listened. The footsteps faded into the distance and were gone. He put his hand on the doorknob, then remembered that Valant had locked it. But to his surprise, as he turned away, the door swung open.

Without thinking about it, he stepped out into a long corridor with a curve in it, so he couldn't see the end. There were red velvet hangings on the walls. He caught a flash of movement down the hall. He hesitated. Valant had wanted him to stay in the room, that was certain. But why had the door been unlocked?

Maybe I can get to the bottom of all this, Danny thought. Who do Fairman and Valant think they are, anyway? Swinging the door closed behind him, he set off.

He didn't remember the corridor being as long when he'd come in, or as spooky. The lights were far apart, and they seemed to flicker as if the electricity was on the verge of going out. There were more doorways than he recalled too. He moved as fast as he could, and once or twice he thought he saw movement in front of him, but he couldn't catch up to whoever, or whatever, it was. At last he reached the end of the corridor. The sign on the doorway in front of him read RECEPTION, and he didn't want to meet Valant again. He stopped. He was breathing hard and he could hear his own heartbeat, but above that was another sound, faint and far away, almost beyond earshot, but most definitely music—and that music was coming from behind the battered-looking door to his left. He weighed it in his head: risk another encounter with Valant, or follow the music? He took a deep breath and plunged through the door.

To his surprise, he found himself right back on the ground floor, even though he had gone down no stairs and the corridor had not sloped. He was in another passageway, with windows looking out onto the graveled front of the building. The passage was dingy, and some of the windowpanes were broken, so that the torn and faded rags that might once have been elegant curtains billowed in the wind. The music was louder, though, and a sign with BALLROOM written on it pointed to the right. He followed it.

The corridor led to a set of double doors covered in faded gilt and scrollwork. The music was obviously coming from the other side. He reached the doors. Hands trembling, he reached out for the right door handle. He eased it open until there was a tiny crack he could see through. Then he put his eye to it. To his astonishment, the ballroom was full of people. In one corner, a small orchestra was playing slightly creaky-sounding waltzes. Many of the people were dancing. Men and women of all ages, many of them with long oval faces, a little sad, perhaps, and all of them with the same strange blue eyes that made them look as if they were dreaming with their eyes open.

Most of the dancers were waltzing slowly around the floor to the melancholy rhythm of the music. Some of those who weren't dancing sat at tables, the women fanning themselves with elaborate fans. The men wore suits that were a little shabby but were brightened up here and there with a handkerchief in a pocket or a colorful tie. The women wore long gowns, the hems frayed and the flower patterns faded until they were almost invisible. They wore their hair piled high on top of their heads.

The people seemed to be a little taller than average. But it wasn't their height that was strange, or their long faces and sad blue eyes. It was the fact that on each back, between the shoulder blades, dusty and graying, sprouted a pair of shapely wings.

THE DEVIOUS ARTS

Danny knew he should go before he was caught, but he couldn't tear his eyes away from the scene in front of him. An elderly couple swung into view close to the edge of the dance floor, and he examined the wings more closely. They were about five feet long and elegantly shaped. But the feathers looked a little threadbare and worn, as if they hadn't been cared for. Danny remembered the footsteps he had heard passing his door. It must have been these people. But where had they come from? Perhaps they were some strange club who liked to dress up as angels. But something told Danny that these wings weren't dress-up. They were real. In fact, every so often a pair of wings would unfold and shake a little, as though to settle the feathers.

There didn't seem to be much conversation between

any of the dancers. Some of them looked very proud, haughty even. The music came to a halt, and there was a little polite applause. The leader of the orchestra, who wore a black tailcoat, turned and bowed, then turned back to the orchestra and began another waltz, as slow and melancholy as the one before it. Danny noticed that people were starting to stand up and gather gloves and handbags. The evening was drawing to a close, he thought, and it was time for him to be out of there. But he had waited too long. As he made to go, something struck him hard from behind. He hit the floor with an impact that knocked the wind out of him. A strong wiry body landed on top of him and an arm snaked around his neck, almost choking him.

"Not a word out of you," a hoarse voice said. "Can't you see there's Cherbs about?"

Despite his shock and fear, Danny looked at the long windows on the corridor and saw that dark shapes were flitting past outside. There was a sudden crash of broken glass and a great commotion from the ballroom. Even with his cheek pressed painfully against the floor he could see that the lights in the ballroom had gone out. People were shouting, some in anger and others in fear.

From outside a reedy and malicious voice yelled, "A message for you!" The voice trailed off into sneering laughter and then Danny saw more shapes flitting across the window, lit from behind by the moon.

"Cherbs. They'll deny it, of course," the person holding him down said. The grip around his neck relaxed. Danny turned around. He found himself looking at a dark-skinned boy with a thin face. The boy crouched beside him, peering out the window where the attackers had disappeared. His eyes were the same strange blue as those of the dancers in the ballroom. He was about the same age as Danny, but there was one difference. As the boy looked down at him there was a fluttering sound, and in the moonlight, Danny distinctly saw the tips of wings flicker briefly over his shoulders.

"Sorry about that," the boy said, reaching behind him in the darkness, offering a hand to help Danny up. "There was no telling what them Cherbs was up to. Who knows what would have happened if they'd seen you through the window."

"Who are you?" Danny asked.

"Les Knutt, at your service," the boy said, giving a mocking half-bow.

"Danny. Danny Caulfield," Danny said. "What . . ." He opened his mouth to ask another question, but realized he didn't know which of the questions crowding his head he wanted to ask. Who were the people in the ballroom? Why did they have wings? Who were the Cherbs? And why was there a low, angry worried hubbub of voices from the ballroom? By the time he closed his mouth again, Les had his eye pressed to the crack in the door.

"Looks like they got somebody," he murmured. Danny looked too. Someone in the hall had lit candles. One of the tall figures was lying motionless on the floor, and others were tending to him. Les kept his eyes to the door and Danny had a chance to study him in the moonlight. The boy was painfully thin, and his ragged clothes seemed to belong to another century. His collar was velvet and there were gold buttons on his jacket. The dirt was ingrained on his small quick hands. Then there were those wings. Almost without thinking, Danny reached out to touch them. The feathers were white, with golden tips that shimmered as they moved. The minute Danny's hand touched them, Les's wings opened wide with a speed that made Danny jump back in alarm.

"Don't touch the wings," Les said, turning to Danny and refolding them.

"S-sorry," Danny stammered.

"That's all right," Les said. "You weren't to know."

"Please," Danny said, "who are you? I mean, all of you? And where am I?"

"Where are you?" Les said, looking baffled. "You're in Wilsons, of course."

"What is Wilsons?"

"You really don't know?" Danny couldn't see the boy's face clearly, but his tone sounded half amused, half pitying.

"Wilsons is . . . ," Les began. But just then, with a shudder and a whir, feebly at first, then growing in strength, the lights came on again. Les stopped abruptly and stared at Danny. His expression changed from amused to alarmed and hostile.

"What is it?" Danny asked, but Les was backing away from him, the light glinting off the knife that had suddenly appeared in his hand.

"Don't try anything," Les said slowly. "The tip of the knife is dipped. You wouldn't last a minute."

"What did I do?" Danny asked, bewildered.

"Your eyes," Les said.

"What about my eyes?" Danny said.

"The hair . . . everything . . . ," Les said, almost to himself. "One of them, right here . . ."

"One of who?" Danny cried. "What's going on?"

"You don't fool me, Cherb," Les said, his eyes hard and wary. Danny took a step toward him, but the knife came up, fast as lightning, the tip of it to Danny's throat. The boy's eyes searched Danny's face.

"I never seen one close up before. Your lot killed my mum and dad." Danny could almost feel the point of the knife.

"I don't even know what a Cherb is!"

"One more inch and there you go, all over." The boy's voice was almost a whisper. Danny backed away slowly until his heels touched the wall behind him. He looked into the thin face held close to his. Les was going to strike. . . .

"Knutt, put up the knife!" A figure dressed in black pushed swiftly between them, and the knife was snatched from the boy's grasp.

"But Mr. Brunholm, he's a Cherb!" Les said.

"No he isn't." Danny breathed out. His rescuer was a dark-haired man with a mustache, wearing a long dark cloak.

"His eyes . . . ," Les said.

"What are you saying?" Danny asked. He didn't like the subject of his eyes being brought up, particularly when it seemed that they had nearly got him killed.

25

"The brown and the blue," Brunholm said musingly, "that belong to the untrue."

"So what if they're different colors?" Danny said. "If it's any of your business, it was an operation that went wrong when I was small. They messed up the iris."

"Yes, yes, of course," Brunholm said, almost chuckling. Suddenly he grasped Danny's chin. "But look, Knutt. The dark hair and the way it sweeps round at the cheekbones, the pointed ears, the eyebrows, the fine bone structure at the chin."

"A Cherb, like I said," Les insisted. Danny glared at him. Although being called a Cherb probably beat being called Danny the Pixie.

"I told you. I was born this way," Danny said. "I'm not a Cherb, whatever that is."

"No, of course you're not," Brunholm said smoothly. "An accident of birth is all."

"If you're sure," Les said grudgingly.

"Yes, I am sure," Brunholm said, "and by the way, the carrying of a knife dipped in venom is expressly against the Tenth Regulation, not to mention extremely dangerous."

"You going to report me?" Les asked. "I can't take any Tenth Regulation offense. They'll throw me out."

"He was using the knife to protect me from the . . . the Cherbs," Danny blurted out. Les looked at him gratefully.

Brunholm looked at them in amusement.

"How very naive and touching. I won't report you," Brunholm said to Les, "but from now on, you are mine, boy."

Les shrugged. Danny thought that it was one thing claiming rights over Les, but enforcing them might be difficult.

"This has been a productive night," Brunholm said happily.

"Excuse me," Danny said, between gritted teeth, "when you two have finished . . ."

"Yes?" Brunholm said.

"Would somebody explain to me where I am?"

"Wilsons," Les said. "I told you."

"But what is Wilsons?" Danny felt his voice rising.

"An academy of the devious arts," Brunholm said.

"Devious arts . . . what are devious arts?" Danny said despairingly.

Brunholm bent down to Danny's face. His eyes brimmed with both amusement and malice.

"Spying, my dear young man," he said. "Wilsons is an academy of spying."

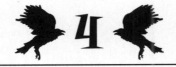

MASTER DEVOY

A school for spying? Danny looked from Les to Brunholm, bewildered.

"Not just *a* school for spying. Wilsons is *the* school for spying," Brunholm said, clapping Danny on the back. "Only the elite, the handpicked few, end up at Wilsons. Knutt here, for instance, is one of the great natural thieves. It's a pity you couldn't meet a few of the others tonight."

"You can," Les said quickly. "We was doing Stealth and Shadows revision tonight. We only just finished. They're all getting something to eat. I was just on my way down to Ravensdale—"

"And thought you might do a bit of quick thieving on the way, no doubt, from those feeble old creatures in the ballroom," Brunholm interrupted. Les looked wounded.

"Now," Brunholm said. "Let's go and meet some of your new friends and classmates."

"Classmates . . . ?" Danny was bewildered. "I don't . . . I mean, I won't . . ."

"Come on," Les said kindly. "We all felt that way at the start." Les started after Brunholm, who had strode off down the corridor. Not knowing what else to do, Danny followed.

Les and Brunholm walked quickly, and it was all Danny could do to keep up with them. Every time he reached a corner, it seemed that they were just disappearing around the next one, or they were concealed by cunningly placed urns and plants. Eventually Les realized what was going on and dropped back.

"It's just Wilsons," he said; "the place is just like that. You'll get used to it."

"I don't want to get used to it," Danny said. "I'm getting out of here in the morning. I'm supposed to be at Heston Oaks."

"I wish you luck, mate," Les said, "but I bet you don't even know where you are." Danny opened his mouth to speak, and closed it again. Les was right. He didn't have a clue where they were. He didn't even know what time it was. There didn't seem to be any clocks at Wilsons.

They rounded a final corner and were faced with a huge pair of dusty purple velvet curtains.

"Ravensdale," Les said. "I'm starving." And he plunged through the curtains. Danny followed him.

If Danny had been expecting anything, it would have been a dining hall like the one at school, with tables in orderly rows, and a serving hatch at the top. But Ravensdale was nothing like that. As he opened the curtain he stepped into what looked like a dark street in a small town. The street was crooked and badly lit, and tendrils of fog obscured blank walls and locked doorways. Shadows flitted across the cobbled passageway in front of him, shadows cast by flickering lamps high above his head. And above the lamps were gnarled and dead tree limbs, with untidy nests of sticks scattered through the boughs. Along the top branches, almost out of sight, he thought he could see the shapes of ravens. There was a single caw, which sounded like a signal of some kind. Other ravens appeared from nowhere and perched on the bottom branches, their heads turned toward Danny. Les and Brunholm were nowhere to be seen.

He turned back toward the curtains, feeling for them with his hand, but his fingers met only rough stone. He took a deep breath and began to walk slowly along the street. There were no windows at street level, only narrow slits high above his head. He could see nothing but darkness above the lamps. Alleyways led off to either side, but they were bathed in darkness and Danny had no desire to venture down them.

After a minute he came to a small crossroads. Each building around the crossroads had a doorway, and each door had a tarnished brass nameplate on it. The one that Danny stood beside read THE KAMIRILLA. The one opposite read THE JEDBURGHS. There was a small stone plinth in front of him with a wooden beam going straight up from it. Danny looked up. He felt a chill go through

30

him. At the top of the beam was a gibbet, and from the gibbet swung a hangman's noose.

Then two things happened. A door with a plate that read CONSIGLIO DEI DIECI opened, and light flooded into the square. Les walked out, sharing a joke with someone behind him.

"There you are," he said to Danny. "I thought you were behind me." He dragged Danny back through the door and slammed it behind them.

Danny found himself in a snug little room arranged around a battered wooden table. The table was covered with dirty plates that suggested that chicken and roast potatoes and gravy had recently been served. There were bench seats with high leather backs on three sides, and on these sat an assortment of boys and girls about the same age as Danny. A fire burned in a hearth set into a whitewashed wall.

It was obvious that Les had been talking about him. The others were all looking at him with open curiosity.

"Looks pretty like a Cherb to me," a tall thin-faced boy in a beret and brown trench coat said dubiously.

"Leave him alone," said a small girl with big hazel eyes and two prominent incisors, which gave her a faintly vampirish look.

"Yeah, Lord Snooty," another girl piped up. "Give him a break. Can you remember your first night here?"

Les had pushed Danny down into the seat beside the door. The closest boy to him was dark-haired, with heavy eyebrows and red-rimmed eyes. He was wringing his strong-looking hands, and muttering to himself.

"Cherbs . . . damn them . . . wring every one of their

filthy necks . . . blood and terror . . ." He turned to look at Danny. His eyes narrowed. He peered hard at Danny's face as if he was trying to remember something. He's going to think I'm a Cherb, Danny thought nervously. But before the boy realized what he was looking at, a girl was suddenly in the empty space between them. Danny looked at her, astonished. He had no idea how she had come to be there. She had curly brown hair and freckles, and a vague manner, as if she wasn't really sure how she had got there either.

"Oh. Hi," she said. "I'm Dixie Cole. I . . . er . . . I . . . oh yes . . . thought it would be a good idea if I got between you and Toxique. . . . He's okay, really . . . comes from a family of assassins, and they want him to learn. . . . Not really up to the job if you ask me. . . ."

"This is Danny, the new boy," Les said with a grin. "Dixie's a good friend of mine. Danny just dug me out of a spot of bother with Brunholm. Cherbs attacked the Messengers' dance. . . ."

Before Les could say any more, the lights went down. High on one wall an old-fashioned black-and-white television set flickered to life. Danny saw Brunholm sitting behind a newsreader's desk. NEWS AS TRUE AS THE DAY IS LONG, a sign on the wall behind him read.

"It's a short day, then," someone murmured, in what sounded to Danny like an old joke.

"Attention," Brunholm said, facing the camera with what he probably imagined to be a sincere expression. "A few notices." He cleared his throat and read swiftly from a piece of paper in front of him.

"A Cherb raid on the ballroom tonight was unsuccessful." Danny and Les exchanged looks. "Tonight's Stealth and Surprise exercise was a resounding success." This time the others exchanged looks. They obviously didn't agree. "And we have a new pupil, Danny Caulfield, who is not a Cherb."

Brunholm put down the piece of paper, stood up, beamed at his audience, then walked off camera and was gone.

"Not a word of truth in the whole thing. Everything that man says is a lie," the tall boy with the beret said.

"You might be right, Smyck," a small boy with large, blinking eyes said. "Except that this boy has all the anatomical characteristics of a Cherb."

"Well," Dixie said slowly, "if everything Brunholm says is a lie . . . and he says that Danny isn't a Cherb"—she appeared to be thinking very hard—"then it means that Danny can't be a Cherb!" And she smiled brilliantly at the others.

"No, Dixie," Les said in exasperation, "what you mean to say is . . ." He looked at Dixie and sighed. She already appeared to have forgotten what they had been talking about. "He ain't a Cherb," Les finished lamely.

"Good argument, Knutt," Smyck said sarcastically.

The others started talking among themselves about the exercise that night. Without warning, a hatch beside Danny slid open and a plate of chicken and potatoes and gravy slid across the table, coming to a stop right in front of him.

"Tuck in," Les said. Danny did as he was told.

It was the middle of the night, or felt like it, but he was starving.

As he ate, he noticed that there were framed photographs of men and women above the bench seats. Some of the subjects were distinguished. Others were wild-eyed, or haunted-looking. There was a particularly beautiful young woman with a long neck and almond-shaped eyes.

"That's old Bob Spetznaz," Les said admiringly. "Seduced kings and all in that getup."

"What about this one?" Danny pointed to an empty frame.

"That's Steff Pilkington. Near as anything invisible. Never managed to get a photograph of him. Every time they tried the film come back blank. One of the greats."

"Where are they all now?"

"Let me see." Les looked at them and frowned a little, then went round the wall. "Steff, he's dead, of course. Bob couldn't resist a challenge. Fell in love with Lydia Steelgate—when he wasn't dressed as a woman, of course. She had him garotted. Let me see. Dead, dead, dead, dead. Cheryl Orr—she's believed to be alive but gone mad." The photograph of Cheryl Orr showed a girl with calm gray eyes and a wide mouth with a smile lingering at the corners. Danny hoped Les was wrong about her.

"Missing, drowned and . . . dead." Les concluded his list.

Danny wasn't sure whether Les was telling the truth or not, and he didn't have time to ask. The door opened swiftly, and Brunholm's head appeared.

"All finished? Good. The master wants to see you,

34

Caulfield." The others looked at Danny with interest. A summons from the master was, it seemed, not something to be taken lightly.

Brunholm took Danny by the sleeve and drew him out the door. He marched him back down the little street.

"What is this place?" Danny asked.

"Ravensdale?" Brunholm said. "Its origins are lost in the mists of time. It was, as you see, a village. The old books talk of a cruel place. Family turned against family. A place of shadows and whispers. Abductions and assassinations were not unknown. And of course information became of the utmost importance, so people became spies. The annals say spies from Ravensdale were much sought-after, the greatest the world has ever seen, and of course strategically placed between the Two Worlds. But they are all gone now, dispersed forever. We don't know very much about them. It is an obscure branch of lore studied by few. Only the ravens are left of that time.

"It lay vacant for many years before we turned it into a place where the cadets can eat. They are split into different houses like the Jedburghs and the Kamirilla to encourage them to plot against each other. But usually they're too busy talking and gossiping. The ravens took a fancy to Ravensdale and built their nests here. We think it's their way of keeping an eye on the cadets. The ravens like to know everything that is going on."

Brunholm appeared to dismiss the subject, and walked ahead rapidly. Danny thought about asking what the gibbet was for, but decided to keep his mouth shut.

The journey to Master Devoy's study was the strangest Danny had yet encountered in Wilsons. There were doors that swung open only with a password. There were corridors that appeared to abruptly end, only for a hidden turn to reveal itself. He and Brunholm climbed a long narrow staircase with no banister in almost pitch-blackness, and halfway up, Brunholm grabbed Danny's arm roughly.

" 'Ware there, boy," he growled. Danny looked down. Where he had been about to step, there was only a dizzying drop. His foot dislodged a piece of stone. He watched until it disappeared, and he did not hear it strike bottom. Cold sweat broke out on his forehead.

"Jump over it," Brunholm said. Danny shut his eyes and jumped. To his relief he landed on solid ground. They continued to climb until, above them, Danny saw a small, plain door with a light above it.

"There we are," Brunholm said. "Master Devoy's study."

Danny started toward it, eager to get off the staircase, but Brunholm took his arm again.

"Look," Brunholm said. He lit a match. Across the top of the stairs was strung a shining wire, which gleamed softly in the flame.

"Put that there myself," Brunholm said, looking pleased. "Piano wire strung at neck level, razor-sharp. Take your head right off." He chuckled in an unpleasant way. He ducked under the wire, then rapped sharply on the door. Three knocks, followed by two, then three again. The door swung open. Brunholm pushed Danny in, then stood behind him in the doorway, nodding and grinning, for all the world, Danny thought, like a dog that had fetched a stick.

"Thank you, Marcus. Close the door, and please don't think about eavesdropping from one of the hidden entrances," a cultured voice said. Brunholm's face dropped in a way that would have been comical if Danny hadn't seen the thunderous look in his eyes. Without anyone touching it, the door closed in Brunholm's face.

It was a medium-size room, shabby in a cozy way, with a battered sofa and chairs and a fire burning in the grate. To one side of the room was a desk, behind which sat a man in a pinstripe suit, his face in shadows. Danny turned around and almost jumped out of his skin. A stuffed weasel stood on a shelf beside the door, its snarl so lifelike, he recoiled.

"The weasel," the man said. "Our equivalent in the animal world. Of the spy, that is." His voice was low and pleasant. He didn't say anything else, so Danny looked around. The room was full of things to do with spying— so many that he thought it might be a museum. On a side table there was a pen that on closer examination contained a gun. There were false mustaches and wigs. There were volumes of Catullus and other Roman scholars, each containing a radio transmitter in its hollowed-out middle pages. A whole shelf was devoted to cigarette packets in various stages of being transformed into a miniature revolver. In a stand in front of him Danny noticed an umbrella with an ornate ivory handle carved in the shape of an elephant's head.

"Pick it up," the man said. Danny did as he said. "Press the elephant's left tusk." When Danny pressed it, a long spike shot from the tip of the umbrella.

"For delivery of poison," the man said, coming out from behind the desk. "Remarkably efficient in a crowd." Danny shuddered. "Invented by the Bulgarians," the man continued examining the umbrella thoughtfully. "Resourcefulness on a limited budget. Sometimes it makes for the best espionage." He stepped into the light. He was a tall man with an intelligent, well-bred face that was entirely expressionless. He did not look directly at Danny.

"It has been a long war," he said, seeming to be speaking to himself, "and a long and uneasy truce. They get stronger, and we get weaker by the day." Master Devoy sighed. He suddenly lifted his head and looked straight into Danny's eyes. Danny felt as if all his secrets had been exposed, and found himself blushing.

"Yes," Devoy said slowly, "Brunholm was right. Not just the physical appearance . . . a quality you have, not quite deviousness, not yet . . . you will have to learn that . . ."

"I don't want to learn anything," Danny said, his voice not quite seeming to belong to him. "I want to go home."

"That's the problem." Devoy's tone was kindly now. "You can't go home."

The fire crackled and spat. Rain spattered against the window. Danny stared at Devoy. There was something final about the way he had told Danny that he wasn't going home.

"Why?" Danny managed, aware of how tired he felt.

"We need a spy," Devoy said, "a great spy who will sit at the very heart of our enemy and reveal what he is thinking."

"But I'm not a spy," Danny protested.

"No," Devoy said, "but you will be. I cannot reveal your mission until you complete your basic training. I will say no more than that, except that we are under great threat."

"Why would I want to help you?" Danny said. His voice sounded petulant, like that of a naughty child, but he didn't care. "You kidnapped me!"

Devoy didn't answer. Instead, he sprang to his feet and went to a cabinet. He opened the glass doors with a small key and removed a globe of the world. He brought it over to Danny and set it down in front of him. "What is it?" he asked.

"A globe?" Danny replied. Devoy waved his hand over it. The globe began to change. The familiar seas disappeared. The landmasses dissolved. Danny found himself looking at a new world with new seas and new lands. The same, but different. Danny examined it. Were the colors harsher, the shapes of the land a little more jagged?

"This is a Globe of the Two Worlds," Devoy said, "a rare and beautiful object."

"Two worlds?" Danny said. "I thought there was only one."

"Two," Devoy said, "occupying the same space and time. You have just crossed from the Upper World into the Lower World. Once it was easy to cross. Men and women of wisdom did it all the time, and there were Messengers."

"Messengers?"

"Like the winged people you saw in the ballroom."

"You mean I'm . . . in another world . . . ?" Danny's voice trailed away.

Devoy replaced the globe carefully.

"Yes. You crossed over with Fairman in the taxi."

"But how . . . school . . ."

"An elaborate hoax carried out by my colleague Mr. Brunholm, without my knowledge, of course."

Danny wanted to ask more questions, but he was feeling sleepier and sleepier.

"The chicken you have just eaten contained a thirty-three-minute sleeping draft," Devoy said, checking his watch. "It is taking effect—that is good. You need your rest."

As if from a great distance Danny heard a knock on the door. It opened to reveal Valant. Devoy indicated Danny.

"You may take him now, Mr. Valant. Please ensure this time that his room is not unlocked. If the Ring get wind of his presence before we are ready . . ."

"The Ring . . . ?" Danny managed. "Who are the Ring?"

"The Ring of Five, Danny," Devoy said, leaning over him. "Be patient! Soon you will know all there is to know about the Ring, that is our hope!"

Then Danny felt sleep wash over him, and heard no more.

ST. AGNES

Danny woke in the small room he'd been given the night before. It was morning, and a cold light shone through the windows. He was sure that a voice had woken him, but when he looked around, he could see no one. Then the voice came again, crackly and far away.

"Breakfast in ten minutes and forty seconds. Please wash and dress." Danny saw that the voice was coming from a device on the wall that looked like an old-time radio. He groaned and let his head fall back onto the pillow, remembering everything that had happened to him. The cab ride, Wilsons . . . it was too much to think it was all a dream, but just in case, he shut his eyes—if he could go to sleep again, perhaps he would wake up in his own bed.

"Breakfast in nine minutes and twenty-three seconds," the voice crackled again. "Cadet Caulfield is in

41

danger of incurring a Section Two Offense if he does not get out of bed."

Danny leapt out of bed and looked around wildly. How did the voice know he was still in bed? Then it spoke again, this time very low.

"Psst . . . Danny?" Without thinking, Danny went over and put his ear to the speaker.

"Jump up like a good lad, don't want a Section Two on your first morning, do you," the voice whispered in a kindly way. Then, resuming its normal tone, it went on.

"Breakfast in eight minutes and fifty-three seconds. Cadet Knutt. Please return the toothpaste you have purloined from Cadet Smyck."

Danny scrambled into his clothes, splashed some water on his face and brushed his teeth, then stepped out into the corridor. He looked up and down. He didn't have a clue where he was going.

"Hello," a voice said. He turned and saw Dixie standing behind him.

"I—I," he stuttered, "where—"

"They sent me to find you to bring you to Ravensdale," she said calmly. "Wouldn't want you getting lost. Come on, or they'll have eaten everything."

"Hang on a second," he said. "I need to . . . I don't know . . ." Dixie looked at him sympathetically.

"Did Devoy give you the old Two Worlds lecture last night?" Danny nodded dumbly. "Thought so," Dixie went on. "I felt pretty strange when I was told that there was another world—it goes both ways, you know."

"But how can there be two worlds?"

"Think of them as being different countries, if that helps." Dixie's tone was kind. "But don't try to think about it too much. It'll make you dotty, like me!"

She linked her arm through his and marched him off down the corridor, which seemed to be going a different direction from the previous night, and did not look at all familiar.

"How do you find your way around here?" he gasped, half running to keep up with her. "I mean, it's different all the time!"

"You have to look for clues," she said. "Takes a while to learn. For instance, the carpet is always red in the north wing." Danny looked down—the carpet was indeed red, patterned with sinister-looking black ravens. "And the ravens always point south. And no matter where you are, Ravensdale is always to the south. Easy."

Danny didn't see anything easy about it.

"I'll take your word for it," he said.

"Oh no," Dixie said, stopping and turning to him, her expression almost comically serious. "Don't take anybody's word for anything around here. That's the whole point!" She started walking again. "I hope they've got bacon this morning," she went on in a conversational tone. "I love bacon."

There was a murky kind of light in the phantom village, which was, as Dixie put it, "all the daylight you're likely to get around here." A low ceiling of cloud hung over the rooftops and a cold breeze blew down the street.

They headed down the dingy street toward the Consiglio dei Dieci, and Danny was glad when they

43

pushed the door open and entered a warm fug of talk and food.

After the bacon there were pancakes with honey and maple syrup, and waffles and toast, all washed down with hot milky tea. Danny squeezed in beside Les and tucked in. Only when he had finished did he remember that someone had put a sleeping pill in his food the evening before. Anger at being tricked began to grow in him. Who did they think they were? Kidnapping him, imprisoning him, then sneaking pills into his food. That seemed to be the way of things in the spy school. But they weren't the only ones who could be sneaky.

"You look chirpy this morning," Les said. "Decided to go along with the whole thing, have you?"

"Yes . . . well . . . yes," Danny said, forcing a smile onto his face. Go along with it, all right—go along with it until I find out where I am, then escape!

"Are you going to class this morning?" the girl with the prominent incisors asked. "I'm Vandra, by the way."

"I'm Danny. But I don't know if I'm going to class or not."

"Danny the Cherb," the tall boy broke in, and laughed unpleasantly.

"Leave it out, Smyck," Les said wearily. "Danny, you got to go to Stores this morning, get yourself kitted out." The rest of them exchanged grins. Danny eyed them suspiciously. What was so funny about going to Stores? But before he had a chance to say anything about it, the voice he had heard from the speaker rang out.

"Three minutes to class."

44

"Give over, Blackpitt," Smyck said.

"I heard that, Cadet Smyck," Blackpitt went on smoothly. "Two minutes to class."

There was the sound of many feet as the inhabitants of the benches got up at once.

"Who is that? Blackpitt, I mean," Danny asked Dixie.

"Blackpitt? He's . . . he's the voice on the speakers!" she said brightly. Les looked at her and shook his head.

"No one's ever seen him, far as I know," Les said, rushing past, "but he ain't a bad sort. Knows everything that goes on. Listen, we'll see you later—you'll be put in our Roosts, I'd say."

"Roosts?"

"Yeah, see you later." And Les was gone. In a moment, so were the others. Once more Danny was on his own. He stood up.

"Stores, Cadet Caulfield," Blackpitt said helpfully. "Look for the parade ground." But when Danny tried to question the speaker further, Blackpitt was silent.

Danny pushed through the velvet curtains and stood in the corridor beyond, looking for clues. He wandered dusty halls for twenty minutes before he found a large oak door. The drafts whistling round its edges suggested that it must lead outside.

The door creaked and groaned, but it opened. Danny stepped outside onto a terrace that overlooked gardens running down to a small river. The gardens looked as if they might be pleasant in summer, but there was a cold wind blowing through the shrubberies, and the large

Italianate fountain in the center was dry and full of dead leaves. Danny shivered. Nothing looked like a parade ground.

Then an ornamental arch caught his eye. It was made from wrought iron, and long-dead creepers clung to it. But it was the shape that caught his eye. It was in the shape of a trumpet. Perhaps . . . He wondered: military bands used parade grounds . . . and they played trumpets. . . .

He crossed the grass to the arch and went through. He was right! Beyond the arch lay a large, empty parade ground, which looked as if it hadn't been used for many years. The surface was cracked and broken, and weeds poked through the cracks. There was a single building at the other side, and above the door, on a peeling sign, was written the word STORES.

Danny walked the parade ground quickly, the wind cutting through his jacket. As he neared the other side the wind began to whip sleet horizontally through the air, and he ran the last few yards, pulled the door of the shabby wooden building open and went in.

Inside, the Stores was warm and muggy. There were folding metal chairs in what looked like a waiting area, with posters overhead. The posters were faded and curling at the edges and said things like *Rationing—It's for Everyone!* underneath a picture of a small boy greedily tucking into a packet of biscuits, and *Turn Out That Light—Save Power!*, showing a girl reading a book under a powerful light.

In front of the chairs there was a counter, and at the

counter was a small man in a brown coat and glasses. He was reading a paper. He did not look in Danny's direction.

"Excuse me," Danny said. The man didn't look up. Instead he pointed to a bell on the counter. Danny went over to the counter and pressed the bell. The man sighed and looked up.

"Chit," he said.

"What?" Danny asked.

"You got a chit? A bit of paper saying you need your kit."

"No," Danny said, "no one gave me one." The man sighed and rolled his eyes to heaven.

"You'd think I'd nothing better to do than hand out kit to youngsters with no paperwork."

"I'm sorry," Danny said innocently. "If you want me to ask Master Devoy . . ."

"No, no," the man said hastily, "no need to trouble the master. Ain't his fault anyhow. I'll make an exception this time, busy and all as I am."

Danny looked along the seats, which were covered in a fine film of dust, as were the shelves behind him. What kept the man so busy?

"Wait here," the man said, and turned away. Danny looked down. The newspaper he had been reading was still lying on the counter. Danny furtively turned it toward him. It was called the *Covertian*. The headline read:

CAPTAIN SRANZER MISSING ON FRONTIER

and underneath a photograph of Devoy was the caption:

47

Ring Points Finger at Wilsons;
Devoy Denies Involvement.

Sranzer, Danny thought. Wasn't that the name of the man who had stopped Fairman's cab the night before?

But before he could read on, the paper was snatched away.

"You want a paper to read, buy your own," the Storeman grumbled. He put the *Covertian* under the counter and went back to his work. First he went to a huge bin full of a white powder, which billowed around him as he scooped it into a tin. When he finished, and stopped sneezing, he put a lid on the tin and slammed it down on the counter in front of Danny.

"Fingerprint powder," he announced. The object he put down beside it looked like a bunch of keys with hooks instead of teeth.

"Lockpicks." The lockpicks were followed by a magnifying glass, a pair of binoculars, a codebook and something that looked like a hairy centipede.

"What's that?" Danny asked, pointing at it.

"False mustache," the man said. "Purposes of disguise." While Danny stared at the false mustache, wondering whether it was a joke, the man placed a small mirror on the counter. "Signal mirror," he said. Danny could understand that, but his eyes widened when the Storeman produced a small silver-plated gun.

"Derringer pistol, no rounds, ammunition on order." This was followed by "Miniature camera, no film" and "Secret transmitter concealed in copy of Bible, no battery."

"You mean none of these things work?" Danny asked.

"Of course they work," the Storeman snapped. "There just ain't been any deliveries for a while."

"How long?" Danny asked.

"Five years," the man snarled, dropping a roll of wire on the counter.

"What's that?"

"Piano wire. For purposes of strangulation." Danny gulped. The Storeman added a razor-sharp stiletto knife to the pile, followed by fake glasses and a ginger wig. With a flourish he produced a long brown coat. It was stained and frayed about the collar, and was about ten sizes too big for Danny.

"Coat with hidden pockets," he announced proudly. Finally, on top of the coat he placed a small blue tablet.

"I'm not even going to ask," Danny said.

"Cyanide tablet."

"Why?"

"Kill yourself if you're captured. Just put it between your teeth and bite. It's sugar-coated. You won't feel a thing." Danny shuddered and decided there and then that he would throw the thing away at the first opportunity.

The Storeman made Danny put on the coat, which smelled of damp, and then put all the kit into the various hidden pockets, which didn't seem very hidden at all. He stood back proudly to admire his handiwork.

"Now," he said, "agent ready for the field. You look the part, young man."

"I look a right twit," Danny muttered under his breath, but the Storeman had, it appeared, finished with him. He took his paper out from under the counter, and turning away so Danny couldn't sneak a look, began to read. There was nothing for it but to leave.

"Thanks a lot," Danny said, not bothering to hide the sarcasm. The Storeman merely waved a hand at him. Danny walked to the door and stepped out onto the parade ground.

As he crossed the parade ground, the wind made the coat flap around him, no matter how tightly he tied the belt around his waist. He felt bulky and ridiculous. He ducked quickly through the trumpet-shaped gate and into the garden. Ravens cawed over his head. He walked up onto the terrace. Where did he go now? The strangeness of his situation washed over him. One day he had been sitting at home, waiting to go to Heston Oaks. The next morning he found himself in a school for spies! This couldn't be happening.

A gust of wind blew through the trees above his head. He shivered, remembering how he had left home the night before, the rain lashing the trees and the sinister black taxi outside. If his mother and father had been there . . . Part of him longed to see them again, but another voice whispered bitterly that they had been too busy to wait to see him off to school, to make sure that he was safe. They have betrayed you, he thought.

He looked down at the brown coat, which hung almost to his ankles. The first thing I can do, he thought crossly, is get rid of this coat.

He took the coat off and flung it on the ground, then sat down on the low balustrade that ran around the terrace.

He would find Devoy and Brunholm, he decided, and demand to be sent home straightaway, and in the meantime he would have nothing to do with their school and their classes and their Cherbs, whatever those were. . . .

"Look out!" A man's voice cut through the quiet of the garden. Danny looked up to see a large object hurtling through the air toward him. He threw himself sideways. The falling object struck the balustrade with a sickening crash, sending debris flying. Something hit Danny on the cheek and drew blood. He looked up through the fine plaster dust that hung in a cloud over the place where he had been sitting. A man was looking down at him. He wore a double-breasted suit and scuffed black shoes. He had a long face and gray eyes, and his mouth turned down at the corners, as if the world had disappointed him once too often.

"You okay?" the man asked. His voice was deep and graveled, with the remains of what might have once been an Irish accent.

"Yeah . . . I think so . . . ," Danny said shakily. The man bent down to the rubble on the ground. He lifted a chipped and broken plaster woman's head.

"Saint Agnes," he said, "patron saint of spies." He stared into the statue's empty eyes as though she might tell him something about what had happened; then he replaced the head carefully on the ground.

"The name's McGuinness," he said. "So maybe you'd tell me who you are and why someone would try to murder you?"

"Murder!" Danny gasped.

"That statue didn't fall on its own," McGuinness said, pointing at a now empty niche high on the wall above them. "Somebody pushed it."

"I'm Danny Caulfield," Danny said, "and I only just got here—to Wilsons, I mean. And I don't know who would want to . . . to murder me."

"New boy, eh," McGuinness said, looking at Danny as if sizing him up and finding him wanting. "Must be more to you than meets the eye. I'll have to look into this."

His eye fell on the coat that Danny had thrown on the ground.

"Just get your kit, then?"

"Mad things, like a magnifying glass and stuff. And that stupid coat," Danny said, feeling a bit hysterical.

"Take it easy, son," McGuinness said. "I wouldn't be surprised if you're not in a bit of shock." He picked up the brown coat, turned it lining-side out and looked at the label.

"S.P.," he murmured. "Steff Pilkington himself must have owned this at one stage. This is one of the Marburg coats, a classic. Wouldn't mind one myself."

"You can keep it if you want," Danny said sourly. McGuinness gave him a weary look, which made him wish he had kept his mouth shut. Then, with one swift movement, the man put the coat on. It was too small for him, and he looked a bit silly, but his face was serious.

"Did you have the pockets filled?" he asked Danny softly.

"Yes—there are loads of things in it."

"Find them. Search me," McGuinness said. Danny

hesitated, then started to search the pockets—or rather, he would have searched them if he could have found them, but no matter how hard he tried, he couldn't find any pockets, and no matter how he patted the lining, there didn't seem to be anything in it.

"Grab my collar, as if you were catching a fugitive," McGuinness said, something like amusement in his gray eyes. Danny did so, and yelped. His hand burned as if he had been stung by a dozen bees.

"And look at this." McGuinness laid the coat on the ground. He pulled at the buttons, which came away, drawing behind them fine but strong wires. Within moments the coat had formed a small but neat dome-shaped tent.

"Don't underestimate these coats. I'd say if it belonged to Steff Pilkington, then it has more features that I don't know about."

Danny picked the coat up with a new respect, and it sprang back to its original shape.

"Are you a spy too?" he asked.

"I am chief executive of the Office for the Enforcement of the Ten Regulations," McGuinness replied, with a mirthless laugh. "In other words, I'm a spy cop. I try to stay out of the proper spy business, and both sides respect that. My job is to investigate crime. Even spies need law and order. Which reminds me, I need to have a look at where that statue stood. You better watch yourself. Here." He took six small bullets from his pocket.

"Keep those for the derringer. Don't use them unless you have to."

McGuinness turned abruptly and walked away across the lawn. When he got to the edge Danny called out to him.

"Excuse me?" McGuinness looked back expectantly. "I just wanted to say . . . thanks," Danny blurted out. McGuinness smiled, a smile that did not touch his gray eyes, and walked on. Within seconds, he was out of sight.

CAMOUFLAGE, CONCEALMENT
AND DECEPTION

Danny went back into the building through the door he had originally used, and was immediately lost again. He might have wandered for hours if Blackpitt had not announced "Break time" from a battered old speaker over his head, and then, in a whisper, "Go left at the top of the corridor and take the second right, Cadet Caulfield."

He did as he was told and was relieved to find himself back in the entrance hall, where the rest of the pupils were milling around, eating chocolate biscuits and drinking lemonade from tall jugs set out on a table beside Valant's desk. As Danny made his way toward Les and Dixie he heard Smyck's mocking tones.

"Nice coat, Caulfield."

"See you got to the Stores," Les said, with a grin. "Got your false glasses and all?"

"They gave me a light brown wig," Dixie said, looking at her own light brown hair and frowning as if she had just realized that a mistake had been made.

"Most of it's a load of old rubbish," Les said, "but hold on to the codebook. You'll need that for Codes and Ciphers."

"I use the mirror to brush my hair," Dixie said. "The mirrors are kind of weird in Wilsons."

"The coat's a bit ripe," Les said, wrinkling up his nose. "Not exactly smart, if you know what I mean."

"Give it to me later," Dixie said. "I'll do something with it." Danny smiled. He wondered what Dixie might do to the coat.

"What happened to your face?" she said. Danny put his hand up. He'd forgotten about the cut. He realized that he felt a bit numb all over. "Sit down." Dixie's voice came from a long way away. Les caught Danny under the arms and helped him into a chair.

"I'll be all right in a minute," he said, taking a deep breath. When he had recovered he told them about the statue, and about McGuinness.

"You mean *the* McGuinness? The detective?" Les looked impressed. "The man's a legend."

"I didn't expect to meet a detective," Danny said. "I thought this was a school for spies."

"McGuinness used to be a spy," Les said, "but he wanted out."

"He took a Vow of Everlasting Truth and Fidelity in the Hall of Shadows," Dixie said, and shivered.

"The Hall of Shadows?" Danny said. "What's that?"

"Nothing," Les said quickly, "but it means that he can't tell lies or anything anymore. Means both sides keep him around to investigate crime. Not that the Cherbs really want someone investigating crime, but it's part of the treaty."

"You'll find out what the Hall of Shadows is soon enough," Smyck put in.

"What is it with him?" Danny asked.

"Never mind him," Les said. "Him and some of the others lost everything when the Cherbs took over the Lower World—all except here. They're kind of sour about it. They think Devoy and his lot were too soft on the Cherbs."

"Are there any other people here from . . . from my world?"

"From the Upper World? I think you're the only one. Reckon that's why they look at you funny."

"Nothing to do with the eyes and the face, then?" Danny asked sarcastically.

"Do you really think someone was trying to kill you?" Dixie broke in, her eyes like dinner plates.

"The statue didn't decide to fly on its own," Danny snapped, then regretted it. But if Dixie was offended, she didn't show it. In fact, she looked as if she was giving serious consideration to the idea of statues that decided to take off and fly through the air.

"We'll have to take a look at this," Les said grimly. "We can't have people chucking statues at our mates, can we?" Danny felt a surge of gratitude toward his new friend. "Take it easy," Les said, patting him on the shoulder.

Danny considered the other cadets. Most of them looked like ordinary young people at break time in a normal school. But he was reminded that they weren't when Les sniffed the air again.

"That coat's a bit musty, if you take my meaning," Les said, and used his wings to fan fresh air across his face. Danny almost jumped out of his skin—it was going to take him a long time to get used to the wings.

"Er, Les . . . ," he started. Les looked at him, but Danny couldn't think of a way of framing the question.

"The wings, dummy," Dixie said. "He's never seen a Messenger before."

"A Messenger?" Danny said.

"Yep," Les said. "Same as them old folk you saw last night. Us Messengers used to carry dispatches backward and forward to the Upper World. You remember them old pictures you would see of angels talking to people?" Danny nodded. "They weren't no angels, they were Messengers. Used to have a bit of status in them days. People looked up to us."

"Do the wings—I mean—do they work?"

"Course they do. You need training, though. I can kind of glide on them. Of course, the old folk you saw dancing, they wouldn't use their wings—it's not supposed to be polite. Most of them wouldn't even talk to the likes of me. Our lot was the branch of the family . . . well, my dad got into trouble and got thrown out of the Messengers. Bit too fond of the bottle, he was. When they voted to stop flying he laughed at them."

"They got it into their heads that flying wasn't

genteel," Dixie said. "If you ask me the old things are a bit ashamed of themselves now that they can't message anymore, and they made up this 'flying is bad manners' lark so they don't have to fly and be reminded of the time when they were useful."

"Class is starting," Blackpitt said testily.

"Come on," Les said. "It's Camouflage, Concealment and Deception. Nothing too tricky about it. It's usually a bit of a laugh—Duddy teaches it. She's mad as a hatter."

Danny followed them through the front door. They turned left and walked down a gravel path between dense shrubberies. They passed an opening in the greenery and Danny, looking in, saw what looked like a maze of yew.

"What's that?" he asked.

"That's the Helix of van Groening," Les said. "It's a maze that changes shape. Kind of dangerous. I'd stay out of it."

The path turned to the left and opened out into a clearing in which there stood an old wooden building with wide eaves and narrow windows. As they emerged from the shrubbery, a figure in a bright red coat dashed across the gravel in front of them. Before anyone could move, the figure produced a gun and leveled it at them. Danny ducked. Les hit the ground, along with most of the others, while Dixie disappeared. The figure pointed the gun just above their heads and unleashed a fusillade, then turned and ran off into the trees behind the stone building.

The cadets got shakily to their feet. There was a long, shocked silence; then they all started talking at once. Dixie reappeared beside them, even paler than usual.

Danny saw a woman approaching them from the building. She had long gray hair to her waist, and wore a brightly colored knitted scarf that reached to the ground. The upper part of her face was obscured by large dark glasses. As she walked she flicked her hair back and shook her head like a schoolgirl, even though she had to be sixty if she was a day, Danny thought. She cleared her throat loudly.

"Silence!" she commanded.

"But Miss," one of the girl cadets said, her voice shaking and tears in her eyes. The woman held up a hand theatrically to silence them.

"That's Duddy," Les hissed.

"You have just been attacked," Duddy said. Her voice was surprisingly deep. "I would like you to describe your attacker."

They all looked at each other. Apart from the red coat, none of them could remember the attacker's face.

"Man or woman?" A grim smile crossed Duddy's face. "You have learned a valuable lesson. There are two reasons why you did not recognize your attacker. Firstly, she was wearing a brightly colored garment in order to distract you. You saw the red coat and nothing else. Can anyone tell me the second reason?"

"The gun," Toxique said quietly. Danny looked around. He had forgotten about the boy who came from a family of assassins.

"That's right," Duddy said. "When someone points a gun at you, you will almost always look at the gun, not at their face. You have learned two valuable lessons."

"It was like a gun in a dream," Toxique went on.

"Leave it out, Toxique," Smyck said. Vandra looked at him nervously.

"Yes, well," Duddy said, then clapped her hands, "inside now."

They all filed into the front room of the building, which was laid out like a classroom, with rows of desks and a blackboard. If Danny expected anything as dramatic as the attack to take place, he was disappointed. The lesson was on the subject of animals that disguised themselves as other things—insects that looked like sticks, fish that imitated poisonous species, chameleons and the like. Duddy's deep voice had a droning quality, and Danny found his mind starting to wander.

"For human beings," Duddy went on, catching Danny's attention again, "this kind of disguise is limited to a handful of people who have what we in the trade refer to as the Quality of Indeterminate Location. Come up here, Cadet Cole."

Dixie stood up and walked to the head of the class.

"Please demonstrate your gift," Duddy said. Dixie smiled and looked a little embarrassed.

"Could I not sing a song or something?" she said.

"Cadet Cole," Duddy warned. "Now, class, watch her carefully." Danny stared at Dixie, who was humming and looking into the air. He could see that Smyck was watching her very closely as well. There was no way she could move without being seen, Danny thought, just as Dixie disappeared! He rubbed his eyes. One minute she had been standing there; the next she was gone! He looked wildly round the classroom. Les was grinning.

"Please come back in, Cadet Cole," Duddy said in a raised voice. The door opened and Dixie came back in, smiling.

"How did you do that?" Danny gasped.

"A variation on what we have been talking about," Duddy said, "and not as big a mystery as you might think. Perhaps not even as big a mystery as someone who looks like a Cherb, but apparently is not." She turned her dark glasses on Danny, who shifted in his seat uncomfortably.

The class ended with Blackpitt proclaiming "Lunch" in a tone that suggested he was looking forward to a good lunch himself. Danny walked back to the main building with Les, Vandra and Dixie.

"Listen," Danny said, "I need to know what a Cherb is. And I want to know why everybody is looking at me in a funny way."

"Cherbs is our enemy," Les said. "Simple as that. They look like you . . . well, everyone knows what they look like, but they're as wicked as anything."

"They were part of the Lower World, and we used to get on okay with them, but that's all changed," Vandra said. "They've got soldiers and stuff—all we've got really is Wilsons."

"The Cherbs and us ordinary people lived together forever and ever in peace in the Lower World," Dixie said, "and then they decided to take over."

"We're on the only bit of territory not under the

control of the Ring," Vandra added. There it was again, Danny thought. The Ring!

"There are a truce and a treaty, but the truce isn't much good—the Cherbs attacked us last night, and Brunholm lied about it. One of the Messengers was killed!" Les said.

"I didn't know that," Vandra said. "I'm sorry. But it doesn't change things. The peace we have is better than no peace at all."

"By the looks of things, we're not going to have it for very much longer," Les said.

"I don't understand," Danny said. The others looked at each other. "What?" Danny was exasperated. "Is anybody going to tell me?"

"There is an island between the Lower World and the Upper World—the Upper World is your home, where your parents are and everything," Vandra said. "The island is us, Wilsons Island. It's part of the treaty that we guard the Upper World against the Ring of Five and the Cherbs."

"Without us," Les said, his tone deadly serious, "the Ring and the Cherbs would take over. Your lot wouldn't stand a chance."

"As it is, it's only a matter of time. The Ring don't care about the treaty anymore," Vandra said gloomily.

Danny looked from face to face. They were all serious, there was no doubt about that. Once again he found the words resonating in his head. The Ring of Five.

"Some people think we are about to fall," Vandra said, "and if that is true . . ."

". . . it'll be curtains for your world," Les said grimly. There was a long silence, which was broken by Dixie.

"Do you think they'll have sausages for lunch?" she said. "I like sausages."

They didn't have sausages for lunch, but they did have steak pie and roast potatoes with gravy. As they were finishing off the last of the pie, Brunholm appeared briefly on the battered old television. He looked a little shaken, and announced briefly that they had the rest of the afternoon off. There was a cheer from the cadets.

"Brilliant," Les said, "that means that we can get you settled into the Roosts."

Danny wasn't sure he liked the idea of a Roost. It sounded cold and drafty. But I won't be in it for all that long, he thought.

They filed out of Ravensdale after a particularly satisfying apple pie and custard. Danny noticed that many of the other cadets would not meet his eye, or edged away from him. And a few times he thought he heard the word "Cherb" behind him.

"Don't worry about them," Dixie said cheerfully. "They wouldn't know a Cherb if one . . . fell on them, or something."

Danny felt someone plucking at his elbow. It was Brunholm.

"Are you all right?" he asked hoarsely. "Are you hurt?"

"No, I'm okay," Danny said.

"Are you sure, boy?" Brunholm demanded. "McGuinness wants to launch a formal inquiry. A mountain of paperwork and him poking his nose everywhere. Are you sure it wasn't an accident? Wilsons is very old. Bits fall off every so often. That's it, I'm sure. Yes, you can tell McGuinness it was an accident."

"I'm afraid I can't do that," Danny said, politely but firmly. "Mr. McGuinness was there and he saw what happened."

Something gleamed deep in Brunholm's eyes for a second, something that made a chill run down Danny's spine. Then he let go of Danny's sleeve.

"Yes, yes, of course," he murmured distractedly, "things must take their course. Very proper of you." He walked away from them, seemingly deep in thought.

7

THE GALLERY OF WHISPERS

Danny followed his new friends to the Roosts, his mind racing. *"Curtains for your world,"* Les had said. But even if it was true, it didn't give Wilsons the right to kidnap and drug Danny.

They turned the corner of the main building and walked across a smooth lawn.

"Here we go," Les said. "The Roosts."

Danny looked up in surprise. The Roosts were two large wooden buildings, each with a crooked chimney and weathered carvings on their corners and eaves. The carvings looked very old, and seemed to depict all sorts of shadowy creatures. But that wasn't what was so surprising about the Roosts. The buildings stood on slender iron legs, intricately wrought with flowers and leaves. Danny reckoned that they must be fifty or sixty feet off the ground. The buildings were joined only by a tangle of wires and pipes at the back, and a balcony at the front. An iron bridge ran from the Roosts across to Wilsons's main building. Two metal staircases soared upward, if they could be called staircases, for they were incredibly light and springy, and when Les grabbed the handrail, the whole thing flexed and bounced. Paying no attention to this, Les ascended at great speed. Dixie followed him. With a nervous glance up, Danny followed, trying not to look down, keeping his eyes fixed on the top of the stairs.

Despite the fact that the cadets' weight made the staircase writhe like a snake as they climbed, it felt more secure than it looked, but Danny was still glad to reach the top. He steadied himself against the rail and looked down. It was a long way to the ground.

"The Roosts used to be quarters for the Messengers," Vandra explained, "before they stopped flying."

Les opened the wooden door and Danny followed them in. It took a moment for his eyes to adjust to the gloom. On either side of the Roosts were rows of beds separated by wooden dividers, so that each bunk was almost in its own room. A large black stove glowed in the middle, surrounded by armchairs and an overstuffed sofa. "This is yours here," Les said, pointing to one of the beds. "You're down our end of the hut. Smyck's lot have the other end, so you're better off here."

"The other hut's for the girls," Dixie said. "Kind of cozy, don't you think?"

Danny sat down on his bed, noticing that his suitcase was already under it. For some reason that he could not

67

explain, the place already felt like home. Stop it, he said to himself; you're getting out of here. First chance.

"Can you get to the school by the bridge?" Danny asked.

"It's supposed to be for the instructors to keep an eye on us," Les said. "We're not allowed to use it."

"We're forbidden from going onto the two top floors of Wilsons," Dixie said. "It's all dark and deadly up there, from what they tell us."

Danny went out onto the balcony. There was a good view of the roof of Wilsons. There were turrets and peaks and gulleys divided by metal walkways. He could see windows and skylights in unexpected places, as well as what looked like antennas and satellite dishes, all pointing in the direction of the glow in the sky he had seen the previous night. He looked that way, but his view was obscured by trees growing on a ridge, so all he could really see was a darkening of the sky, as though smoke was drifting up into it.

"I expect you'll be inducted tomorrow," Dixie said.

"What's that?" Danny turned to her.

"Inducted. They have to ask you do you want to be a cadet at Wilsons . . . and . . . some other stuff."

"They have to ask me?" Danny said. "I could say no?"

"It's up to you," Les said.

"So all I've got to do is tell Brunholm and Devoy to stuff it!" Danny exclaimed. "That shouldn't be hard."

He saw his two new friends exchange a look.

"What is it?" he asked. "They kidnapped me."

68

"They shouldn't have done that," Les said slowly.

"No, that was very bad," Dixie said. Danny felt that he had said something wrong, but he didn't know what.

"Listen," Les went on, his smile returning. "There's another way to get down from here." He looked around swiftly to make sure no one was watching.

"Go on," Dixie said, smiling.

"Turn your back to me," Les said. Danny did as he was told. Les put his arms under Danny's armpits, then locked his hands behind Danny's head.

"Ready?" Les said.

"Ready for whaaa—" Before Danny had a chance to react, Les had launched himself from the edge of the balcony.

Danny had never been so scared in his life, the ground rushing toward them at a hundred miles an hour. Then he felt the arms around him take his weight, and he could hear a rustling, whispering sound as his friend's wings cut the air.

"We're flying," Danny gasped as the wind blew through his hair.

"More like gliding," Les shouted over his shoulder, "but I kind of like it. If the old Messengers saw me doing this they'd have kittens."

It took seconds, really, but it felt like much longer. They had almost reached the ground when Les shouted again.

"Hold on tight!" he said. "I've never been any good at landing."

"Now you tell meeeeeee . . ." Danny hit the ground

face-first and plowed along for several yards before Les bounced back into the air again and flipped over, so that Danny was looking straight up at the sky. Les tried to turn around again but only succeeded in doing a somersault, then a double flip, before both boys came to a crashing halt upside down in a holly bush.

"Ouch," Danny groaned, picking himself gingerly out of the bush. "You need to practice."

"Sorry about that," Les said ruefully. "Thought I had it cracked just before we hit."

"Wouldn't it be great," Dixie said, coming down the stairs, "if we all had wings?"

And she wandered off across the lawn, flapping her arms like a bird. They watched her until she reached the edge of the lawn, then disappeared from sight behind a privet hedge.

"Isn't she a little . . . unusual . . . to be a spy?" Danny asked.

"She is a bit barmy, all right," Les said, a tone of admiration in his voice, "but she ain't stupid. Just sees the world a different way from the rest of us."

"I suppose so."

"Listen," Les said a bit awkwardly, "I got something I need to do. Will you be all right for a few hours?"

"Yes, no problem," Danny said. He didn't mind the idea of a few hours on his own. He could plan what he was going to say tomorrow at the induction. He might even find a way to escape before then. And even if he didn't find the means to escape, he had the right to refuse

70

to be inducted, and after that they would hardly force him to stay.

"Brilliant," Les said. "I'll see you later, then. You need anything, ask Vandra. She might have a bit of a family history, but she's the salt of the earth."

Danny wondered what the family history might be. He remembered Vandra's two vampirelike teeth. . . . Surely not.

It was still cold, but the sun had come out and he thought he would explore the grounds of Wilsons. He could get an idea of how you got in and out of the place and what lay beyond it.

Devoy watched Danny from the library of the third landing. One of the other cadets had probably told the boy about the induction, he thought. And that he had the right to accept or refuse. Devoy wondered if Brunholm had considered that Danny might say no when he had paid Fairman to bring the boy across the frontier.

To be fair to Brunholm, his plan had a lot to recommend it. On the downside, though, it was dangerous, especially for Danny. Brunholm's plans never took any account of the fact that they had to be carried out by people of flesh and blood.

Danny seemed intelligent, and capable of learning, though whether he could learn what he needed in the short time available remained to be seen. And he could still refuse. That was the big difference between Wilsons and the Ring: with the Ring you had no option. Devoy sighed. Sometimes he thought that was the only difference.

Danny started by finding a gravel path that led away from Wilsons. It was lined with old lime trees. He walked for a long time, moving further and further away from the building, and deeper and deeper into the trees. The limes gave way to ancient oaks covered in moss, and the dense canopy of branches above his head cast a deep gloom, despite the fact that there were no leaves. He was relieved when the oaks were replaced by lime trees again, and then amazed when he reemerged in exactly the same spot where he had set out!

He went out into the garden and heard tea being called from a speaker concealed in the bushes somewhere. He saw some other cadets ahead of him and followed them to Ravensdale at a discreet distance.

Ten minutes later he was sitting at the table in Ravensdale with Les and the others. He smiled at Vandra, but she looked away.

"You missed it," Les said excitedly. "Brunholm was in a right old strop about that statue that nearly hit you. Took us all in one by one and asked us to 'account for our movements.'"

"I said there was no accounting for my movements," Dixie told them. "I just . . . flow." Danny looked at her to see if she was joking, but her face was serious.

"Then there's the statue supposedly falling on this

boy who has the anatomical features of a Cherb," the boy with large, blinking eyes said.

"Yeah, well. Exspectre, you have all the anatomical features of a bush baby, but it don't mean you are one," Les said.

Dixie stifled a giggle. Exspectre looked at Les without expression, then turned away.

"Not a whole lot of fun, that one," Les whispered to Danny. "Ah, here comes grub."

They ate in silence, although Danny was aware of eyes on him. Vandra, perhaps, or Smyck. Or even Exspectre, blinking over his plate.

When they were finished, Blackpitt came on the speakers and announced, "Study," then, in a not-very-low whisper, added, "Did you hear we had Inspector McGuinness in today? Verrrry exciting."

"Poor old Blackpitt," Les said, "he does love a good bit of gossip."

Danny followed Les up a set of marble stairs. The cadets chattered among themselves as they walked. Danny got some unfriendly glances, and some openly curious ones. He tried to work out how many cadets thought he was really a Cherb, but gave up. He wouldn't be here long enough for it to worry him.

They walked through a curious domed marble room with a walkway around the top of it, about twenty feet above their head.

"What's that?" Danny asked.

"The Gallery of Whispers," Les said. "They say that if you ask a question at one side, your voice will travel all

73

the way around the room and return with the answer. They also say that there is always a snare in the answer."

"It comes in your own voice too," Dixie said, putting on a spooky voice herself.

"You can't get to it from here," Les said, seeing the way Danny was eyeing it. "If you're thinking of trying to ask it who tried to drop a statue on your head, it's forbidden to go up there. Unauthorized entry to the gallery is a Ninth Regulation offense. The answers are supposed to be really tricky, so I suppose Devoy thinks we're not bright enough to work them out."

They passed under the Gallery of Whispers and emerged into a long, high-ceilinged study hall. There were desks in rows, and a high table at the top, where Miss Duddy sat scrutinizing the students as they entered.

"Desk number seventeen, Caulfield," she piped up. The high desk had new books piled on it.

"We do an hour's study," Les whispered, "then we're free."

Danny looked up and saw something moving in the dim-lit rafters. There was a fluttering sound, and then another. Shadows of wings were thrown against the wall, huge and dark.

"What's that?" Danny whispered.

"Only the ravens," Les whispered back. "They're kind of the symbol of Wilsons. They say that the ravens were a gift from the Fifth himself!"

"Caulfield and Knutt, a First Regulation offense each," Miss Duddy intoned. "Whispering in Study."

Les groaned and turned his eyes to heaven. He pointed Danny to a desk and sat down at his own, which was covered in an untidy sprawl of books and papers. One by one the other cadets took their seats, and silence fell over the hall, broken only by the rustle of paper.

Danny looked at the pile of books in front of him. There were titles like *From the Bosporus to Oxford: One Spy's Journey; Basic Inks; How to See and Not Be Seen; Political Assassination: A Brief Guide;* and *Spycraft: An Intermediate-Level Reader.*

He opened the most promising-looking one, which was called *Poisons: A History.* An upbeat introduction promised "an introduction to the marvelous world of poisoners and poison." He soon found himself lost in a world of queens murdered by asp bites, and hollowed-out rings for holding poisons. There were drawings of people writhing in agony and turning black while still seeming to have a cheerful smile on their faces, as though it was a privilege to be poisoned by some new and wonderful strain of deadly nightshade. He looked up and saw that Toxique, the trainee assassin, was watching him. He pointed wordlessly to the cover of Danny's book and nodded grim approval.

Danny then picked up a dull-looking book on the nature and composition of invisible inks, which seemed to be full of mathematical symbols for the chemistry of inks. Above his head there was more fluttering. He looked up to see a line of ravens. They were sitting on a beam almost directly above his head looking at him, heads cocked to one side, their beady eyes unblinking. He started to feel uncomfortable. Why were they watching him? Perhaps they thought he was a Cherb as well.

He looked around the hall. Les had his head buried in a book, but was so still that Danny thought he must be asleep. Dixie was making strange movements with her hands, as though building an imaginary structure in the air. She flashed him a quick smile and went back to her work.

He couldn't concentrate on any of the books, and the minutes stretched out. It was a relief when Blackpitt announced, "End of study. Take your weary brains off to bed. Pay attention to flossing and oral hygiene. Prevention is better than cure," he added bossily.

Danny stood up to go. As he did so, something fell from the rafters above and landed with a splat in the middle of his desk, narrowly missing his head. He looked up. There was only one raven left, but it had its beak open, and if he hadn't known better, he would have said it was laughing.

The cadets made their way toward Ravensdale. As they walked, Les grasped Danny by the elbow.

"Quick. I need you for a minute."

Danny followed Les to the entrance hall. Valant stood at the desk, laboriously copying something into a huge ledger.

"Distract him," Les whispered, then darted off into the shadows beside the fireplace, giving Danny a shove in the back that sent him staggering into the middle of the floor.

"Yes?" Valant said, raising an eyebrow. Danny thought frantically. Out of the corner of his eye he could just see Les creeping toward the desk, clinging to the shadow of the wall, moving silently.

"We must be careful, Mr. Valant," Danny said. His voice came out slow and grave. "There are shadowy forces at work out there."

Valant looked at him suspiciously.

"Of course there are shadowy forces at work," Valant said, "this is a school for spies, Cadet Caulfield."

Danny was aware that Les was moving quickly toward the open door behind Valant's back. He hesitated. He knew that to keep Valant's interest, he had to give him something interesting. Otherwise the man would just dismiss him as a show-off. He put one elbow on the counter and leaned forward confidentially. Valant looked around and moved closer. Danny kept a straight face, but his mind was searching desperately for something that he could use. Then the headline in the paper he had seen when he was at the Stores came into his head. He beckoned Valant closer. Behind the man, Les had reached the shelves, his wings only a foot away from the back of Valant's legs.

"I hear," Danny said in a low voice, "that Sranzer is still missing."

The effect on Valant was electric. One wiry hand shot forward and grabbed the front of Danny's shirt.

"What do you mean?" Valant said, his voice low and furious. "What do you know about Sranzer, boy?"

Danny gasped. Both because Valant was half choking him and because he had seen Les climb up the shelves with incredible speed, then turn so that he was hanging upside down with his ankles hooked over the top shelf. His fingers riffled through the keys that were hanging on a board directly behind Valant's head.

"I . . . I . . . ," Danny gasped as Les selected a key and, with a quick thumbs-up, swung himself upright again and pocketed it.

"I . . . I only saw it in the paper . . . at the Stores . . . ," Danny managed to squeeze out. Valant regarded him with deep suspicion, but loosened his grip.

"You'd better be careful what names you bandy around here, boy," Valant said. "There's many a one would dearly love to know what happened to Sranzer."

Valant looked around and put his face so close to Danny's that Danny could smell the musty odor of the man's breath. "Don't let me hear you mention that name again. Do you hear me?" Danny nodded. With relief he could see that Les had made his way to the corner of the room. Danny backed away. Valant's burning eyes fixed on his face. Danny kept backing up until he got to the door, then turned and bolted out of the room.

Les was waiting for him in the corridor, grinning and dangling a large iron key.

"Good work, Danny," he said. "Kind of funny, though, the way Valant jumped at you when you said that name—what was it? Sranzer?"

"Don't ever do that to me again," Danny said furiously, rubbing his neck. "He nearly strangled me!"

"Worth it, though," Les said. "I got the key."

"What key?" Danny snapped, still cross.

78

"The key that opens the upper floors of Wilsons. We need to get a look at how that statue fell on you."

"We don't know what's up there. It could be dangerous."

"What? Dangerous like someone dropping a statue on your head?"

Danny hesitated, but part of him did want to get a look at the mysterious upper floors.

"Okay, but just me and you," he said firmly. Les nodded quickly.

Danny went to bed fully dressed, and tried to stay awake, but he must have dozed off, for the next thing he knew, Les was shaking him by the arm.

"Wake up!" Les whispered. Danny sat up in bed and swung his legs out. He slipped on his shoes. Outside, rain drummed on the roofs of the Roosts and the wind howled.

"Are you sure about this?" Danny whispered.

Les grinned. "Let's go." On tiptoe they crossed to the door, eased it open and slipped out into the night. Rain whipped across Danny's face, and below them the tops of the trees tossed like a stormy sea.

"Come on!" Les shouted, his voice almost drowned by the wind. Danny moved round to the front of the Roosts, and felt the full force of the storm. His clothes were soaked in seconds. Les bent to the gate that protected the gangway to the main building. Within seconds it sprang open. He handed Danny a torch.

"You'll need this," he yelled. "It won't be seen. There'll be nobody about in this weather anyway."

Les stepped onto the gangway. Danny followed, grabbing the handrails as he felt the bridge flex and sway in the howling wind, which was doing its best to snatch him and propel him into the darkness below.

It got worse as they crossed. The gangway dipped in the middle and the two boys' weight set up a pendulum effect in the wind, so that all they could do was cling desperately to the rails, moving neither forward nor back. The torch beams swung wildly in the dark. Danny could feel his arms start to ache from holding on. The wind rose to a crescendo, then momentarily fell away.

"Now!" Danny shouted. "Run!"

Pushing Les hard in the back, he ran after the winged boy, who slipped and slid on the wet planks. As the wind lashed at the gangway, they reached the door at the end. Les fumbled for the key and with numbed fingers put it in the lock. Although the lock looked old and rusted, the key turned with ease, the door opened and the two boys fell into the gloom on the other side. The door slammed shut behind them. They were in.

But they had not been unobserved. Down below, a pair of shrewd eyes had followed them, and had watched the torch beams in the darkness. Now McGuinness stepped back into the partial shelter of the wall behind him. The two boys might find more than they bargained for in the upper floors of Wilsons, but that wasn't his concern. His job was to stop crime, nothing more.

8

THE MAID OF THE NORTH SHORE

Danny shone his torch around the room. It had bare walls and a high vaulted ceiling.

"Turn off the big torch," Les said, taking a smaller flashlight from his pocket.

"So what now?" Danny asked.

"All we got to do," Les said, "is to get to the floor above this one. That's where the statue was."

Danny looked around him doubtfully. Who knew what secrets the upper floors held?

"All right," he said, "let's get this over with."

Danny went to the door in the wall opposite and eased it open. Beyond it was nothing more sinister than a corridor lined with doors, dimly lit by a single bulb in the middle. Each door had a nameplate on it. There was MR. M. BRUNHOLM, and MASTER DEVOY, MISS R. DUDDY, and on a shabby disused door, MR. S. PILKINGTON. Danny remembered the photograph of the legendary spy in Ravensdale, and realized with a pang that he had thrown the spy's coat aside without a further thought.

They crept past Brunholm's door carefully. Les paused at Duddy's door. From within there came the sound of loud snoring. Stifling a laugh, they crept on.

The corridor opened into a dining room that was obviously used by the instructors, and continued into another room with comfortable leather armchairs. There were piles of exercise books sitting around, and report cards on the polished wooden table. The room looked just like the staff room at school, Danny thought, apart, that is, from the display of blowpipes on the wall, over a case full of brightly colored darts with a notice saying POISON! DO NOT TOUCH!

At the far end of the room Danny spotted a staircase leading up.

"That looks like the one we need," he whispered. His nervousness was now replaced with a growing sense of dread. "Les, come on!" he said. Les had stopped in front of a small silver-colored door with a barred window.

"I wonder what's in here," he mused.

"Les, please," Danny begged. With a strange reluctance and several backward glances, Les moved away from the door.

The two boys climbed the staircase, which seemed to be barely used. Thick dust rose from the boards each time they put their feet down. Halfway up, there was a window. Danny peered out and could see the niche where the statue had stood.

"That's funny," he whispered, withdrawing his head and staring at the floor.

"What?" Les said.

"Look at the floor." Danny pointed. The floor was covered with undisturbed dust. "Whoever pushed the statue wasn't standing here. They would have left a foot-print."

"We better take a closer look. Maybe there's some kind of opening we can't see."

The staircase ended at a landing. Again, it looked as if nobody ever came this way. Old furniture and carpets were stacked in one corner, and great sheets of cobwebs hung from the ceiling. A single door led off to the left. Les gently turned the handle. The door swung silently open.

"Look at this," Les said quietly. The hinges had been recently oiled.

"I don't like this," Danny said. "We should go."

"One quick look," Les said, "since we came this far."

Feeling the hairs rise on the back of his neck, Danny stepped into the room, followed by Les.

The furniture was covered in white dust sheets, ghostly in the flickering beam of the torch. The two boys made their way to the window. Danny had been right. There was no way that anyone could have got near enough to the statue to topple it toward Danny far below. And yet it could not have fallen on its own.

"A mystery," Les said. "Might as well take a quick

look around the room, doesn't look as if anyone would miss anything. . . ."

"I hope you're not thinking of . . . of . . . taking anything that doesn't belong to you," Danny said.

"You mean stealing it," Les said cheerfully. "Only if it looks as if nobody has any use for it. . . ." He flicked back one of the dust sheets and froze.

"Look at this." Danny went over and found himself looking at a long iron bed with shackles at each corner. There was a large handle at one end.

"What is it?"

"A rack." Les looked pale. "They have them in the Lower World. You put a prisoner on it and stretch them until they confess."

Les threw back another sheet to reveal a shelf of vicious-looking instruments.

"Thumb-screws, teeth pullers, flesh pincers . . ." Les ran his fingers along the shelf.

"Look at this." Danny threw back another sheet. There was an electrical generator with bull clips on the end of wires. "They don't . . ."

" 'Fraid they do, Danny."

There was a brazier under another sheet, with branding irons neatly stacked in it. A sheet hung over a large upright object. Danny knew that it wasn't a good idea, but he caught a corner of the sheet and pulled.

"I think I've seen this on TV," he said queasily. It was a hollow iron figure the size and shape of a man. His hand trembling, he took hold of the catch at one side. The front of the figure swung open. On the inside, long spikes pointed inward. "What . . . ?" Les began.

"It's an iron maiden," Danny said. "They make you stand in it, then close it. The spikes . . ."

"Even the Ring never did that," Les said quietly. "Let's get out of here."

They threw the sheets back over the torture instruments and left the room quietly. Danny was shivering, even though it was not cold. His friend's face was pale. Neither of them looked up, or they would have seen the sign: DEPARTMENT OF INFORMATION EXTRACTION.

Moving swiftly and silently, the two boys went down the stairs. They were halfway across the dark staff room when they heard the voice. Danny froze in his tracks, an icy hand running down his spine.

"Help me," a woman said, low and desperate.

Les had stopped dead as well. The two boys looked at each other, the whites of their eyes showing in the dark.

"Help me, please." It was a low, musical voice, sad and full of despair. Les was first to react. He went to the little silver door. The barred window framed a woman's face. A pale face, a little careworn, perhaps, but still beautiful. She had long blond hair and deep green eyes, which she kept cast down. Her small hands gripped the bars as if they were the only things holding her up. Danny could feel his heart go out to her. She glanced up at them quickly, then looked down again, as though she scarcely dared hope that someone would help her.

"Brunholm," she murmured, "he is holding me

85

prisoner here—a hostage. He means to send me to the Cherbs. I do not need to tell you boys what might happen to me there." A tear ran down her cheek.

"But who are you?" Danny said. "Why is he keeping you locked up like this?"

"It is a long story," she sighed. "Brunholm and Master Devoy are suspicious of anyone they can't control. I suppose that is what happens in time of war."

Danny found that he was only half listening to her words. She glanced up at him again, holding his eye until he felt like telling her everything that had happened to him since he had got to Wilsons, knowing that she was the only person who would understand. He could see that Les was enthralled as well.

"If only I could just slip away into the night, far away from here . . ." She gulped back a little sob.

Les had his lockpicks in his hand and was working dreamily at the lock on the door, all the time staring into her big green eyes. Danny vaguely felt that he should stop his friend, but that feeling was overridden by a longing that she would switch her gaze from Les to him. . . .

With a gentle click the door swung open. The two boys stood back as though a queen was about to enter the room. Smiling, she stepped forward. She was small, about the same height as Danny, and she wore a green dress that shimmered as she moved. There was something girlish about her, even though Danny suspected that she was much older.

"That's better," she purred. "And to whom do I owe my freedom?"

"I—I'm Danny, and h-he's Les," Danny stammered, feeling his face redden.

"Thank you, Danny and Les."

"Who . . . who are you," Les stuttered, "if you don't mind me asking . . ."

"Me? I'm Victoria, Maid of the North Shore, the Siren of the Two Worlds. But you can just call me Vicky—that's what my friends call me."

"Siren of the Two Worlds . . . ," Danny said. "Isn't a siren a woman who . . ."

"Yes, yes," she said dismissively, "lures ships onto the rocks, drives sailors mad with love so that they throw themselves overboard and drown—that sort of thing. That's kind of my stock-in-trade, keeps things ticking over, so to speak, but I've been trying my hand at a bit of spying and treachery this past while. Things are a bit slow in the drowned sailors line."

There was no sign of the sorrowful voice and the downcast eyes now, and Danny was beginning to feel that perhaps they had acted a little hastily in letting the siren out of her prison.

"Now," she said briskly, "I'll just take a few minutes to do for old Brunholm, and I'll be out of here."

" 'Do for old Brunholm'?" Danny could feel his heart sinking to his boots. "What do you mean?"

"It's just too good a chance to miss," Vicky said, picking up a blowpipe and running her eye along the row of poison darts.

"I don't think that's a good idea, really," Danny said. Vicky turned to him and raised one eyebrow. Les gave

Danny a look that said, Don't argue with a siren with a blowpipe in one hand.

"Who made you the boss around here?" Vicky said, her eyes narrowed in a way that made him think she was measuring the distance between them.

"No one," Danny said quickly, "it's just that the last person I saw hit by a poison dart . . . well, they turned black and swelled up and squealed really loudly. If the whole place wakes up, you might end up back in the cell."

"Not that we wouldn't fight for you," Les added. "But there's only two of us."

Vicky looked regretfully at the blowpipe in her hand.

"I suppose you're right," she said. "Never thought of that. I could strangle him, but you never know with Brunholm—you don't really want to get close to him. . . . I suppose I'll leave it for now."

Danny almost collapsed in relief. He wasn't very fond of Brunholm, but he didn't want to see him hit by a poison dart.

"Well, I suppose I better be making tracks," Vicky said, tossing the blowpipe onto the floor. "All I can say to you two is, I owe you one."

She glided over to them and planted a kiss on each of their cheeks. Danny smelt a perfume that was sweet, but with an undertone of dark fishy ocean depths.

"Bye," she said, and in a moment she had disappeared into the gloomy corridor.

"Phew," Les said, "that was close. When was the last time you saw somebody hit by a poison dart?"

"Never," said Danny. "I had to make up something."

"I thought I was supposed to be the liar around here," Les said. "But at least she's gone."

"Yes," Danny groaned, "she is gone. What have we done?"

"Yes indeed," a grave voice said behind them, "what have you done?" The two spun around. Devoy was standing in the doorway wearing pajamas and carrying a candle.

"Come with me, boys," he said.

They followed Devoy to his office. Danny could see the whites of Les's eyes in the dark corridor.

"Mr. Blackpitt?" Devoy spoke out into the darkness.

"Who's that?" a sleepy voice said from a speaker mounted onto a beam overhead. "What do you want?"

"It is Devoy," the master said. "I am sorry to wake you, but the siren has escaped. I want you to see if you can locate her in the building."

"Yes, Mr. Devoy, I'll let you know," Blackpitt said politely. But just before the speaker crackled and went silent, they heard him mutter something about "If they can't keep a siren under lock and key, what hope do they have against the Ring?" If Devoy heard it, he gave no sign.

They reached Devoy's office. The two boys stood in the middle of the floor. Devoy sat down behind the desk. He folded his hands.

"Does either of you know what disinformation is?" Devoy said.

"It's like in a war—you tell lies to the enemy to make them think . . . things, sort of . . ." Danny started well but ended lamely.

89

"Yes, well, you are going in the right direction," Devoy said. "You lead the enemy to believe that you are stronger than you actually are. Spreading disinformation is a very great part of spying. Take Wilsons. Our survival depends on the Ring thinking that we are stronger than we in fact are."

Danny watched Devoy with a sinking feeling in his stomach. There was more to their release of the siren than they had thought.

"The siren operation was my idea. We captured her last week. We were going to feed her false information. Then we would let her escape. She would go to the Ring and sell them the false information, thus helping to protect Wilsons."

There was a long silence in the office. Danny could feel the tension in Les's body beside him.

"Your intervention has prevented that. Now the siren is loose in the building. She was very difficult to capture first time round. I have several nasty scratches to prove it."

"We were only trying to find out who was trying to kill Danny," Les cried.

"Perhaps," Devoy said. "Did you find anything useful?" There was a long silence.

"We found out that the statue couldn't have been pushed," Danny said.

"Mr. McGuinness has already established that," Devoy replied. "Anything else?" Another pause ensued. "I thought not. For you, Mr. Caulfield, this is a first offense, although grave, and it does not merit a Tenth

Regulation offense. For you, Mr. Knutt, it is different. You do deserve such an offense. You are expelled from Wilsons."

Danny looked at Les. His face had gone ashen, and he swayed and would have fallen if Danny had not taken his arm. He wet his lips as if he would speak, but although his mouth opened, no words came out.

"No," Danny said slowly, "the whole thing was my idea."

"Really?" Devoy said. "So it was you who stole the key from Mr. Valant, was it?"

Danny shook his head.

"How . . . how did you know about the key?" Les said, finding his voice.

"It is the only way you could have got in. The lock is unpickable."

"If he goes, then I go," Danny said firmly.

"Don't do this, Danny," Les said. "I'm not that important."

Danny took a deep breath. "If you expel Les, I won't go on your operation against the Ring of Five. I mean it."

Devoy's eyes fell on Danny's face and stayed there for a long time. Danny felt a bead of sweat trickle down his back. He knew that Devoy was a proud and complicated man, and that he had crossed a line with the master.

"Very well," Devoy said. His expression as usual did not change, but his voice was like ice. "Knutt stays, for the moment. Return the key to Valant in the morning. Remember that this is more than a school. This is the front line against an enemy that could destroy us all."

Devoy watched the door close behind the two boys. Danny had stuck up for his friend. It showed admirable loyalty, he thought—probably too much. But then, neither of them had mentioned the Department of Information Extraction, which showed an encouraging tendency toward concealing facts. The instruments in the department had not been used since Longford had deserted and betrayed Wilsons. If Devoy had his way, they would be destroyed, yet Brunholm had a way of working their existence into conversation. . . .

When they got out of the room, the two boys ran as fast as they could to the bridge.

"Thanks," Les said, panting. "I really thought I was a goner that time."

"You would have done it for me," Danny said. There was a quaver in his voice. He had not been as confident as he looked in facing down Devoy.

"You don't know how much it means," Les said.

There was a strange tone in his friend's voice, and Danny looked over at him, but couldn't see his face in the dark.

They reached the door to the bridge and unlocked it. Les stowed the key in his jacket as they stepped out. The storm had subsided a little and the gangway was easier to cross. But this time two pairs of eyes watched them as they crossed. Below, McGuinness watched without expression from under the dripping brim of his hat. And from her perch high on the rooftop, the siren watched them.

THE UNKNOWN SPY

The morning was a blur of rising and getting dressed and teeth brushing, with an irritated-sounding Blackpitt muttering through the speakers about how the place was going to the dogs and in the old days cadets were up and dressed before dawn.

"Never mind him," Les said. "He's always grumpy in the morning."

They raced down the stairs and across the lawn to Ravensdale, where they wolfed down bacon and pancakes.

"Did you sleep okay?" Dixie asked Danny.

"Fine, thanks," he said.

"I dreamed about a faraway world," Dixie said. Danny waited for her to go on, but she didn't, just sat with her fork raised and a thoughtful look in her eyes. Danny grinned to himself. He was getting used to Dixie.

"What class do we have this morning?" Danny asked. He tried to look eager, as if a morning of invisible inks or codes was just the thing.

"Double maths and geography," Vandra said shortly.

"Oh," Danny said. "You get to do that stuff here as well?"

"Course we do," Smyck said. "You wouldn't be much of a spy if you couldn't read or write, would you?"

"How do you spell 'Cherb'?" Exspectre said, making a wheezing, gasping sound that Danny realized was a laugh.

That's it, Danny thought, I'm definitely getting out of here.

He followed the others out of Ravensdale. They turned left and went through an archway in the hall. Danny stayed toward the back of the group, looking for a chance to get away. He got his opportunity when he saw two doors side by side. One had a male figure on it wearing a cloak and a top hat, the cloak pulled up so that his face was concealed. There was a revolver in his hand. The other had a woman on it, with a scarf concealing her head, and a long stiletto blade in her hand. The signs were a bit over the top, Danny thought, but the toilets would be an ideal place to hide until the others had gone ahead. He let them walk on for a moment, then ducked in.

He closed the door carefully behind him, and stood there listening. Not a sound. When he was sure that the others were gone, he turned to take stock of his surroundings, and realized that the place did not look remotely like a toilet. In fact, it looked like only a small hallway, with a hat stand in one corner and a door, which, as he watched it, began to swing open. Moving slowly, reluctantly, yet as if compelled to do so, Danny stepped through the door.

He found himself in a darkened room. He could dimly see a large bookcase to his left and a marble fireplace to his right. In front of him, large curtains hung from ceiling to floor. And in front of the curtains was a large mahogany desk, behind which sat a shadowy figure.

"One more move," a man's voice said, a voice that was educated but weary beyond measure, "one more step into the room and I'll blow your treacherous head off."

Danny froze. Even by the standards of Wilsons, he hadn't expected this. He peered into the gloom and realized that the man sitting behind the desk looked just like the figure he had seen depicted on the door: the same hat and cloak drawn up over his face, the same deadly-looking revolver in his hand.

"So the Ring has taken to sending Cherbs against me." The man gave a harsh laugh. "They think I have dropped my guard after all these years."

"I'm not a Cherb," Danny said quickly, "really I'm not, I only look like one. My name's Danny Caulfield."

The man sat up. His dark eyes scrutinized Danny.

"Not a Cherb," the man said, as if thinking aloud. "Perhaps the boy is telling the truth. It would be strange if a Cherb denied what was plain to see. Yes, it could be true."

Danny's heart leapt. He stayed very still, not wanting to sway the man's thinking.

"But then," the voice went on tiredly, "perhaps it is a

bluff. A Cherb pretending not to be a Cherb, knowing that it is so unlikely that I will accept it. No, better to shoot and be damned."

The man sat up and raised the gun.

"Wait," Danny said desperately. "If . . . if somebody was trying to bluff you, would it not be unlikely that they would send a real Cherb who was pretending not to be one, and would not realize that you would see through it?"

"That is true," the man said thoughtfully. "But then, they could send a Cherb pretending not to be one, expecting me to see through it, and you to point out to me how transparent it is, so that I would then be fooled that a real Cherb pretending not to be real is so see-through and clumsy that I would come around to believing that you are not exactly what you look like, which is in fact a Cherb."

"But anyone with any intelligence would expect you to work that out exactly," Danny said, his brain beginning to overheat, "and so . . . so that proves that I'm not a Cherb . . . I think . . . ," he finished lamely.

"I know, it's hard to work out all the possibilities," the man said, almost a kindly tone to his voice. "It's easier just to shoot you now and then we won't have to worry about it anymore."

"I'm not a Cherb!" Danny cried. "I just can't prove it."

"You know," the man said, "I nearly believe you. You're really very good, aren't you? But you see, if there's even the tiniest chance that you're a Cherb—you have to understand, the odds just aren't in your favor." The man sighted along the barrel. Danny shut his eyes, but just as he did so, he heard the door behind him open. Help at last! he thought. But that was before something cold and hard touched the nape of his neck.

"Don't move a muscle," a stern voice said— McGuinness!

"Who's there? Who's there?" the man behind the desk demanded, something like panic in his voice. "Don't move. I have bullets for the two of you."

"It's all right, sir," McGuinness said, holding up a badge beside Danny's ear. "Lower World Police, detective division. We'll take it from here."

The man peered at the badge in the gloom.

"How do I know you are who you say you are?"

"You may remember we sorted out a . . . situation for your wife last year." McGuinness coughed delicately.

"Ah yes, that was you? All right. You are who you say you are. But watch yourself. These Cherbs are pretty slippery."

"Don't worry, sir, I have the tip of my umbrella at his neck, loaded with class-one venom. He'd be dead before he hit the floor."

"Excellent, excellent. Well, Detective, be alert."

"I will, sir," McGuinness said smoothly, "and thank you for apprehending this villainous-looking sneak. We'll make sure he is taken care of."

"Very good, very good," the man said, keeping his gun trained on Danny as McGuinness backed him out the door. The last thing Danny saw was the man lowering the gun, and as he did so, his cloak slipped, revealing for a second a long mournful face—a face that was somehow familiar. . . .

But that was all. The door closed behind Danny. The umbrella was removed from his neck.

"Phew," Danny said. "Good bluff, about the poison in the umbrella tip."

"It wasn't a bluff," McGuinness said. Danny gulped.

"Who is he?" Danny asked. "The man in the room."

"The Unknown Spy," McGuinness said. "He and his wife were in deep cover on the other side for so long that they have both forgotten who they originally were."

"Deep cover?" Danny asked.

"I forgot, you're new. It's when a spy pretends to be someone else and goes and lives that person's life— sometimes for years—until they're needed by their spymaster. The Unknown Spy and his wife were gone for many years. When they came back they couldn't pick up the threads."

"He was pretty strange."

"What were you doing in there?" McGuinness asked, not raising his voice.

"The . . . the bathroom . . . ," Danny stammered. The detective wheeled to look at the door, then smiled grimly.

"Yes . . . I suppose I can see how the mistake could be made. But it should not have been made."

"I just . . . I had to go," Danny said, boldly building on the lie.

"Not that," McGuinness mused. "The fact is, this

door is always kept locked. But now it is open. The question is . . . was it unlocked for your benefit?"

McGuinness looked at Danny, who had the uncomfortable feeling that the policeman knew exactly why he had ducked into the room. Then McGuinness knelt to look at the base of the door, where there was a padlocked brass bolt that Danny hadn't noticed. The padlock was open. McGuinness took a magnifying glass from his pocket and scrutinized the lock. Danny leaned over until he could see through the glass, but all that was visible was a larger lock, with tiny scratches on it.

With a click McGuinness locked the padlock again and stood up.

"It's time you got to class," he said. "But I have to warn you—you must be alert. You may have been meant to go in there by someone who knew how dangerous the Unknown Spy can be in his confused state. Could be the second time you were meant to have an accident in two days."

"But who wants something to happen to me?"

McGuinness shook his head with a weary look as if to say there was no explaining the wickedness abroad in the world.

"If Detective McGuinness is finished," Blackpitt announced stiffly, "Cadet Caulfield is late for double maths. Take the first left, Cadet Caulfield."

"Wait a second," Danny said as McGuinness began to walk off. "What were you talking about in there—the bit of bother with the Unknown Spy's wife?"

"She got out through the window with that knife of

99

hers," McGuinness said without turning round, "just as a Cherb raiding party was coming across the lawn."

"What happened to them?" Danny asked.

"There was a lot of paperwork." McGuinness spoke over his shoulder. Danny watched until he was swallowed by the gloom under the arch.

TEXAS HOLD 'EM

The maths teacher was a small sallow man called Docterow, with a barely understandable accent, who motioned Danny to his seat with an irritable wave of his hand. Danny felt his heart sinking. He had never been any good at maths, and Docterow looked like the kind of teacher who couldn't understand why everyone wasn't as brilliant as he was. Danny sat down at a chipped desk and waited to be bored. Les gave him a questioning look.

"Tell you later," Danny whispered.

"What is your name?" Docterow demanded.

"Danny. Danny Caulfield."

"Mr. Caulfield. You will learn to think defensively and offensively. You will learn to feint, when to hide, when to stand and fight. Have you played these games?" He reeled off a list of names machine-gun style.

"Backgammonchessblackjackgocontractbridgetexas-hold'em."

"Er, chess, a bit," Danny said, surprised.

"Chess, a bit." Docterow looked down at him as if there was a bad smell in the room. "You either play chess or you don't. Which is it?"

"Er, play," Danny said.

"Get a chessboard from the cupboard," Docterow commanded. "Toxique? Make sure Miss Cole deals the cards fairly."

Danny looked over. Dixie was dealing a game of poker—probably the Texas hold 'em Docterow had been talking about. He watched her as she riffled the cards expertly from hand to hand and dealt to a group of other cadets. Les was at another table, holding a hand of cards. He looked over at Danny and grinned.

"Bridge," he mouthed. Danny was surprised. He thought bridge was a game for old people.

Toxique sat down opposite Danny and set out the chess pieces. He didn't look Danny in the face, and kept muttering under his breath. Danny could hear words like "death" and "suffering."

Danny wasn't really a chess player. He knew that the bishop moved diagonally, and that the pawns were the least important pieces, and that the object of the game was to capture the king, but apart from that he wasn't very good, and he could see straightaway that Toxique was an expert player. He cut apart Danny's defense from the start, and Danny thought that the game would only last for minutes. But then he noticed something. Every time Toxique had the opportunity to capture one of Danny's pieces, he turned aside. It was almost as if he couldn't bring himself to knock them off the board. Once Danny saw this he was able to attack Toxique's king with ease and soon had won the game. The next game went the same way, except that Toxique's muttering increased. Docterow watched the game for a minute and raised his eyebrows when Toxique passed up a chance to take Danny's queen.

"You have to be ruthless, Toxique." He hissed the word "ruthless."

Danny started to feel sorry for the boy. He had stopped muttering now, so when he spoke, Danny almost jumped out of his seat.

"You're not a Cherb, are you?" he said in a low voice.

"No," Danny said, "of course not."

"I can tell these things. Just by looking at your face. Look at Les. He's going to cheat Spectre. He's going to slip a card out of his sleeve and deal it to him. I can see it in his face."

Danny looked. Les's face was absolutely still and un-readable. Yet Toxique was right. Watching carefully, Danny could see that when Exspectre asked for a card, Les swiftly and expertly shook one out of his sleeve and into his palm.

"Vandra's got a terrible hand," Toxique said, "but she's bluffing that she's holding aces. Dixie knows she's bluffing and she's about to call her out."

Exactly as Toxique had forecast, Dixie called Vandra's bluff and won the hand.

"That's incredible!" Danny exclaimed.

"Not very," Toxique said. "I can tell something else from your face."

"What?"

"That you're trying to get out of here."

Before Danny had a chance to reply, Docterow came up behind them again. He moved Danny to the poker game. To Danny's surprise, he found that he was good at it.

"Poker is a game of the mind," Docterow said. "You have to learn how to read your opponent's face while concealing your own thoughts."

"Danny's too good at this," Dixie said, "I don't know how to read his face."

And indeed Danny found that he could keep his face very still. Soon he was winning hand after hand.

The next class was geography. As Danny began to file into the classroom he saw a woman with bushy hair standing at the head of the class. She was wearing old-fashioned goggles pushed up onto her forehead. When she saw Danny she reached behind herself and snatched up a wooden-backed blackboard duster from under the blackboard. In the same smooth movement she threw the duster at Danny's head. It ricocheted off his temple with a resounding thwok, half stunning him and sending him staggering several paces backward.

Beside him he could hear Les's low whistle at the aim and execution of the throw.

"That Spitfire," Les said, his voice full of admiration, "what a woman!"

"Get that boy out of my classroom," the woman said, her voice clear, almost musical in contrast to the violence of her actions. "There should be no uninducted cadets in this class." She peered into the gloom at Danny. "Are you all right, dear? I threw underarm since you're a new boy." Danny nodded groggily. "Good, good," she went on. "Now kindly leave the room. Knutt, replenish the ammo." Les hesitated, then picked up the duster and brought it back to her. He came back to Danny and steered him by the arm out the door.

"See you after class," he whispered apologetically.

Danny stood uncertainly in the corridor. Every time he went somewhere on his own something happened to him, and he was getting a little tired of it, so he resolved not to move. There was a comfortable-looking armchair with a strangely shaped back in a little alcove off the corridor, so he sat down in that to wait for the others to finish.

He found a pile of well-thumbed magazines on the table beside the chair, and he picked up the top one and began to look through it. It was called *On Wings of Gold,* and it was full of photographs of Messengers getting awards for things like ballroom dancing and quilt making and flower arranging. There were advertisements for ointments to rub on aching wing joints, and a product promising to "bring out your natural feather color," with a lady Messenger half turned and smiling broadly as she showed off a very unnaturally bright pair of silver wings. Danny particularly liked the ad that said "Fed up with carrying those heavy wings around all day?" and showed a grumpy Messenger sporting what looked like a corset worn backward.

The next magazine in the pile was called *Perils of the*

Air and seemed devoted to showing how dangerous flying was. There were drawings of spindly Messengers plummeting to the ground, or in midair collisions, or being struck by lightning as they flew perilously near to thunderclouds. There were pages of stories about real-life disasters—whole squadrons of Messengers who took off and were lost over the "Bodminster Triangle," and a tale of a flight of Messengers lost in snowy peaks who survived for days—with dark hints that some of the survivors were driven to eat the others.

The back pages of *Perils of the Air* were given over to handy hints on what to do if someone closed a car door on your wings, and how to avoid getting sucked into the intake of a jet engine. Danny was so fascinated that he didn't notice when a tall shadow fell over him.

"Errr . . . hem!" The throat clearing was like a gunshot, and Danny leapt to his feet in surprise, scattering magazines all around him. A Messenger stood in front of him. He was tall with long sideburns, and wore a threadbare lounge suit with black shoes that might once have been elegant but were now scuffed and battered. He had a long nose, and he looked down it at Danny as though he was sighting along the barrel of a gun.

"I knew things had gone to pot at Wilsons," he said, his voice like that of a professor who has found his prize student cheating, "but I didn't think we had gone so far as allowing a Cherb to sit in my chair, reading my magazines."

"I'm not a Cherb," Danny said, hurriedly picking up the magazines.

"I suppose not," the Messenger said. "If you were I would have had a knife in my throat by now. Where did you come from, anyway?"

Danny hesitated. He wasn't really sure where he was, which made it difficult to say where he had come from.

"Never mind," the Messenger said with a mirthless chuckle, "you're probably one of Brunholm's nasty little schemes. Excuse me, please."

He sat down in the chair and breathed a sigh of relief as he sank into it.

"Much better."

Danny could see now why the back of the chair was strangely shaped—it was so that the Messenger's wings would fit.

"What's your name?" Danny asked.

"Gabriel," the Messenger said, "if it's any of your business. Come here; at the very least you can make yourself useful."

Danny moved closer. Gabriel pulled his own lower eyelid down, revealing an expanse of red-veined eyeball.

"Look closely," he growled. "Any sign of illness, yellowing or pus?"

Feeling a bit queasy, Danny peered into the eye.

"Looks okay to me," he said, withdrawing as soon as decently possible.

"Okay?" Gabriel barked. "Are you a doctor? How could it be okay?"

Gabriel, looking exhausted from his outburst, opened a magazine entitled *Wing and Feather Diseases* and commenced to ignore Danny.

Half relieved, Danny sat down on the floor. After a few minutes he decided that Gabriel wasn't going to speak to him again, so he cautiously slid a magazine from the bottom of the pile. This one was much older than the others. The paper was brittle and the colors were faded, and it was a moment before Danny realized he was holding it upside down. He turned it round the right way and squinted at the title.

Epic Journeys, he read. Must be epic journeys to the bathroom, he thought, if this lot were involved. He looked at the cover. At least on this one the Messenger was actually flying and wasn't about to crash or burst into flames or something. In fact, the Messenger looked exhausted but determined. He was wearing goggles, and ice had formed on them and on the edges of his wings. There were singe marks on the feathers as well, and orange bursts of flame in the background, as though someone was firing on him. Then Danny's eyes widened. He rubbed them and stared again.

"It's you," he exclaimed, "on the cover. It's you!"

"What? Eh? How did that get there? Give me that!" Gabriel snatched the magazine from Danny's hand and stuffed it into his pocket.

"You were flying!" Danny said. "And people were shooting at you . . ."

"You are mistaken, young man," Gabriel said stiffly, "and if you repeat this allegation of, of flying, then I will speak to Master Devoy himself."

"You can speak to him all you like," Danny said, "I'm out of here tomorrow."

Gabriel looked around, then bent down to Danny.

"Listen, boy," he whispered hoarsely, "what will you take to keep quiet about this?"

He straightened and began to fish in his pockets, but no matter how frantically he looked, he only came up with fluff and old tissues and a tube marked *Feather Gel*, which he stuffed quickly back into his pockets.

"Wings are decorative—that's all," he said, and Danny could see that he was upset. "All this flying nonsense . . . it's all in the past. It's not talked about. Simply not talked about."

"You've nothing to be ashamed of," Danny said.

"I'm not ashamed of anything," Gabriel said, looking anxiously up and down the corridor to see if anyone was coming.

"If you don't want me to mention it, I won't," Danny said.

"Really?" Gabriel seemed surprised.

"Honest."

"Well, thank you," Gabriel said, eyeing Danny suspiciously. But before he could say anything else, Blackpitt announced, "Class over," in a bored voice, and the door of the classroom burst open, the corridor filling with chattering cadets.

"Hello, Gabriel," Les said with a grin, "how's the wings hanging?"

Gabriel gave him a disgusted look and turned away. Les shrugged. It was obvious that Gabriel didn't think very much of him.

"Tell you what," Les said, not seeming particularly

worried by Gabriel's low opinion, "why don't we go outside for lunch. I've, er, come across a bit of grub."

"I've got some things to do," Dixie said, with a mysterious look. "I'll see you later."

Danny looked around. He wasn't sure if he really wanted to go outside, but no one else seemed to be taking Les up on his offer.

"I'll go," he said, and was rewarded with a pleased look from Les.

Danny followed Les out onto the lawn, half regretting his decision as the wind flung a handful of sleet into his face.

"Come on," Les said. "I want to show you something."

Les plunged into the trees opposite the lawn and Danny followed him. It was dark under the trees, and it was a while before Danny realized that they were following an overgrown path. The gravel had grass growing through it.

"I think I'm the only person who ever uses this," Les said, pushing branches aside and holding them to let Danny through.

After about five minutes the path emerged into a clearing. The trees surrounded it, cutting out the icy wind, and pale sunshine broke through so that the air felt warm. In the middle of the clearing was an old summerhouse, its wooden walls faded and its windows cracked and cobwebbed. Les made his way toward it.

The door of the summerhouse was stiff and squeaked in protest when Les put his weight against it, but inside the house was surprisingly warm and dry. It was dusty, and the windows were so dirty they were hard to see through, but there were faded cushions on the window seats, and two battered armchairs arranged in front of a stone fireplace. It smelt pleasantly of sun-warmed planks and wood fires.

"Here," Les said, producing a package from his inside pocket. There were cheese and pickle sandwiches and a large slice of chocolate cake, along with a bottle of lemonade.

When they had finished Danny lay back on a window seat, basking in the warm pool of sunlight coming through the window.

"Good place, this," he said. "How did you find it?"

"I don't remember," Les said.

"What do you mean?"

Les stayed quiet for a minute, then spoke in a low voice, staring out the window.

"When my mum and dad were killed I ran away from our house. I just kept running and running. I didn't know where I was going. Don't even remember that much of it. I was found here the next morning. Wilsons took me in."

Les had mentioned his parents' death before, but Danny had barely registered it. Now he looked at his friend and could see the pain in his eyes.

"What happened?" he asked gently.

"I don't really know," Les said. "The Cherbs came in the night. My mum or my dad must have got me out. All I remember is the Cherbs cheering and the house burning and me running as fast as I could. It was during the Uprising."

"The Uprising?"

"It's what they call the time when the Ring of Five emerged and joined up with the Cherbs. The Ring were looking for control of the Lower World and all. My mum and dad and the other folk there rose up against them. They thought they would win the fight. They didn't. They were put down by the Cherbs, and the Ring got control of most of the Lower World."

"I'm sorry about your mum and dad," Danny said quietly, a sudden wave of homesickness washing over him. His mother and father didn't seem very good at being parents, but he would have given anything to see their faces.

"You want to go home," Les said. "I don't blame you. I probably would too. I suppose Wilsons is my home now. Most of the cadets lost someone in the Uprising."

"Dixie too?"

"Her mum and dad died in the fighting. The Cherbs near broke through into the Upper World. Her mum and dad held out for hours till help arrived. She don't talk about it."

"What about Wilsons?"

"It's kind of all that's left. There's a ceasefire and an agreement that nobody crosses the border into the Upper World. But Master Devoy, he reckons the Ring is only waiting for an excuse to attack."

That name again. The Ring of Five. Danny didn't

know anything about them, but every time he heard the name a shiver of fear ran down his spine. And there was something else—a dark thrill that made him turn his head away in case it showed on his face.

"Who are they? The Ring, I mean?" Was it his imagination, or did the sun suddenly dim slightly as he spoke the name? Les looked troubled.

"The Ring," he said, almost under his breath. "I . . . I think I'd better let Master Devoy tell you about the Ring."

"Why?" Danny could see that Les was picking his words carefully.

"The Ring . . . well, nobody from the Upper World is supposed to really know anything about the Ring, and when . . ."

"When I go back home, you mean, after this evening?"

"It's not that I don't trust you," Les said, looking embarrassed.

"What you're saying is, if you told me, I might not be allowed to go back?" Danny said.

"That's what I was trying to say." Les breathed a long sigh of relief.

"Don't worry," Danny said. "I won't make you tell me if it means that I have to stay here!"

"Okay," Les said. "Time we were heading back."

"What's on this afternoon?"

"We just got one class this afternoon. IE."

"IE?"

"Illegal Entry. How to break into a place."

The two boys made their way back to Wilsons through the trees.

"So—you're kind of adopted by Wilsons, then?" Danny asked.

"Sort of."

"What about Dixie?"

"Dixie? She has an aunt and uncle at home she could stay with."

"Why doesn't she?"

"Dixie wants to be at Wilsons. When her mum was dying Dixie promised she'd help to put an end to the Ring. She's here because of that promise."

11

THE KNIFE
OF IMPLACABLE INTENTION

They cleared the gloom of the trees and emerged onto the lawn just in time to hear Blackpitt announce the beginning of the IE class.

"I didn't realize the time," Les said anxiously. "We better get going!"

They sprinted across the lawn and in through the side doors and plunged down a stone staircase.

"All the good stuff is in the basement," Les shouted back over his shoulder as they took the steps three at a time.

They raced along a corridor with doors opening off it every ten feet or so. Danny caught glimpses of a laboratory through one door; from behind others came the sounds of machines, and in one case what sounded like gunshots. Les skidded to a halt in front of a forbidding black door studded with brass nails.

"We're late," Les said.

"We can just apologize," Danny said.

"It mightn't be as easy as that." Les fished in his pocket for a set of lockpicks. As he flicked through them, Danny reached out for the brass door handle. It turned and the door swung silently open.

"See," Danny said, "easy." Les gave him a strained look, and as Danny made to step into the dark corridor beyond, Les pushed him back.

"I'll go first," he said. He moved gingerly over the threshold, checking each step before he put his foot on the ground and feeling the walls with his hands. Danny looked at him as if he had lost his mind. It was just a little corridor, and all they had to do was go through it into the classroom, where they could just apologize to the teacher. He opened his mouth to speak, then heard a small metallic sound. He looked up at the ceiling. A heavy metal spike that tapered to a deadly point was plummeting from the ceiling, heading straight for the top of Les's head.

"Look out!" Danny shouted, and dived forward. His shoulder caught Les in the small of the back, just below the wings. With an "Oof!" Les was thrown forward through the curtains at the other end of the little corridor, while behind them, Danny heard the spike strike the ground with a clang.

Danny slowly lifted his head. They had landed at the front of a class, right beside the instructor's desk. Danny could see faces looking down at him—Dixie grinning, Vandra looking stern and Smyck smirking.

"This must be our new pupil," a smooth voice said. Danny raised his eyes to see an oily-looking little man standing over him. His black hair was brushed over to one side and flattened down, and his beady eyes shone with malice and amusement.

"He and his thieving little friend," the man went on, "have provided us with a valuable lesson: when one is breaking into a premises, one must be ready to react to added defenses. Boys and girls, you do not drop your guard just because you are in the house and ready to plant your listening device or steal your secret documents. Take a seat, Knutt and Caulfield, and next time try to be prompt. My name, by the way, is Exshaw."

As they picked themselves up Les grinned at Danny. Danny didn't return the grin.

What sort of a place is this, he thought, where the punishment for being late is a spike through the back of the head?

The two boys dusted themselves off and sat down at desks at the front of the class.

It was a review class, and most of the cadets looked bored, but Danny was fascinated. It was all about finding hiding places in someone else's house. Danny would have thought of under the bed as a hiding place, or under the floorboards. But he would never have thought of hiding a gun in the toilet cistern or important top-secret papers in the freezer. Exshaw talked about things being hidden in plain sight. How he had searched in vain for a secret document in a house one night, only to find out afterward it had been framed and hung on the wall. His eye had passed over it, thinking it was a certificate for something or other.

There was a test then. Each person in the class was given a silver disc the size of a large coin. Then Exshaw stood up and went to the door.

"Now, my little minions," he said, "I am going to turn out the lights and count out one minute, which is the time you will have to conceal that silver disc somewhere in the classroom." Without any more warning Exshaw pressed the light switch and the room was plunged into total darkness. There was dead silence, save for the odd faint rustle. For the first time Danny truly realized where he was—the children around him really were trainee spies! They were moving in silence and stealth in the darkness where ordinary children would have giggled or cried out in fear.

There was no time to waste, he decided. Instinct once more prompted him. He moved forward in the dark, toward the front of the class.

Thirty seconds later the light came back on. All the cadets, including Danny, were back in their seats, varying expressions of innocence on their faces. Exshaw prowled around the classroom. He seized discs from light fittings, from behind pictures, and from between the pages of books. Then for several minutes he didn't find any.

"That's the easy meat out of the way. This is where it gets interesting." He grinned, showing neat little teeth like a row of pearly white buttons. Vandra was the next to be caught. Danny gasped when he realized that the silver pendant she wore around her neck was in fact the disc. Dixie was caught next. Danny thought that her disc was in plain view, standing on its edge on her desk. Then he realized what she was doing. She was turning it gently with a pencil as Exshaw moved around the classroom, so that the thin edge was always toward him, making it invisible. Finally she touched it a little too hard and it fell to the desk with a clatter. In the end there was only one disc left unfound.

"Show me where it is," Exshaw said. Every eye in the classroom was fixed on Danny. He stood up, his heart in his mouth. He didn't know what instinct had prompted him to do as he had done. He walked up to the head of the class and stood in front of Exshaw.

"Put your hand in your left pocket," Danny said. Without removing his eyes from Danny, Exshaw reached into his pocket and removed the disc. He raised one eyebrow a millimeter.

"Of course. The best place to conceal something is on the person of the searcher. But how would our little newcomer know that? Unless of course he has the soul of a spy to begin with. Do you have the soul of a spy, boy?"

"Er, no . . . well, I don't really know," Danny stammered. Exshaw stared at him intently for a long moment, then looked at his watch.

"Class over for today. Let's finish up before that tiresome twit Blackpitt starts to pontificate at us."

The cadets streamed out of the class. Danny was in a slight daze. Why had he thought to plant the disc in

119

Exshaw's pocket, and how had he known to move so swiftly and silently in the dark?

"The evening meal will be early," Blackpitt intoned in his best crackly station announcer's voice, "on account of an induction this evening at eight o' clock. All welcome. Reservations not required."

The cadets headed for Ravensdale, where each table had an array of cold meats, chicken wings, pickles and bread fresh from the oven. Danny didn't feel particularly hungry and picked at the food. If anyone made any remarks to him about being a Cherb, he didn't notice. He murmured thanks when Dixie told him how she loved the way he had put the disc into Exshaw's pocket.

"Looking worried there," Smyck called across the table.

"Worried by what?" Danny said.

"The Hall of Shadows won't like a Cherb," Exspectre said, his pale eyes fixed on Danny.

"What is the Hall of Shadows?" Danny asked, with an uncomfortable feeling that he hadn't asked enough about the induction.

"Not allowed to tell you," Les said. He would not meet Danny's eyes.

"All you have to do is tell the truth," Dixie said, "or at least don't tell a straight lie. The shadows always know."

"Gone a bit pale, Cherb," Smyck jeered.

When they were finished, Danny decided to wander out of Ravensdale and into the school on his own. He was aware of ravens watching him, but he was already used to it. He looked around and saw Les and Dixie in conversation. When he was sure they weren't looking his way, he nipped around the corner and walked quickly to the front door.

Outside, sheets of fine sleet were blowing across the grounds. It was so cold that the sleet was lying on the grass without melting. He had intended to walk for a while and have a last look around before he left, then go to the boys' Roosts and pack his suitcase, but the sleet was falling so heavily that soon he found himself blundering around the lawns, hardly even able to see the gray bulk of Wilsons.

He had just made up his mind to go straight to the Roosts when his shin struck a rock.

"Ouch!" he exclaimed. As he put his foot to the ground, he realized too late that he had struck the stone parapet at the top of a set of decorative steps. His foot slid out from under him, and two things happened very quickly. The first was that he slid down the steps with an ugly series of impacts that drove the breath from his lungs. The second was that a long black knife whistled through the air above his head and buried itself with a thwunk in the trunk of a tree just behind where he had been standing. In the sleet Danny could see a shadowy figure moving swiftly away.

"I've had enough!" He'd been kidnapped, forced into spy school and almost murdered three times, all in two days. With a roar he leapt to his feet and raced toward the spot where he had seen the figure.

Whoever it was had left clear tracks in the sleety

ground. Danny plunged on, his eyes and mind fixed only on the tracks. Wet hail gathered under his collar and drove into his eyes.

The ground sloped downward, and Danny skidded on the wet, icy grass. Something about the tracks suggested an even, unhurried gait. The person he was following was not fleeing in panic. Danny snatched a heavy wet branch from the ground for a weapon as he followed the tracks into some shrubbery.

In and out the footprints weaved, always purposeful. The trickle of melting sleet down the back of Danny's neck had cleared his mind a little, and he moved with more caution now, checking before each turn in case his attacker was waiting. The sleet was starting to ease. The tracks were becoming less well-defined, fading away to muddy marks in places. Then, with a final rattle of icy drops on the leaves, the sleet stopped completely. Danny looked around. Wet, dark green laurels and yews stretched off in every direction. There were marks on the ground in front of him, but there was no way of telling which mark might be a footprint.

Danny was suddenly aware that he was holding the branch so tightly that his fingers had gone numb. The attacker had escaped. He relaxed his grip. It was then that he saw a gate in the yew hedge in front of him, lying open as though in invitation. Swinging the stick in front of him, he made his way toward it.

There was no one on the other side—at least, not as far as he could see. But someone had been there recently.

He could tell by the fresh flowers placed on the rows of graves enclosed by the rustling yew hedge.

Danny moved forward, afraid to disturb the quiet of the place. There was a tarnished brass plaque set into a stone pillar just before the first grave. Danny bent to read it.

THIS MARKS THE FINAL RESTING PLACE
OF THE VICTIMS
OF THE SECOND GREAT PURGE.
VICTIMS OF THE RING
REST IN PEACE.

Danny felt a shiver run down his spine for the second time that day. He looked at the first grave. There was a name and a photograph of a smiling couple on what looked like their wedding day. Danny looked closer. The couple had wings. He read the name: Knutt!

Danny went through the graveyard. Dixie's parents were there, her dad making a funny face, her mum staring off into space with the same vague look Dixie wore most of the time. There were other faces he recognized from cadets he had seen around Wilsons. At the very end of the last row he found what he thought must be Vandra's parents, for they looked identical to her, down to the two incisors that protruded over her lips. The inscription read

C. V. VAUNT, PHYSICK AND HEALER
GLADYS VAUNT, PHYSICK AND HEALER

Danny leaned on one of the headstones. There were so many graves. . . .

"Yes, Wilsons is virtually an orphanage," a voice said, as if reading his thoughts. "You can tell why so many of them are against the Ring."

Danny wheeled around. The detective McGuinness was standing at the gate, with the black knife that had been thrown at Danny in his hand.

"You shouldn't be out on your own," McGuinness said, "although this time you were safe enough."

"Safe enough?" Danny retorted angrily. "That knife was meant for me!"

"Meant for you? That is one thing we can be clear about. It was not meant for you."

"You could have fooled me," Danny said. McGuinness looked at the knife thoughtfully.

"If it had been meant for you, it would be buried in your heart by now. This is a Knife of Implacable Intention."

"A knife of . . . what?"

"Implacable Intention. It means that it will do whatever the person who throws it wants it to do. If they had wanted it to kill you, then you would be dead. These knives are quite a rare thing, thankfully."

"So it was meant to miss me? It doesn't make sense."

"Everything makes sense on some level," McGuinness said. "You need to learn that. Now, they will be looking for you. You had better go back. Here, take this."

He held out the knife. Danny took it from him. It was smaller than it had looked earlier, and it felt cold but almost alive in his hand. Without thinking, he slipped it into his jacket pocket.

"If I have the knife now," he said, a sudden thought springing into his mind, ". . . does it mean that I'm meant to have it, then?"

"You might be right," McGuinness said with a grim little smile. "Now you're beginning to think like a spy." Danny wasn't sure whether it was meant as a compliment or not.

12

THE HALL OF SHADOWS

An anxious-looking Brunholm was waiting for Danny when he got back to Wilsons. "Where have you been?" he demanded. "Are you all right?"

Danny opened his mouth to tell him about the knife attack, then closed it again. For some reason he didn't want Brunholm to know.

"They're almost ready for you in the Hall of Shadows. Come quickly." Danny felt a wave of dread wash over him. What were the shadows? Had he not been threatened enough?

"I'm not going."

"Of course you are," Brunholm said.

"No," Danny said obstinately. Brunholm's smile was a cold affair.

"Yes you are. If I were you, I know what I would be

thinking. I have been kidnapped against my will and brought to a place where people have tried to kill me. I don't want to be here and yet I don't know how to get back home. Meantime, I am told a mad story about Upper and Lower Worlds and Cherbs and all sorts of things until my head is spinning. I am offered a chance to get out, although there may be danger attached. All I have to do is go into the Hall of Shadows and say no. No one will force me to say yes, and then I will be able to go home."

Danny stared at Brunholm. It was as if he had read Danny's thoughts. Except for one thing: a picture of his home formed in his head, an empty home, his father's coat gone from the coat stand at the door, his mother's car keys missing.

Brunholm hurried Danny through the front door. He stopped in front of a black door that Danny had never seen before and pushed some buttons in the wall—it was an elevator. The doors opened creakily and Brunholm shoved him in.

The elevator interior was wood, old and scarred. A brass panel held a row of buttons, but there were no numbers. Brunholm stabbed at them quickly and the elevator jolted to life, but Danny could not tell whether it was going up or down. The lighting was low and Brunholm did not speak. Danny was starting to get nervous.

"What is the . . . the Hall of Shadows?" he asked. Brunholm shook his head and grinned. In the dimly lit elevator Danny could see his teeth shining unpleasantly in the dark.

The elevator lurched to a halt and they stepped out

into a foyer. The floor was made from black wood, and there were black velvet hangings on the walls. As Danny looked up and down, Brunholm seized one of the hangings and threw it aside. With the other hand he thrust Danny in behind the hanging. Danny gasped and turned to try to get back out, but he could feel only stone under his fingers. Trying to keep back the rising tide of panic, he looked slowly around.

He was standing on a balcony, as if he was in a theater. He had the impression that the darkness below him was full of people, but he could not see or hear them. There were other balconies stretching out to either side of him, and these seemed to be full—if not of people, then what? Shadows? Certainly something stirred in them, and there was a low whispering coming from that direction. And not just to either side of him. With a gasp he realized that they were behind him as well, cold, whispering shadows that were closing on him so that he had to move forward to get away. They were whispering of dark things— schemes, plots, betrayals—so that he felt he would do anything to get away from them.

The edge of the balcony came closer and closer, and below it, the darkness. He could not go back, and yet there would soon be no room to go forward. He looked desperately about him; then he saw it: a narrow wooden plank, black, like everything else in this place of shadows, that arched up into the darkness. He put one foot on it, and then the other foot. The shadows behind him were close enough to touch. He imagined clawing hands, and he shuffled forward a little more.

Then the other shadows in the balconies joined in the whispering, and this time it was as if they were telling stories—of friendships betrayed, of kings and governments overthrown, lies told, secrets revealed. He struggled to keep his balance, desperate to get away from them and knowing that his only hope was to go forward. Then he started to hear actual voices, snatches of actual plots. ". . . betrayed them all, I did . . . ," a man's voice said, full of wicked triumph. Then a woman's voice: ". . . I planted the knife right between his shoulder blades, the traitor." He heard a girl's plaintive tones: "I was next in line. . . . They put the poison in an apple. . . . Ah, the pain . . ."

The voices were all talking about him now. He put his hands over his ears, but they would not be shut out, these tales of murder and betrayal. Blindly he stumbled forward, deceit and misery flooding his mind. Who are you? The question formed in his mind, and it was answered by a thousand whispering voices.

We are the cheats and liars and traitors. The betrayers of home and family and country. We cannot rest. We cannot rest.

At last he reached the end. The plank led to a small platform. The voices faded away, and a light came on above his head, so that the shadows shrank back. Devoy sat on another balcony in front of him, and down below him were the cadets. He could see Les looking anxiously up at him, and Dixie and Vandra.

"You have walked the gauntlet of shadows," Devoy said, "and have not been put off course by the whispering.

Now is the time to answer the question. Will you join the fellowship of the shadows, always to work in the dark, forever to be wary, to walk in the vale of deception? Will you be a spy? Answer!"

Danny could see his parents' faces in his mind's eye. His friends at school. He thought of the times that someone had tried to kill him since he had come to Wilsons, of the looks he got from cadets who despised him because he had the appearance of a Cherb. He remembered all of this and his lips formed the word "No." But then another image came into his head, of the graveyard where the parents of his new friends lay. How could he let these friends down when they had given everything to fight the Ring of Five?

The Ring! Once again he felt a dark thrill at the very name! Even now they were out there, sunk in plots he could not even imagine, weaving webs of intrigue that were beyond the minds of ordinary people to understand.

"Answer!" Devoy said again. Danny could feel the eyes of all the cadets on him. Even, he thought, the eyes of the shadows were watching him. And from the shadows it seemed he caught a faint scent of perfume—the perfume his mother wore! Anger and self-pity stabbed at him—he was left alone with the frightful shadows at his back and a terrible decision before him. He looked Devoy in the eye and felt his mouth move as if it did not belong to him.

"Yes," he said. "I will join the fellowship of the shadows. I will be a spy." And as his friends whooped with delight below him, thoughts of the Ring and of his

130

parents jostled in his head. Had he joined because he cared about his friends, or because he was drawn to the Ring? Had he joined because his parents had betrayed him?

"Take you the oath of the shadows? That under the multitudinous roofs of this academy of the devious arts, you will keep faith, tell no secret, commit no perjury, countenance no fraud, unless in the service of Wilsons, or may the shadows consume you and count you among their number for eternity?"

"I take the oath," he said faintly, and the shadows clustered around him.

When Danny was brought into the library of the third landing by Valant, Devoy was standing at the window looking out, his hands clasped behind his back. Valant left. Danny stood awkwardly in the middle of the room, waiting for Devoy to turn around. Sleet came down the chimney and hissed in the fire.

"Look above the fireplace," Devoy said without moving, his voice so quiet that Danny could barely hear him. Danny turned to the portrait.

"Suzerrain Longford," Devoy said, "once principal at Wilsons, now head of the Ring." Danny looked up at Longford. Head of the Ring? The man was almost boyish-looking, with a flap of hair that fell forward over his eyes, and yet those eyes followed Danny around the room, a hint of mockery in them.

"He waited until he knew everything about us, every

131

secret, before he revived the Ring. Quite brilliant, really. It was only by a miracle that we survived at all."

"What have I got to do with this?"

"Tell me." Devoy swung around. "Why did you say yes in the Hall of Shadows? Why did you agree to join Wilsons?"

"I . . . I saw my new friends . . . what happened to their parents. I felt I would be letting them down."

"Is that it?" Devoy demanded. "Is that all? Did you perhaps feel something more than that? A thrill in your veins? The dark appeal of treachery, the desire to deceive, to feel the power of that deception, to betray?"

Devoy's face as always was expressionless, but his eyes searched Danny's as though they would see into his mind. Danny remembered the poker lesson and let all expression drain from his face, feeling as if someone had drawn a veil over his thoughts. At that moment he knew that he could fool Devoy. He could feel the eyes of Longford in the portrait on him. He had of course felt an attraction to the Ring, but the words that came out of his mouth sounded sincere.

"No," he lied, "I just wanted to help."

Devoy stared into his eyes for an eternity; then he nodded in what looked like satisfaction.

"Sit down," he said. "You need to know the history of the Ring of Five." Danny sat.

"Once the Two Worlds lived in harmony. Or in balance, I should say. A balance between good and evil. The Cherbs represented the evil side of the Two Worlds, but

132

they were kept under control by the Ring of Five. Sometimes they would break out and do harm in the Upper World. Those who saw them thought of them as devils—but they weren't; they were just the cruel side of living beings. The head of the Ring, the Fifth, was one who embodied the qualities of both sides. To qualify as the Fifth, one must have the faith of both sides—and thus must be half man, half Cherb.

"I will not trouble you now with the history. Suffice it to say that the Ring was corrupted and dissolved and the Fifth was lost—no one knows where. Evil began to come to the fore. Still, perhaps we would have held the line if Longford had not gone bad and sought to revive the Ring. He secretly organized the Cherbs, and planned to overthrow the Lower World and invade the Upper. There were massive casualties on both sides, but the Upper World was not invaded. We who resisted him barely escaped with our lives, and retreated to this place, Wilsons Island, which has long guarded the crossing place between the Worlds. We are all that is left."

Something stirred in the rafters. Danny looked sharply up. He found himself looking into the beady eyes of a raven, its head cocked to one side.

"The ravens tell no tales," Devoy said. "For many years we on Wilsons watched for danger, keeping in contact with the Upper World. It was a place of culture and learning."

"What happened?"

"We stopped watching. Wilsons declined into what

you see now, a run-down old building on an island, full of child spies and people like the Messengers who have nowhere else to go.

"The Ring corrupted the Messengers it held and set them to work, not pleasant work. . . . The Seraphim . . . But I wander."

"What has this got to do with me?" Danny said. His voice was shaky with nerves, but there was a growing excitement as well.

"Longford has done well in reviving the Ring. Including himself, they are four. But they cannot regain their strength until they have replaced the final member. Until they are five again."

Devoy was looking directly at Danny. The fire crackled. Devoy's eyes bored into him. Then the realization dawned. It was so ridiculous that Danny felt like laughing in the man's face. And this time he did not veil his thoughts.

"Yes, Danny," Devoy said, his face unchanging but his voice eager, "you are the one. You are the person they think they are looking for. You will join the Ring but serve the good, and betray their innermost councils. The fate of this world and yours may rest on it!"

Danny was aware that his mouth was hanging open. He was afraid that he would start babbling hysterically.

"Why . . . what . . . ," he mumbled, "why me?"

"Because you are the person they are looking for. A boy who lives in the Upper World. According to the lore, the Ring must have a person of half-human, half-Cherb blood. Only then will its power be complete."

"But you don't know anything about me!" Danny protested. "And my parents are both human."

"We know much about you." Devoy went over to a carved desk beside the bookcase. He carried over a large wooden box and tipped the contents onto the floor. Danny gasped in astonishment. He could see copies of his school reports, dental records, even a copy of what looked like the cardboard medical file from his doctor. There were photographs of Danny in the schoolyard, in the car with his mother. There were even some of his schoolbooks.

"Brunholm has been watching you for several years, apparently," Devoy said. Something in the man's manner told Danny that Brunholm hadn't told him what he was doing.

"He was able to furnish me with all this information on you. He should be here any moment."

As Devoy spoke, there was a flicker of movement in the corner, and when Danny looked, Brunholm was standing on the carpet.

"Good that you joined us," he said, smiling and rubbing his hands together. "Welcome aboard. Indeed, welcome aboard."

"I've just been telling our young recruit the reasons why we need him."

"Need him." Brunholm was grinning. "Yes, of course. Need him."

Danny looked from face to face. Devoy expressionless. Brunholm's eyes darting about the room. He thought he could feel the power of the Ring reaching out to him, drawing him in. The enormity of the mission that Devoy had outlined was just starting to come to him. He, Danny Caulfield, was to go out and become part of a ruthless spy ring, concealing his identity and mission from its members. He remembered how Les had gone through the photographs of the spies in Ravensdale, how many of them had lost their lives. He thought of the Unknown Spy and his wife, who were unable to remember their own names.

"What makes you think," Danny said slowly, something in his voice making the two men turn around, "what makes you think that I can do this, that I won't crack, or be found out the first time I open my mouth?"

"That depends on many things," Devoy said, watching Danny carefully. "How we instruct you, for a start, and how much you learn. You must have some spycraft. It will depend on the team we send with you. But most of all, it will depend on your courage and your mind, whether you can outwit Longford and the others."

"And whether you can betray what is dearest to you when the cause is worthy," Brunholm broke in. His eyes glittered in the gloom. Danny only half understood what Brunholm was saying. He knew that he should refuse. And if he did, would they send him home?

"I can't . . . ," Danny went on.

"It is too late to refuse!" Brunholm said sharply.

"You have made your decision and have spoken in front of the shadows. There is no turning back!" Brunholm went on. The stumbling, grinning character that had come into the room had gone. This was a much harder creature.

"Now, now, Marcus," Devoy said gently, "you're frightening Danny. What Mr. Brunholm is trying to say is that you are the last and best hope of this world and of your world. We know that an attack is imminent, but we do not know where or how. Think of your friends. Think of your family."

"But how can I do this all on my own?" Danny cried, feeling responsibility settle on him like a great weight.

"You won't be on your own," Devoy said. "Would you like to meet your team?"

13

A PATH OF INFINITE RETURN

Danny followed Devoy and Brunholm out of the library and down a corridor to a pair of wooden doors. In the darkness above, something fluttered. Danny thought he saw a raven hopping from rafter to rafter.

"The anteroom to the library of the third landing," Devoy murmured and opened the doors. It was an elegant room with long windows through which the last rays of the setting sun cast shadows across the polished floors. Danny could see three shadowy figures sitting around a fire, and his heart dropped. He was going to be sent out with strangers—or even worse, with some of the inhabitants of the Hall of Shadows. As he approached, they stood up.

"Les!" Danny breathed in relief. "Dixie, Vandra!" Les

and Dixie grinned at him. Vandra watched Brunholm, a wary look in her eyes.

"A thief, an airhead and a . . . a . . . ," Brunholm said.

"Physick," Danny said, remembering what it had said on her parents' gravestone.

Vandra's eyes widened, but she smiled at him gratefully. If Dixie was offended at being called an airhead, she didn't show it.

"A real live mission," she said, "what fun!"

"Children!" Brunholm exclaimed.

"Perhaps," Devoy said quietly to his cohort as the four friends chatted excitedly, "but there is a real friendship between them."

"Friendship?" Brunholm looked as if he was about to spit. "Where's the friendship that can't be betrayed?"

"Indeed," Devoy said sadly, "in our line of work . . ."

"We weren't allowed to say nothing to you until after the Hall of Shadows," Les said. They were walking across the lawns toward the Roosts.

"I can't wait," Dixie said excitedly, and as if to underline her point, she disappeared, only to reappear a second later beside a lime tree on the lawn, then standing on one of the academy's windowsills.

"Stop that, Dixie," Vandra said crossly, "you know it gets on my nerves."

"Sorry." Dixie reappeared beside them.

"Why've you got that look on your face, Danny?" Les asked.

"Well . . ." Danny rubbed his chin. "It's just that

you're all . . . well, kind of normal, yet you can do these crazy things, or you've got wings or, or . . ."

"Fangs," Les put in helpfully. Vandra glared at him.

"It's just a different world, is all," Dixie said. "It doesn't mean we're all that different."

"Although I'll make an exception in your case," Les muttered under his breath, grinning.

"I never knew this stuff about the different worlds— Upper and Lower."

"The ancient Greeks in your world knew about it," Vandra said, seriously. "You know, when they wrote about crossing over the river Styx and the underworld, people thought they meant dying . . ."

"Yes, yes, Vandra, we get the idea," Les said, "you pay attention in Myths and Stories of the Upper World."

"It's really very interesting," Vandra said. "If *you* paid attention you'd—"

"Would you like to see Westwald?" Dixie broke in, an innocent expression on her face.

"What's that?" Danny said.

"The city of the Ring, is all," Les said, "and it's not a good idea."

"I only said look at it," Dixie said, "not go there. It's this way." Dixie pointed to the very path that Danny had taken the previous day. Les and Vandra looked at each other and shrugged.

"No harm in him getting a look," Les said.

"But every time I took that path I ended up back where I came from," Danny said. "It was driving me mad."

"It's a Path of Infinite Return," Dixie explained

140

patiently, as if she was talking to someone very slow. "You have to confuse it."

"How do you do that?" Danny asked.

"Walk backward, of course," Dixie said. "Come on!" Looking comically serious, she started to walk backward along the path. Les and Vandra followed. Feeling extremely silly, Danny followed them.

As the path swooped under the trees, Les spoke up.

"You know, me and the others have been talking . . . we need to start taking a look at whoever's having a go at you. I mean, you could have got killed a couple of times."

"McGuinness, the detective, he's supposed to be investigating," Danny said.

"McGuinness is a good sort—for a cop, that is," Les said, with the air of a man who had experienced a few brushes with the law in his time, "but he's got a lot on his plate. I mean, between here and Westwald there's a fair bit of crime—particularly in Westwald."

"What do we do?"

"I don't know." Les frowned. "But we can't have them trying to bump off a mate without us doing something about it, can we?"

They walked backward for another five minutes or so: then Dixie spoke.

"That should do it."

With relief Danny turned around the right way. They were in a part of the wood that he hadn't seen before. The path was cut through sheer rock, with trees forming a roof overhead so that they were walking through a green tunnel. There were the remains of old walls and what looked like a small, deserted castle above them.

The tunnel opened out into scrubland. In places the trees had been burned but had started to grow back, and there were deep holes and rusting barbed wire running across the land. In the distance Danny could see several houses, but they were fire-blackened and roofless, and the foliage had started to cover them. His friends didn't make any comment on it, but Danny thought it looked as if an army had passed this way.

They turned a corner in the path and suddenly Danny could smell the sea. More buildings came into view, this time with walls blown out, and debris lay scattered around them.

"The war," Les said curtly. The path turned into a road, the surface pitted and scarred. The burned-out remains of cars and trucks had been dragged to the sides of the roadway and lined its edges like some strange traffic jam. Old telegraph poles tilted drunkenly. Danny looked about him. Wilsons had somehow seemed unreal, but this felt very real.

"Cherbs kept attacking in the early days," Les said. "When we get to the top of the hill, keep your head down."

The smell of the sea was stronger now. The road breasted a small rise. Danny followed the others as they got down on their hands and knees to crawl to the top. When they got close they lay on their bellies and peered over.

Danny found himself looking down on a long beach

littered with burned-out boats and jeeps and trucks. There were rolls of barbed wire everywhere, and a sign said, DANGER: MINEFIELD.

Waves crashed on the strand and on the abandoned boats. Waves tumbling from a dark, angry-looking inlet of the sea. All along the beach watchtowers stood on long legs, looking out toward the other side of the inlet. Beyond the wharfs and piers on the far shore was a city over which there hung a grayish haze, making it hard to distinguish streets and buildings. Much of the haze seemed to come from high redbrick factory chimneys in the distance. But despite being hidden by smoke—or perhaps because of it—the town exuded mystery, beckoning to Danny. The smoke was stirred by a gust of wind, and he had a quick glimpse of narrow winding streets.

"Westwald," Les murmured.

Looking up the inlet, Danny could see a long iron railway bridge, its delicate arches spanning the angry water below. The iron was damaged and scorched, sagging in places, missing whole girders in others. But still it stood grimly above the current.

"Hard to think that all you had to do once was jump on a train to get across. The bridge runs to Tarnstone on our side." Vandra sighed.

"A bridge?" Danny asked.

"We were on the last train across from the lower side," Vandra said. "The Cherbs bombed us as we crossed." Vandra's dark eyes turned watery. Dixie put her hand on Vandra's pale hand sympathetically.

"The two cities face each other across the sea,

143

Tarnstone and Westwald. Cherbs come across in boats at night to attack," Les said. "The guards in the watchtowers try to keep them out, but they still get through. There are thousands of Cherbs."

Vandra pointed and Danny saw for the first time that there were towers on the other side as well. "Look," she said. As they followed her finger they could see a glint of light from one of the towers.

"Coming off binoculars," Les said. "They spotted us. Better get down. Don't want them recognizing Danny when we get over there."

The shadows were growing and it was almost dark by the time they got back to Wilsons. Their return trip had taken longer than the walk out due to Dixie's insistence on spinning round and round "to really confuse the path." She had succeeded, and the path had ended up crossing itself several times before they could persuade her to stop. They were late getting to Ravensdale. When they entered the abandoned village, rain was pelting down on the narrow main street, and they were soaked by the time they got to the Consiglio dei Dieci. Most of the other cadets had finished dinner, and the only food that appeared was cold stew. They wolfed it down, however, and Danny yawned a yawn that made his jaw crack.

"Sorry," he apologized, "it's been a long day."

Twenty minutes later they were standing on the balcony outside the boys' Roosts.

"Just one thing, before we go," Vandra said. "When

we were in the anteroom to the library of the third landing, you said I was a physick. How did you know?"

"I . . . I saw it on the headstone. Your parents' headstone."

"What headstone?"

"In the graveyard, where all your parents are buried . . . ," Danny said. They were all staring at him now.

"There is no graveyard, Danny," Les said.

"All our parents were left behind—in the Lower World," Dixie said.

"But I saw it," Danny cried. "There were flowers on the graves and everything!"

"Welcome to the world of spies," Vandra said with a grim little smile. "Somebody desperately wanted you to say yes, so they thought up a way to make you feel our pain. The graveyard was a fake."

Danny stared at them. Of course. Under his jacket he felt the outlines of the knife that had been thrown at him. That was why it had missed. He'd been meant to follow the pretend assassin and find the fake graveyard.

"The whole thing was a setup," Dixie said with a sad little grin. "It was a fake, Jake. Now our boy with the multicolored eyes won't stay with us."

"He has to," Les said, "he said it in front of the shadows. But will he want to now?"

"The reasons I said yes haven't changed," Danny said firmly, although he wasn't sure, "even if I was set up. But there's something I need to know."

145

"What?" Les asked.

"If I'm supposed to get into the Ring, then no one is supposed to know that I'm not really the lost member."

"Yeah?"

"But everyone in Wilsons knows me—who's to say that one of them isn't a spy who'll go back and tell . . . Longford or somebody that I'm not who I say I am?"

"Do you remember the oath you took in front of the shadows?" Les sounded serious. "The Oath of the Shadows? It binds every cadet. The shadows would have you in a second if you told something like that. Don't worry, mate. Your secret is safe."

The boys said goodnight to the girls and went into the Roosts. The first person they met was Exspectre.

"Must be the first time a Cherb has joined Wilsons," Exspectre said, blinking his big eyes.

"Push off, bush baby," Les said, shoving Exspectre aside. Smyck sat at the far end of the hut, saying nothing but keeping his eyes fixed on Danny. Some of the other boys came up to him and murmured, "Good to have you on board," and, "Congrats." They looked half ashamed as they did it.

"They're afraid of Exspectre and Smyck," Les said. He and Danny sat down by the stove. Danny could feel his eyes start to close.

"What is a physick, anyway?" he asked.

"Like Vandra?" Les said. "She's a healer. . . . Those teeth—they work, you know."

"What?" Danny said, sitting up in alarm. "She really is a vampire?"

"No, no," Les said, "she doesn't take blood out of you. A physick puts stuff into you—like medicine. They drink it and use their teeth to bite it into you. They got their own healing stuff too. They got special glands. A physick's a good thing to have around. Only problem is that what's wrong with you sometimes moves to the physick—it's hard on them."

Ten minutes later Danny lay in bed. Outside, rain began to fall, and he pulled the blankets up around him. An image of Vandra's pale face appeared in his head, and he felt a great pity for her. Then suddenly the realization gripped him: he was a spy! For a moment the world was full of danger, and he felt a jolt of fear at the mission he was to be trained for. Then he heard Les's voice.

"Good night, Danny."

"Good night," he whispered back, feeling better. He wasn't on his own, and was safe for now, at least. He closed his eyes and felt sleep steal over him.

In fact, he was safer than he thought. Outside, in the shadows under the wall of Wilsons, stood McGuinness. Rain dripped from the brim of his hat. His eyes were fixed on the wooden building high above his head, on the window beneath which Danny slept. If anyone, or anything, moved in the night, McGuinness would see it.

14

INKS

The next morning as they were leaving Ravensdale after breakfast, Blackpitt summoned Danny to Brunholm's office. Les raised an eyebrow.

"None of us ever been to Brunholm's office before. Didn't know he had one."

When they reached the main building, Danny watched his friends walk off toward class, and suddenly felt very alone as the corridor emptied. Above his head a raven stirred in the dark rafters.

"Door to your left," Blackpitt said gleefully, "the one with the skull design."

The door did indeed have skulls etched on it, and it opened onto a long dark staircase. There were stuffed antelope heads on the wall, and Danny felt that their glassy eyes were following him as he mounted the stairs. There were no windows, but a cold draft made him shiver. Up and up the staircase went, bending round on itself, until Danny thought he must be right up at roof level. But when the stairs opened onto a landing, he saw through a low barred window that he was only twenty feet above the ground. The twisting and unreliable stairways and corridors of Wilsons were starting to make him feel a little bit unreal, and he felt even more unreal when he stepped into Brunholm's office.

At first he thought the gloomy room was full of people, and that wary-looking boys gazed at him from every corner. Then he realized that all the available space in the room was covered with mirrors—plain bathroom mirrors, mirrors with gilt frames, distorting mirrors like the ones you saw in a fairground, shaving mirrors, vanity mirrors—and from all these mirrors a thousand Danny Caulfields looked back at him.

"I like to come here to be reminded what the world of spying is all about."

Danny spun around to see where Brunholm's silky voice was coming from. The small man's face was reflected back at him from many directions, so that it was impossible to tell which was the real one.

"In our world, Danny, do not believe that anyone is telling the truth. You must suspect everything you hear, question it, wonder what advantage or disadvantage might be gained by a lie."

"But the world isn't really like that," Danny said. "There are things like friendship . . . family . . ."

"Friendship? Family?" There was a sneer in

149

Brunholm's voice. "Have your friends never betrayed you? Has your family never let you down?"

Danny hesitated. It had been one of his friends in school—Mark Dealey—who had started the Danny the Pixie nickname, had whispered it behind his back. And then his mother and father . . . why did they never have time for him?

"You see?" Brunholm said triumphantly. "It is true. The only person you can trust is yourself, and sometimes . . ." Brunholm must have moved, for his face loomed large and sinister from a distorting mirror in the ceiling. ". . . you cannot even do that."

Danny took a step backward, but Brunholm's eyes fixed on him.

"When you are out there in the field, all on your own, distrusted, hunted, perhaps, then you start to mistrust yourself. Were you wrong about this or that person? Perhaps they could be trusted after all. You seek their confidence, tell them the truth, and then"—Brunholm clapped his hands together with a noise like a pistol shot—"you are caught! The person you have put your trust in is an agent for the other side."

Brunholm's face appeared in another mirror. This time the distortion in the glass made him appear like an older relative, sympathetic and concerned.

"You are missing your family now, your home, your school friends, perhaps? And they miss you. It is a lonely life, being a spy, lonely and hard." And indeed Danny did feel a wave of homesickness wash over him.

"Your instruction starts now," Brunholm said. "We have to build quickly toward this mission, but afterward . . . afterward we will be able to work on the greatest art of all."

"What's that?" Danny asked.

"Betrayal," Brunholm whispered, from yet another mirror, his face now a picture of treachery. "The art of betrayal."

"But if you betray everybody you know," Danny said, "then you can't trust anybody."

"Precisely." Brunholm rubbed his hand together in delight, "the ideal condition for a spy. You are dismissed boy."

After lunch Danny went to Inks and Ciphers with the rest of his class.

"Inks is okay," Les said. "The teacher's a bit mental. Bartley kind of thinks in code sometimes, which is a bit tricky. They say that during the war he was spying in the Lower World. There was no way to get an important message out, so they shaved his head and tattooed the message on his skull, then let the hair grow back. He got across to Wilsons and Devoy himself shaved the hair back off to get the message. So they say, anyway."

"The hair grew back again," Vandra said, "but if the light is right you can see the blue ink on his head."

Bartley was a tall man with a long white face and thick black-framed glasses. His shock of wiry black hair stuck straight up. Danny found himself peering at the man's head, trying to see the secret message tattooed on his scalp.

"Good afternoon," Bartley said. "The shepherd has deserted his flock, and the wolf has lain down with the lamb." He beamed at the baffled cadets.

"Today," he went on, "we will be doing some basic inks, or as the seagull said to the fishing boat, let us both cast our nets and to the victor the spoils."

"What is he talking about?" Danny whispered to Les.

"Who knows?"

It went on in the same vein with Bartley talking about invisible inks. Danny had to admit some of it was interesting, when you left out the strange bits. There were inks that were invisible until they were warmed up. There were inks that you could only see under special lights. Then Bartley produced a jar of luminescent blue that shone like a thousand sapphires. He dipped a fountain pen into it and wrote on a sheet of paper. The ink glowed blue, then gradually disappeared. The cadets tried everything they knew to bring the writing back, but failed. In the end Bartley announced triumphantly that it only responded to a particular word.

"Prudence!" he cried, and the writing appeared and blazed like blue flame. He showed them other inks, all with unique qualities and all responding to different things. One particularly sludgy green-brown ink would only reappear after a live frog had been rubbed over the paper.

"No time for ciphers today," Bartley said, his eyes

huge behind the bottletop glasses. "The wind blows through the wheat field and the robin flees her nest! Next week we start to learn how to make these inks, and of course we shall begin our ciphers course."

After Inks Danny let the others walk on ahead. A thought had been growing in his head. The truth had been right in front of him, if only he had thought to look for it! When the others were almost out of sight, he doubled back.

It was very still in the Gallery of Whispers. The smooth stone dome curved high above his head and was lost in the gloom. Every sound Danny made was unnaturally loud. When he swallowed, it sounded like a gunshot. What was it Les had said about unauthorized entry? A Ninth Regulation offense. He had no idea what the punishment for that would be, but he knew it would be serious. It didn't matter. Nothing mattered except that he find out the truth about himself. He moved forward, his footsteps ringing out as though an army was marching in the echoing room.

There was a raven etched into the stone in the middle of the floor. Danny stopped there. It had to be the place. He looked up. He felt an air of expectancy in the gallery, as though his question had been long awaited. Danny peered up into the dome.

"Who am I?" he asked, his voice quavering. For a moment there was no response; then a whispering sound began. His question seemed to be repeated and then repeated again, a thousand times, in his own voice, yet at different pitches, at one point high and girlish, at another deep and rumbling. Round and round the Gallery of Whispers his question went, the sound rising and falling, ebbing and flowing, until he despaired of an answer. Then, slowly, the sound began to die away, as though a crowd was walking away from him, a crowd that would be swallowed in a gathering dusk. Danny waited. The voices faded until he could hear nothing, and the gallery returned to stillness. Finally, right in his ear, in an everyday tone that made him start, his own voice spoke.

"Ask the ravens," it said. Danny looked around wildly. How was he supposed to ask the ravens? As though the gallery had heard what he was thinking, another whisper echoed in the dome. He could not make out the words this time, but the tone was low and mocking.

A GRAVEL-VOICED DWARF

The following morning as they made their way to Ravensdale for breakfast, they found the hallway full of Messengers milling around, in a state of high agitation.

"What is it?" Danny asked Gabriel.

"An outrage," Gabriel spluttered, "an absolute outrage."

"What is?"

"An affront to our dignity as Messengers," Gabriel went on. "We demand that something be done about it. Eluda Fanshawe is completely beside herself, and I can't say I blame her."

No matter how much Danny questioned, Gabriel would not tell him what had happened. But Les had slipped into the crowd and listened in to their conversations. He came up to the others with a big grin on his face.

"That siren we released from prison. She's been hanging around the place since. She got ahold of this Eluda Fanshawe early this morning. You know the way she got me and you to open the door and let her out? Well, she charmed old Eluda into flying around the rooftops three times chirping like a canary!"

"You shouldn't have let her out," Vandra said.

At that moment the door opened and an elderly and particularly miserable-looking Messenger with a handbag over her arm came in. The other Messengers rushed forward and began to commiserate with her.

"I would have given a lot to see that," Les said gleefully.

"Poor old thing," Vandra said reproachfully. "They really think it's terribly vulgar to fly, never mind chirp like a bird while they're doing it."

"Poor old thing, my eye," Les said. "She needs a bit of livening up, by the look of her."

Brunholm appeared, and the Messengers clustered around him. He made a beeline for Eluda, and although Danny could not hear what was said, he could see that Brunholm was oozing oily charm.

The cadets went into Ravensdale and had breakfast. Danny heard talk and laughter about the siren loose in Wilsons. Some of them had seen the Messenger flying around the building.

"I heard the siren sank a hundred ships," a small girl with frizzy black hair said as she passed them. "Thousands of sailors got drowned. And now she's loose again."

Danny said nothing. He found it hard to believe that

156

Vicky, for all her mischievousness, was capable of sinking hundreds of ships.

After breakfast Blackpitt told them that they were to go to Miss Duddy's class.

"Lots of excitement this morning," he intoned dryly. "I don't think."

But in fact the morning turned out to contain much more than Danny had bargained for.

When they got to Duddy's class she announced that they were to spend the day studying surveillance techniques.

"But first," she said, "I have been advised by Master Brunholm that Cadet Caulfield is not to be allowed out of the grounds unless he is disguised."

There was some excited whispering among the cadets at the idea of being out of the grounds.

"Quiet, please," Duddy said. "This will give me an opportunity to demonstrate my artistry in the matter of disguise."

Les rolled his eyes and groaned. Duddy's dark glasses swung around to Les.

"Alas, my art is not sufficient to disguise your ugly mug, Knutt," she snarled, slipping into an accent that was much less refined than the one she normally used. She paused and drew a deep breath.

"Please take a seat, Cadet Caulfield," she said in her normal voice. Danny sat in the chair she had pulled into the middle of the room. Duddy went to the corner and returned with several large boxes brimming with makeup and false beards and fake glasses and even a device that tied one leg behind your back so you looked one-legged. There were artificial ears and noses and jars of hair dye marked "blondish" and "ginger" and "mousey."

Duddy studied Danny's face. "If I had time," she murmured, "what a work of art I could accomplish here. A masterpiece! As it is, I will have to make do. . . ." She grasped Danny's chin and turned his head from side to side. "Yes," she said, "a gross feature might do the trick, something to draw the eye."

Danny didn't like the sound of "a gross feature." Out of the corner of his eye he could see Les settling down on a sofa with an interested expression on his face.

Duddy worked at Danny for half an hour. He could feel her applying something that felt like cold plaster to his face; then she ordered him to sit still while it dried. She worked for ages with brushes and sponges. She squeezed an ointment into his eyes that stung badly, but he wasn't allowed to rub it. Any time Danny caught a glimpse of Les, the Messenger grinned and gave him a thumbs-up, but there was something worrying about the twinkle in his friend's eyes. In fact, the whole class was watching with grins on their faces, particularly Smyck and Exspectre.

At last Duddy stood back and gave a nod of satisfaction. Dixie clapped her hands.

"Magnifico!" she shouted, and then, "Encore!"

From the rest of the class came murmurs of amusement. Danny refused to look at them.

"Not a masterpiece," Duddy said, pleased. "A minor work of art, perhaps, but a work of art nonetheless. Voilà!"

She grabbed Danny's arm and propelled him to his feet in front of a gilt-framed mirror. Danny had braced himself for what might come, but he still didn't expect the wizened little gnome with red eyes looking back at him—not only that, but the gnome had an enormous nose with a large hairy mole growing out of the side of it. He heard a muffled snort behind him, and knew that he couldn't turn around to look Les in the eye.

"The ointment in your eyes makes them red, thus helping to conceal the different colors." Duddy said, "An intelligent solution, don't you think?"

"Excuse me, Miss Duddy," Les asked, his face innocent. "You remember you said that people will only look at a prominent feature and won't remember any of the rest of the face? Well, is that why you did the nose that way?"

Danny could see Les in the mirror now. The Messenger could barely contain his mirth.

"Excellent, Knutt." Duddy beamed.

"It might be a good idea to take a photograph so that others can learn from this excellent disguise," Les went on. Danny shook a silent fist at him.

"A wonderful suggestion," Duddy said. "I shall fetch my camera."

But Danny was to be spared. At that moment the door burst open and Brunholm bustled in.

"I have to say," he announced, "I think this is a very bad idea, but if we are going through with it, then we'd better get on with it. Have you finished, Rosemary?"

"Er, er . . . yes, Marcus, almost . . ."

"Then chop-chop, let's get on with it."

"Oh yes, of course." Duddy picked up a large bag of makeup the wrong way round and emptied the contents onto the floor. Then she tripped over a box of wigs.

"What are you doing, woman?" Brunholm snapped.

"I—I'm sorry, Marcus," Duddy stammered. Danny could see that she was flustered around Brunholm, and wondered if she felt more than professional respect for him.

"I'm just looking for the voice dye . . . ," she said.

"Voice dye?" Danny said dubiously.

"Yes, it was here a moment—"

"Here it is," Les piped up, holding up a little device that looked like an asthma inhaler. Danny glared at him suspiciously.

"Open your mouth," Duddy said. Danny didn't move.

"Come on, boy," Brunholm growled, "we haven't got all day."

Reluctantly, Danny opened his mouth, and Duddy sprayed an acrid-tasting liquid into the back of his throat. Danny choked and coughed, his eyes watering and his tonsils stinging. Duddy waited patiently for him to stop spluttering.

"Try saying something now."

"I've had just about enough of this . . . ," he began crossly, but the voice that came out was not his, but a particularly musical and high-pitched girl's voice. The class collapsed in laughter.

"That's not the right one!" Duddy exclaimed crossly,

examining the writing on the side of the spray. "This is Spring Coquette." Les was doubled over with silent laughter, and Danny realized that his quick thief's hands had switched the spray canisters of voice dye.

"Here it is," Duddy said, "Gravel-Voiced Dwarf."

"I don't want to be a gravel-voiced . . . ," Danny began indignantly, before realizing that his girlish voice had risen to an alarmingly high pitch. The class laughed harder. Even Brunholm seemed to be grimly amused.

"I don't think you have much choice," he said, "unless you want to sound like a schoolgirl for the rest of your life."

Danny opened his mouth once more and felt the acrid sting again. When his eyes had stopped watering Duddy told him to try out the voice.

"I hope this stuff doesn't last forever," he said. The voice was deep, rasping and surly. But it was better than Spring Coquette.

"Now, class," Duddy said, "today we'll be practicing two techniques: switching tails and the box pursuit."

Drawing a diagram on the board, she explained how spies tailing a subject should switch the person following every so often, so that the subject didn't get suspicious.

"The box pursuit is different. In the box, you have at least three people. One behind the subject, one in front and one on the other side of the street. It requires great skill. Now, if you follow me, a charabanc awaits to take you to Tarnstone, where you will practice your skills."

There was another buzz of excitement.

"What's Tarnstone?" Danny growled. Les tried to

answer, but Danny's voice and appearance were too much, and he spluttered with laughter.

"It's the nearest town," Vandra said, "remember? Across the water from Westwald—kind of a funny place. Full of smugglers and people on the run for one reason or another. But it beats school. And stop laughing, Les. It's very immature. If you had to walk around with these teeth, you'd think more about other people's feelings."

Danny felt a warm surge of gratitude for the physick. Les tried to compose his features.

"All right, all right," Danny said in resignation, "I'm a gravel-voiced dwarf. Let's get going."

They walked after Duddy to the front of the building, and there waiting for them was an ancient bus with Valant at the wheel. The bus was painted black, with what might once have been gold trim. The windows were the kind of dark glass that you could only see through from the inside. The engine was running, and the bodywork shuddered and rattled while noxious gases poured from the exhaust.

"It's not very undercover, is it?" Smyck said sarcastically. "Might as well have *Wilsons School for Spies* written on it."

Danny said nothing. In fact, over the driver's head at the front of the bus, a sign said WILSONS.

"Yes, well," Duddy said, nonplussed, "a remnant of happier days. We weren't always in the middle of a war, you know. Spying used to be a much more gentlemanly pursuit."

"What, no girls?" Vandra said.

"Spying wasn't seen as a . . . suitable job for young ladies," Duddy said, in her most exclusive voice.

"Then what are you doing teaching it?" Les grumbled, taking care to keep his voice down.

"Women make the best poisoners," Toxique said. "It's in the blood."

"Do they really?" Dixie said with a look of interest. "I didn't realize. Do have some strychnine, Maud, you really must."

Toxique gave her a wild look and, climbing onto the bus, took a seat at the back on his own, casting dark bloodshot-eyed looks at anyone who tried to sit beside him.

"Mad as a bleedin' hatter," Les said.

"I wonder . . . ," Danny said. He took a seat beside Les as the rest of the cadets climbed on board.

"Now," said Duddy, standing in the middle of the aisle. "I want no fighting, no singing, certainly no spitting in the aisles . . ."

The engine roared, and with a jolt, the bus shot forward. Duddy flew backward and landed with a startled yelp on the floor. The cadets cheered. Danny looked around. It felt strangely like a school outing to the beach or something—well, it felt like that until he saw the collection of physicks and winged Messengers and poisoners accompanying him.

The bus shot off down the tree-lined drive, black smoke billowing out behind it, threads of steam escaping from under the hood. Like everything else at Wilsons, the trees were dark and inward-looking, and Danny caught glimpses of mysterious paths leading off into dense forest. Then the bus went under an arched gate with two semi-ruined turrets towering above it. As Valant steered the bus into the road beyond, Danny saw, in sagging and rusted metal lettering above the gate, the single word WILSONS, the "S" at the end looking as if it was about to fall off.

The road was narrow and winding, passing over little bridges and around hairpin bends. The trees grew right up to the road, and there were small slate-roofed houses here and there, some with smoke coming from their chimneys, although Danny didn't see any people. After fifteen minutes the road widened and there were other vehicles—trucks of the same vintage as the charabanc, and a few cars with long hoods that might once have been modern and streamlined but now looked shabby, covered in dents and rust spots. Every so often there was an old-fashioned limousine, the driver sitting in the open and black curtains hiding the occupants.

Duddy had produced a crackly microphone from somewhere. She coughed and cleared her throat and said, "One, two . . . One, two . . . ," several times.

"Now, cadets," she said. "Tarnstone is . . . well . . . not exactly a dangerous town, not if you're careful, but it is full of . . . spies and renegades and quite unsavory types, so do stay together. I'll appoint one person from each group to be the subject—the person to be followed—and another three to rotate to pursuit."

Danny was hoping to get Vandra, Les and Dixie, but to his surprise and annoyance he was put in a group with Smyck, Exspectre and the frizzy-haired girl, Frieda.

"Caulfield," Duddy said, "you can be the subject—the rest of you follow him."

"We won't let him out of our sight," Smyck said, with a wicked grin. "Stick to him like glue, we will."

The bus approached the outskirts of the town. The road was lined with three- and four-story houses, all a little higgledy-piggledy, seeming to lean up against each other, the chimneys crooked and the windows small and dark like spyholes. There were people walking at the side of the road—men in trench coats with the brims of their hats pulled down over their eyes and women with scarves wrapped round their faces and collars turned up. As the bus slowed to a crawl, a red car with the longest hood Danny had ever seen, with great silver exhausts springing from it, cruised past, driven by a tall woman wrapped in furs. She was wearing a black lace veil, but beneath it Danny caught a glimpse of long dark hair and ruby-red lips, and as she drew level with the bus she glanced up, seeming to see Danny through the dark windows and dismiss him with a haughty flash of her blue eyes.

"Cor," Les said, "who was that?"

"I don't know," Danny said, his eyes following the car into the distance, until with another great shudder, which threw him against the seat in front, the charabanc came to a halt.

Danny picked himself up off the floor. There were groans from some of the other cadets, and Duddy had once more found herself flat on her back. Danny felt a thump on his shoulder.

"Okay, let's go hunting," Smyck said.

16

THE PAINTED WALL

When they got off the bus Danny could see they were in a town surrounded by crooked buildings. There were market stalls in the center, and bars and restaurants on the ground floors of the buildings. The market was in full swing. Right, Danny thought, time to lose the pursuit! Without looking back, he plunged into the crowd. Immediately it closed around him and he found himself in a babbling, jostling mass of people. There were fishermen and farmers mingling with the townspeople, but mostly it was the same kind of folk Danny had seen on the road, keeping their hats well pulled down and their scarves up high, although he caught sight of scarred faces and fierce suspicious eyes. Here and there people wore cloaks or large dark glasses. The whole effect made Danny feel that everyone was up to no good of one sort or another.

And people kept beckoning him over—he realized that his appearance made them assume that he too was up to something. A man selling apples whistled at him and pulled back a sheet to show a box full of revolvers.

"Good quality," the man hissed, "very good price."

A woman offered him a bottle of "top-drawer sleeping draft," and men with darting eyes were selling what looked like false documents and forged passports, opening long coats to show their wares attached to the lining. Danny kept his head down and moved fast, but each time he looked up he could see Smyck's pale cold features, or Exspectre's ghostly face, or the frizzy top of Frieda's head. They hadn't bothered with alternating the pursuit. They were keeping in what Duddy had called the box pursuit, and were doing it well. Danny could see Smyck's triumphant look, and was determined to wipe it off his face. Without really thinking, he seized a crate of apples when a stallholder's back was turned, and dived into one of the restaurants lining the square.

The contrast with the bustling street outside was instant. White-coated waiters with large drooping mustaches moved smoothly among the tables, where women in fur coats and men in expensive suits dined. A small orchestra played mournful Hungarian music in the background. As the door swung to behind Danny, a dark-haired man with a red face wearing an evening suit strode toward him.

"What do you think you're doing?" he whispered furiously.

"Apples for the kitchen," Danny said innocently.

"There's a back door for that!"

"I'll just nip in . . . ," Danny said, skipping nimbly between the tables, avoiding the man's outstretched arm. The waiters wore almost comical expressions of horror as an ugly little gnome ran past their tables, and Danny caught a glimpse of an elderly man dining with his wife, his mouth open, gaping like a walrus. Just as Danny reached the kitchen he glanced over his shoulder and saw Smyck's face appear at the door, where the black-suited man descended on him with a look of thunder. Danny couldn't help grinning. There was no way Smyck was going to be able to follow him.

He burst into the hot steamy kitchen, and a white-hatted chef stared at him in puzzlement. Above the cacophony of crashing dishes and bellowing waiters and rattling saucepan lids Danny shouted, "Wilsons apples, sweetest of all." And he dumped the apples on a worktop. Spying the back door, he made a run for it before anyone could react.

The door opened with a protesting creak and Danny stepped out into a dark dank alley. Restaurant rubbish bins and crates of bottles were stacked high against the walls, and there was a smell of rotten vegetables and gone-off meat. He glanced quickly up and down the alley. Which way should he go?

He took a few steps. Then he saw a shadowy figure cross the entrance to the alley, moving stealthily and speedily, yet not so speedily that Danny did not recognize the furtive gait and the luxuriant mustache. Brunholm!

As Brunholm disappeared without a glance into the

alley, Danny ran to the entrance just in time to see him turn onto a narrow cobbled street. Danny hesitated. He remembered Duddy's warning about Tarnstone and its dangers, but there was something about the way Brunholm had moved. He was sneaky at the best of times, but there had been an added urgency to his sneakiness this time that made Danny suspicious. Taking a deep breath, he followed.

Brunholm managed to stay far enough ahead to make the pursuit difficult. Danny would catch a glimpse of a heel or the end of a flapping cloak rounding a corner just as he entered the opposite end of a street. And the cobbled streets got narrower and quieter, so quiet that Brunholm must have heard the pounding of Danny's heart. The buildings to either side looked like warehouses, their windows barred and dark.

Then Brunholm disappeared. Danny rounded a corner into a small empty square. There was no sign of Brunholm, nor was there any way out of the square, unless Brunholm could walk through the forbidding stone walls or fly up to the small patch of blue sky visible above Danny's head.

Puzzled, Danny looked around. Where had he gone? He examined every inch of the square, but there did not appear to be another entrance. He was about to give up when a cough right beside him made him jump. Then, without warning, a section of wall beside him was swished aside and a stocky man in a striped shirt strode out, wiping his mouth with his hand. Ignoring Danny, he stalked off down the street.

Danny stared at the wall. As far as he could see it was solid stone, but when he put his hand out to touch it, it felt soft, like cloth! He lifted an edge. There was a dark entrance behind it, and further in, a dim glow and the murmur of voices. With a fluttering feeling in the pit of his stomach, Danny stepped inside. As he did so, he saw a neon sign that flickered and fizzed as though it was about to go out at any moment. The sign read: THE PAINTED WALL, and underneath, DRINK SCRAWNINGS FINEST ALE.

Danny moved cautiously toward the light, which was coming from a brick archway directly in front of him. He paused at the archway and peered cautiously in. The Painted Wall was a dark windowless bar. A man in a white shirt stood behind a high wooden counter. Other men were sitting at the counter with drinks in front of them. Along the wall there was a row of snugs, and just visible in one of these, Danny could see Brunholm, bent forward in urgent conversation. With his heart in his mouth, Danny stepped forward. No one as much as glanced in his direction. He looked in the mirror behind the bar, and seeing the disreputable faces of the men and women sitting there, he realized that his new features fit right in.

He strode to the bar and picked a spot where he could keep an eye on Brunholm. He pulled out a stool and clambered awkwardly onto it. When he saw the barman coming toward him, he realized that he hadn't thought his approach through. He could order a drink, but he hadn't any money.

"Well, what do you want?" The barman eyed Danny suspiciously.

"A . . . a pint of Scrawnings," Danny stammered. The barman went off to fetch the beer. Danny thought about making a run for it, but at that very moment, Brunholm turned toward the bar, so that Danny would have to cross his line of sight in order to get out. The barman returned with a tankard, and slammed it down on the counter. Danny fished desperately in his pockets and was just about to blurt out something about leaving his wallet at home when he heard a man speak.

"Here, let me get that," the smooth voice said, and a hand placed several coins on the counter.

The barman grunted and scooped up the coins.

Danny turned to see a young man with blond hair and steady gray eyes. He was wearing a scuffed black jacket with the collars turned up. His gaze was level and appraising, but Danny noted the little lines around the eyes and the wary look of someone who doesn't always trust what they see.

"Th-thanks . . . ," Danny said.

"That's okay, it's always good to help a stranger. It can be a little . . . difficult around here, until you know the ropes." There was a slight tone of mockery in the man's voice that annoyed Danny.

"Can't a man have a drink in peace?" Danny growled.

"Sorry." The man held up his hands. "I didn't mean to intrude."

Then Danny saw that Brunholm had stood up and was walking toward the door, taking a path that would bring him close to the bar. Danny swung around. Brunholm had seen him in his disguise back at Wilsons. He was fairly sure that the bar was too dark for Brunholm to recognize him, but he turned his back nonetheless.

"What's your name, anyhow?" he demanded.

"Starling."

"And how come you're so generous with your money?" If it hadn't been for the proximity of Brunholm, Danny would have quite enjoyed getting into character as an ugly little man with a growling voice.

"I'm always interested in strangers," the man said, "particularly those who might have come from Wilsons Island."

"Then I'm no good to you," Danny said, his chin sinking into his collar as Brunholm swept past.

"That's a pity," the man said, "but if you ever have need of my services, here's my card." Danny looked at the card. It read: *Jonas Starling. Importer and Exporter.*

" 'Importer and Exporter,' " Danny read, letting a sneer creep into his voice. "And what exactly do you import?"

Those steady gray eyes met his again, and when Starling spoke, his voice was soft.

"Hope," he said. "I suppose you could say I import hope."

There was something very familiar about the eyes, but Danny couldn't quite put his finger on it. He swung around to make sure Brunholm was gone, then turned to the alcove where Brunholm had been speaking to the stranger. The stranger was just getting to his feet, and

172

when Danny saw his face it drove all thoughts of gray-eyed men from his mind. For a moment it seemed that he was looking into his own face—but older, with a mouth turned down at a cruel angle, and eyes, one brown and one blue, that were full of corruption and deceit. He shared Danny's pointed ears, high cheekbones and sharp chin, but there was nothing about him that could be described as pixielike. His face was coarse and savage, and Danny recoiled. The man's cruel gaze swept the room, and then he threw a scarf over his face, hiding all but his eyes.

"Well might you stare," Starling said, his voice barely audible. "That is Rufus Ness, chief spymaster and cruelest of the Cherbs. If he dares to show himself here, then things are worse than I thought. I must go."

As Ness entered the tunnel, Starling got off his stool and followed him. Danny barely registered the catlike grace with which Starling moved; his mind was focused on only one thing: what was Brunholm doing having a secret meeting with the chief spymaster of the Cherbs?

It took Danny a long time to find his way back to the bus, and when he did, he found that all the other cadets had already returned. Smyck glowered at him. A team of girls were lying on a patch of grass, exhausted after having tried to shadow Dixie, who had disappeared and reappeared in unlikely places to such an extent that two of the girls had been reduced to tears. Les looked very pleased with himself, having availed himself of the opportunity to fill his pockets with all sorts of sweets and delicacies from the stalls.

Duddy, looking harassed, was trying to shepherd the cadets onto the bus when Danny heard Frieda's high-pitched voice rise above the general hubbub.

"Please, Miss," she said, "Cadet Caulfield stole something." The rest of the cadets fell quiet. Duddy turned toward Frieda.

"What do you mean?" she said.

"He stole these apples from one of the stalls. There was an awful fuss when the man saw they were gone. We saw it all. Danny took them and ran into a restaurant."

"Is this true?" Duddy asked sternly. "Are you a thief, Caulfield?"

"Well, kind of," Danny said, his gruff voice shaking a little. He was already in enough trouble with Devoy over being caught on the upper floors of Wilsons and releasing the siren.

"What happened?" Duddy demanded. So Danny told her about using the apples as a decoy to get through the restaurant and out the back door. Duddy stared at him, unblinking, as he stammered through the story.

"Well," she said softly as he finished, "who would have thought it." Danny fell silent. He could see Exspectre, a cold grin on his moon face.

"Who would have thought," Duddy said, "that a cadet in his first field lesson would use such a textbook example of the Bolivian bistro feint. Well done, Caulfield, we'll make a spy of you yet."

Danny bowed modestly, trying to keep the grin off his face at Frieda's and Smyck's crestfallen expressions. Then

174

he remembered—Brunholm! Drawing Les and Dixie aside, he told them what he had seen. Les's face hardened at the mention of Rufus Ness.

"If I could get my hands on him," he muttered through clenched teeth.

"What about Starling?" Dixie asked. "What did you think about him?"

"I don't know," Danny admitted. "He's up to something, anyway, no doubt about that. But he didn't seem to be any friend to Rufus Ness."

"Then he's a friend of mine," Les said.

Les didn't speak all the way home on the bus. He seemed lost in memories.

"Leave him alone," Dixie said as the bus screeched into Wilsons on two wheels. "Leave him alone and he'll come home, dragging his tail behind him."

"Sometimes, Dixie," Danny said, "you're just plain daft."

"Maybe," she said, "but you do realize something— if Brunholm's carrying tales to Rufus Ness, then maybe he's told Mr. Ness about our mission. We could be walking into a trap. Bang!" Her hands snapped together in imitation of the steel jaws of a trap, making the dozing Duddy jump in the air and exclaim, "Do put the gun away, Marcus dear!" before looking owlishly around her and muttering something about a bad dream.

When they went inside the school, Duddy removed Danny's makeup and gave him a foul-smelling liquid that got rid of his voice dye. Danny was relieved to get the makeup off his face, but he watched carefully. He had a feeling that the gruff dwarf disguise might be useful in the future.

Back at the Roosts he sought out Les and Dixie and Vandra. He told Vandra about Brunholm and Rufus Ness.

"What do we do?" Vandra asked. "Do we go to Devoy?"

"No," Danny said, "we don't have enough evidence—and me and Les aren't exactly the apples of Devoy's eye at the moment. No, we keep an eye on Brunholm, follow him when we can, wait for him to make a mistake."

"Spying on the spy, in other words," Les said. There was a cold light in his eyes.

"It's getting dark outside," Dixie, who had been staring out the window, said in a stern voice making them all look around.

"Well, it is," she said.

AUTUMN

The days passed quickly. The weather was blustery, the trees in the grounds of Wilsons turned gold, and frequent gales sent great clouds of leaves blowing up and down the gardens and courtyards of the old buildings. Danny couldn't believe how easily he had settled into the rhythm of life at Wilsons. In a way it felt as if he had never been anywhere else. The days were a routine of classes and study. At night they studied in the great hall, the ravens fluttering about in the rafters. They did not see Devoy at all, and Brunholm only rarely, muttering distractedly to himself as he passed them in the corridors. Danny thought this was odd—he had expected some form of special training for his mission. And all the while the thought of the Ring of Five gnawed at him, the knowledge that they were out there somewhere, scheming.

He had the impression that McGuinness was there in the background, not showing his face. Danny tried to be wary—there had been three attempts to kill him, after all—but sitting around a warm stove in the Roosts, eating muffins with his friends, it seemed ridiculous that someone might be plotting to take his life.

He had stopped playing chess in maths class and had taken up playing Texas hold 'em with Vandra and Dixie. Les couldn't be tempted away from his game of bridge. Danny had his first class in ciphers with Bartley, working out very basic codes. But even that was maddeningly hard to get to grips with, when you had to listen to Bartley's strange pronouncements.

In his second week he had his first geography lesson with Spitfire. Danny had never seen anything like her great living map of the Lower World. The rivers were real water, and the forests appeared to be real, although the trees were in miniature. Westwald was clearly visible, as was Wilsons; you could see the great inlet separating the island from the rest of the Lower World, and a sea of darkness on the other side.

"So there is water on one side of Wilsons," Danny said slowly, "and what is this?" He pointed to the darkness.

"Don't touch!" Spitfire warned. "That is the Darkness. An unmapped void of space and time separating the Upper World and the Lower. Few know their way through it, and even if they do, the treaty forbids all but a few like Fairman from crossing it. Wilsons is unique among islands. Water on one side, Darkness on the other. But look. Here is Westwald."

The city of Westwald was often obscured by low cloud and smoke from its many factory chimneys, which swirled around so that it was difficult to get a proper look at the narrow streets and tall houses.

Spitfire explained that the map was kept up to date every day, with movements of forces of the Ring clearly marked, and it was increasingly obvious that Wilsons was in dire straits. As far as Danny could see, there was simply a complex system of bluffs and feints, including putting lights on at night in the watchtowers on the beach so that the enemy would think they were occupied. Danny began to see how the siren's false information would have been very valuable to Wilsons in helping to persuade the other side that the defenders were well armed.

In contrast, the Cherb positions were well manned, each division of troops indicated by a blue and brown marker.

"Top-secret info, Caulfield," Spitfire would bark. "See that you keep it to yourself!"

Every night, Danny and Les would meet with Vandra and Dixie after dinner in Ravensdale, and they would talk about the mission. Danny tried to gather as much information as he could about the Lower World from them, but it was clear that most of Les and Vandra's memories were of their families, and that it was too painful to talk much about them. Instead, the cadets tried to imagine the situations they might find themselves in. Dixie talked about "Cherb tickling," although Danny could see a fiercer light in Les's eye when Cherbs were mentioned.

Twice Danny was called alone to the library of the third landing to meet with Devoy. No matter how much Danny asked, Devoy would not discuss the mission. Instead, he would talk about the great spies of history. The people who had infiltrated the courts of kings, or the halls of governments. The terrible risks they ran, the loneliness and distrust, and the strain that sometimes broke them. He hinted darkly at other things as well—dungeons, and torture. But no matter how much Devoy talked about the harshness of a spy's life, Danny could not suppress a dark thrill at the idea of being at the center of a web of espionage.

Devoy did not talk about his own career much, although he hinted at missions undertaken, colleagues lost. And sometimes, Danny noticed, his eyes strayed to the portrait of Longford, who looked down on them.

Smyck and Exspectre mostly ignored Danny, or seemed to be sharing a secret joke at his expense when they saw him.

"Watch them, though," Les said, "they're not stupid." And as the days went on, Danny found that more and more of the cadets crossed to the other side of the corridor to avoid him, and sensed that a whispering campaign against him was gaining ground. A campaign with the word "Cherb" at the heart of it, he thought sourly.

On a lighter note, reports came back daily of the outrages committed by Vicky the siren on the hapless Messengers. They came down to their dance one evening to find that she had decorated the ballroom with stolen photographs of Messengers in full flight. To their fury, she had enchanted one of the older Messengers, and had been interrupted as she attempted, in Gabriel's words, "to pluck him like a common fowl."

For the most part, she left the cadets alone, although sometimes when she was bored she would enchant the younger boys into declaring their love to her in the most lavish terms, usually in front of their classmates. Several attempts had been made to catch her, but she evaded them with ease. There were rumors that Valant had strung nets through the trees and spread glue on tree branches so that she would stick to them.

18

THE APOTHECARY
OF THE SECOND LANDING

Called again to the library of the third landing, Danny found that his eyes strayed to the portrait of Suzerrain Longford on the wall.

"Could you tell me about him?" he asked Devoy. The master leaned forward and put a log on the fire before speaking.

"We were cadets together here," Devoy said finally, "cadets and friends, or so I thought. That is the great and terrible thing about the art of betrayal. It makes you doubt everything that has gone before. When did the betrayal start? When you thought you were sharing something special with a friend, perhaps that friend was secretly laughing at you."

"But why? Why did he betray you?"

"The reasons for betrayal are always the same.

182

Love—whether for friend or family—or the opposite of love: hatred, money, power and pride."

Which one of them would make a parent abandon you? Danny thought sourly.

"With Longford, it was the last two, I think," Devoy went on. "He would wield more power by joining the Ring than he would ever acquire here. But there was more to it than that. He wanted to see if he could take on and defeat the might of Wilsons, as it then was. He has almost succeeded. One of his great triumphs was to take the Cherbs and change them from a disorganized rabble into a fighting force."

"But he was your friend!"

"Yes. And nightly we do battle with each other in our heads, trying to work out what the other's next move might be. His betrayal claws at my soul. As his own knowledge of what he has done must tear at his."

"I'd never betray a friend like that," Danny said indignantly.

"You think not?" Devoy turned expressionless eyes to him. "Do you really think not?"

Devoy let Danny go early that night, and he was one of the first into Ravensdale. The street was dark and deserted as he made his way toward the Consiglio dei Dieci. He sat at the table, listening to the ravens moving unseen in the rafters overhead. Often now he caught them watching him. "Ask the ravens," the Gallery of Whispers had said, but how did you ask a raven a question, and how did it reply?

The table was set for supper—there were jugs of hot

chocolate and a plate of biscuits at each place. Just as Danny reached for a biscuit, the door opened and Smyck came in. His eyes narrowed when he saw Danny.

"What are you doing here, Cherb? Don't have to study like the rest of us?" Danny kept his head down. He didn't want a showdown with Smyck.

"I'm talking to you, Cherb. You act like you own this place." Danny could feel his face getting red. "This is supposed to be a school for the elite," Smyck went on, "not for some Upper World street trash."

Finally Danny got to his feet, fists balled. But before he could move, the door opened, and Vandra and Les came in. Les took in the situation at a glance.

"Don't do nothing, Danny, he's trying to get you into trouble. Leave him be, Smyck. I can make trouble for you like you wouldn't believe!"

Smyck gave a sneering laugh, but he turned away. As he pushed past Danny, his hand snaked out and he grabbed a biscuit from Danny's plate and rammed it into his mouth. He made his way to his seat, where his sneer turned to a snarl.

"Leave it out, Smyck," Les said, "or I'll have to . . ." The snarl grew louder and turned into a choking sound. They saw Smyck reach up to his throat; then the tall boy was flung from his chair in a great spasm. He landed on the ground, his back bowed at an impossible angle, while his hands clawed at his throat, an anguished gurgling sound coming from his wide-open mouth.

"His lips are turning black!" Danny said. Les said nothing, his eyes round with horror. Danny felt Vandra

184

push past him. She knelt beside Smyck, her face even whiter than usual. Ignoring the terrible noises he was making, she rolled up his sleeve to expose his wrist. She slapped the inside of his arm hard several times, and Danny could see the vein under the skin swell upward. Vandra's two sharp incisors had grown longer, curving down over her lower lip.

"Hold my hair back," she instructed Danny. He leapt forward and held her hair away from her face as she bent to Smyck's wrist. Without hesitating, she plunged her teeth into his arm. Smyck writhed as if some new agony was being visited on him. Vandra kept her head bent, and Smyck thrashed violently from side to side.

"It's not working, Vandra," Les whispered, his voice hoarse. But the physick kept her teeth firmly sunk in Smyck's arm. Gradually, very gradually, the spasms grew less. The black started to fade from his lips. The agonized sounds were replaced by gasps, and then deep breathing. Kneeling close to Vandra, Danny realized that her breathing had become shallow and labored, and he could feel tremors running through her body. A violent shudder almost loosened her teeth from Smyck's wrist, and she grasped Danny's arm hard, her fingers twitching. Danny put his other arm around her shoulders, which were heaving.

"Enough!" Les called out. "Enough, Vandra—he's coming round. Let go!"

For a moment Vandra did not seem to have the strength to break free. Then, with a great wrench, she flung herself backward and lay on the ground, wracked by spasms. To his horror, Danny saw that her lips were now black and that blood trickled down her chin. When he saw her hands claw at her throat Danny started toward her, but a voice rang out.

"Leave her!" It was Brunholm. The master moved swiftly to Smyck's side. The boy's face was pale and his breathing shallow, but there was color coming back into his cheeks.

"Never mind him," Les said, "what about Vandra?"

"Leave the physick alone. What if you go near her and she coughs some of the poison toward you? You have to give her body time to absorb it." He peered at Vandra's face and swollen, blackened lips. "It's the way of the physick. They have to take on the poison or the illness, endure it and vanquish it if they can."

"She looks pretty bad," Les said. It was too much for Danny. Vandra wasn't going to fight the poison on her own. He slid across the floor to her and took her hand.

"Boy!" Brunholm warned, but he dared not approach.

"It's okay, Vandra, I'm here," Danny said soothingly. Her eyes opened and met his and he felt her grip momentarily tighten before another spasm wracked her body. Les came over and knelt beside Danny, followed by Dixie, who appeared from nowhere.

For two hours they knelt beside her, with no one else coming near. Valant had slung Smyck unceremoniously over his shoulder and carried the groaning boy upstairs to the apothecary of the second landing, as instructed by Brunholm.

With agonizing slowness the black faded from Vandra's lips, the spasms became less frequent and her breathing slowed. By midnight she was able to sit up, looking frail and dazed, and only then did Brunholm act.

"Take her up to the apothecary," he commanded. "Use the lift if you must."

"And then I would thank you to leave, Mr. Brunholm," another voice put in. McGuinness was standing in the doorway. "This is a crime scene," he went on, hunkering down to lift crumbs from the floor with a pair of tweezers and putting them in an envelope.

With Vandra's arms draped over their shoulders, Les and Danny made their way to the lift.

"You do realize, of course," Dixie said to Danny, "that the poisoned biscuit was intended for you."

"I know," Danny said, grimly.

"And that whoever it is has only got to be lucky once. You have to be lucky every time they try," Les added.

"I know that too," Danny said. "The problem is I don't know what to do about it."

A button on the control panel with a bubbling flask on it indicated the apothecary. As the lift creaked and groaned upward, Dixie spoke again.

"You've never been to the apothecary before, have you?" Danny shook his head.

"Is it like a clinic or something?" he asked, thinking of the clinic at home with its clean examination rooms and kindly nurses.

"Er, it's something like that," Les answered as the

doors of the lift clanked open. They stepped out into a dark corridor lined with wooden cases. Danny peered into them. Each one was stacked high with glass jars. He looked closer. They were full of murky fluid, and things were floating in them, strange fleshy things. Could that gray whorled object possibly be a brain? And could those discolored leathery objects connected by a tube be a set of lungs? Danny wasn't watching where he was going, and recoiled as he collided with something hard and bony: a skeleton hanging from a stand—but not an ordinary skeleton. This one was small and could have belonged to a child, but for the way the bones of the face were slanted.

"Is that a . . . a Cherb?" Danny asked.

"It is indeed," Les said. "Could be a relation, eh?" Danny glared at him.

The corridor widened into a large room dominated by a table made from white marble with drainage channels down either side. It looked like the kind that was used for dissecting dead bodies. On one side of the room were large metal drawers like the ones in which cadavers were kept in on television.

At least the rooms where bodies were cut up on television were clean, Danny thought. Here the white tiles were stained and broken, and there was what looked like dried blood on the floor and nameless dried-out gobbets of matter under the table. Danny shuddered and tried not to think of what they might be. The air smelt of chemicals, but there was an underlying odor of decay. . . .

Dixie and Les didn't look at all worried by the place. Dixie crossed the tiled floor and pushed through swinging doors, holding them open so that Les and Danny could help Vandra through.

The room they entered next was much cozier than anything Danny had seen so far. Beds and divans were scattered about. There were thick rugs on the floor and Middle Eastern hangings on the walls. A fire blazed in a stone fireplace. Smyck was in a bed at the far end of the room. The man who stood over him straightened as they entered and rushed over. He was wearing a coat that might once have been white, but was now covered in nameless stains. He had lank gray hair, a domed skull and huge black-rimmed glasses.

"What do we have here?" he cried. "Goodness, a physick, such a specimen!" He whipped a tape measure out of his pocket and put it around Vandra's head.

"Fourteen point three," he said. "It would be the biggest physick skull in my collection!" Then he spotted Danny.

"Aha, the sham Cherb—I've heard about you—let me see . . ." He whipped an enormous magnifying glass out of another pocket and set to examining Danny's face.

"Er, Mr. Jamshid, we got a poisoned girl here," Les said.

"Nonsense," Jamshid said, glancing at Vandra, "she's a physick. She'll be right as rain in the morning. Just needs some sleep. Put her in the bed by the fire."

"By the way, I'm not a sham anything," Danny said, annoyed.

"Don't take offense, boy," Jamshid said, "it's an

anatomical description—you'll find it in all the textbooks. It's very difficult to tell the difference. Perhaps if I were permitted to examine your buttocks, there are points of difference between—"

Dixie snorted with laughter as the magnifying glass was angled hopefully downward.

"No, you can't!" Danny felt his face go red. Les looked the other way, trying to hide the grin on his face. The two boys carried Vandra to a bed and put her down.

"Thanks," she managed to murmur.

"You're welcome," Les said.

"Now, let me have a look at her." Jamshid pushed them back and bent over Vandra, looking in her ears and nose and eyes.

"He's a bit strange," Les whispered, "but he's a brilliant doctor. Vandra's in good hands."

"You reckon," Danny said, a bit sourly. "You sure we're not going to come back here tomorrow morning and find her head in a jar?"

"Now, now," Les said, "don't be bitter."

"Just because Les is too weedy to put in a jar," Dixie said.

"Not like him," Les said quietly, looking upward. Danny followed his gaze. At first in the gloom he could just barely see huge, outstretched wings; then he began to discern a gray outline in the darkness. As his eyes grew accustomed to the shadows he took a step backward. Hanging from the ceiling was a skeletal Messenger, wings spread, fully twenty feet from tip to tip, still covered in feathers, although the flesh was long gone. Its empty gaze was severe and mournful. The bony arms seemed poised to seize them, and Danny had to tell himself that the Messenger was fixed in place and would hang there forever, magnificent but melancholy.

"Not sure if I approve of the ancestors being hung from the roof," Les said. In the distance a bell tolled. Suddenly Jamshid was pushing them out of the room.

"Quickly, quickly—leave now! Come see your friend in the morning." Before they had a chance to protest he had hustled them out of the room and through what Danny thought of as the dissecting room. Glancing back, Danny saw a small door in the wall open, the front of a trolley carrying a prone, bloodied figure being wheeled in by unknown hands.

"Must have been a skirmish with the Cherbs tonight," Les said as Jamshid shoved them into the hallway and slammed the door behind them without further comment.

Danny felt light-headed. He couldn't quite take in that someone had tried to poison him earlier on, and the smell of chemicals and decay from the apothecary still stung his nostrils. They got into the lift, Dixie yawning as they did so, sparking off matching yawns from Danny and Les.

"I'm dead beat," Les said.

"No wonder," Dixie said. "It must be past one in the morning."

But if they thought bed awaited them, they were wrong. As the lift doors slid open, they found Brunholm standing in the cold and dark hallway.

191

"Devoy needs to talk to you. Now."

Devoy and McGuinness were waiting for them in the library of the third landing. Devoy paced up and down restlessly in front of the fire as Danny, Les and Dixie filed in after Brunholm.

"Mr. McGuinness will brief us on the unfortunate events of this evening," he said without preamble. McGuinness moved to the center of the room.

"You all know that an attempt was made to poison Cadet Caulfield tonight. I have managed to isolate the poison used, but I have not been able to identify it. Cadet Toxique is assisting me in working on it. I have questioned possible witnesses. Nobody saw anything untoward regarding the poisoned biscuits."

"Thank you, McGuinness." Brunholm nodded none too subtly at the door. McGuinness inclined his head to Devoy, then left. Nothing was said until the door closed behind him.   .

"If it had not been for the swift intervention of the physick, we would have lost Cadet Smyck," Devoy began. "Your presence in Wilsons is a danger not only to yourself, Danny, but to those around you, until the person or persons who are trying to kill you are identified."

"What are you going to do?" Danny said worriedly. "I mean, are you going to send me home or something? I want to go on the mission!"

Devoy's empty gaze rested on him for a long time before he spoke. Danny was aware of the fire crackling, of a rook moving in the rafters above his head.

"I am glad," Devoy said eventually, "that you show so much enthusiasm, though you obviously have not been listening to anything I have told you, if you are so eager. However, we have decided that the best plan for the moment is to bring the mission forward."

19

A SECRET

The three cadets looked at each other. The fire threw long shadows on the library walls. Rain spattered against the window. Suddenly the walls of Wilsons seemed strong and comforting, and the mission they were to go on, an act of folly.

"We had intended to give you as much training as possible," Devoy went on, "but circumstances have changed. Cadet Caulfield, you will go to the city separately from your companions. They have trained in blending into alien surroundings. They will each be given a new identity, a cover story and false documents."

"What will I do?" Danny asked.

"Mr. Brunholm will take you into Westwald and infiltrate you into the counsels of the Ring."

"But what am I supposed to tell them? I don't even know who they are!"

"I cannot give you that information," Devoy said.

"Don't worry. The great art of telling a lie is to stick as close to the truth as possible." Brunholm curled one end of his mustache with a finger.

"But . . . ," Danny cut in. "You can't just send me in there. . . . Longford will never believe that I'm, I'm . . ."

"What?" Brunholm looked amused. "That you're wicked enough to be in the Ring of Five? He'll believe you—everyone can be wicked if they want. They only have to release it in themselves. Now. It's very late and you've all behaved with great courage and all of that. Time for bed!"

And before the puzzled cadets could react, they were being hustled out the door.

"What was that all about?" Les asked as the door slammed shut behind them.

"Doesn't matter." Dixie danced up and down, hugging herself. "We're going on a mission, a real live mission!"

Les saw the look on Danny's face.

"Don't worry, mate," he said, "Devoy's pretty smart. He'll have things worked out. And we'll be there keeping an eye on you. Old Longford won't know what hit him."

Danny grinned weakly. He felt more confused than at any time since he had arrived at Wilsons. And he had seen the look that passed between Devoy and Brunholm when he had asked what he should say. It was different for

Les and Dixie, he thought. They had undergone years of training for what they were facing. He was running from danger into danger. He would have his friends nearby, he hoped, but most of the time he would be alone among dangerous spies. How would he cope?

And yet underneath everything there was the strange attraction that he felt every time the Ring of Five was referred to. A secret desire that was almost too shameful to admit, even to himself.

They entered the silent Roosts, which were lit only by a faint gleam from the stove. Danny took off his clothes and tumbled into bed. He shut his eyes. Visions of poisoners and great flying skeletal Messengers skulked and zoomed through his exhausted mind before sleep finally overtook him.

In the library of the third landing, Devoy stood at the window, a glass of cognac in his hand.

"This time you have gone too far, Marcus."

"It was the only way. Longford would break him like a twig otherwise."

"He may break him like a twig anyway. Wilsons was not set up to act like this. We're as bad as the Ring, if not worse."

"We cannot survive unless we make sacrifices."

"That's the problem, Marcus. We are not the ones who have made the sacrifice. It is young Caulfield who must bear the pain. I wish there were another way."

"It's too late now." Devoy looked at Brunholm's

reflection in the windowpane. The glass had originally adorned a Mirror of Truthful Portraiture. Longford had placed it in the window so that he could more clearly read the thoughts of the person reflected in it. Brunholm didn't know about it, Devoy believed. There were still some things that he did not know. Devoy studied the face behind him, its characteristics exaggerated by the glass. He could see the cruelty there, and the cunning, as well as greed and ambition.

"Wilsons may have sunk lower than the Ring this time," he said.

"If that is the case, it is worth it—millions are kept safe by the unsavory doings of people like us. You can't make an omelet without breaking eggs, Devoy."

There was an air of excitement in Ravensdale the next morning. Everyone knew about the poisoning, and the news spread quickly that some of the cadets were going on a mission. There was disbelief too when it was learned that Danny was among their number.

"He's only here a wet week," Dixie overheard Exspectre telling a group of young cadets in the hallway, "and already he's being sent on a mission. They obviously don't think very much of the rest of us."

Danny found Les outside the door of the Consiglio, surrounded by a group of girl cadets, obviously basking in his newfound and unaccustomed celebrity.

"Well," he was saying, "old Devoy was obviously in a bit of a spot, so of course I couldn't refuse. I can't tell you what it is, naturally, but it is risky. Some of us may not come back. . . ." He broke off, embarrassed, when he saw Danny grinning at him.

There was no sign of Smyck at breakfast, but they were surprised to see Vandra come in late. She was pale and very quiet, and just shook her head when they gathered about her to ask how she was.

"I had to leave the infirmary," she said. "There were major casualties from the front line. A battle with the Cherbs."

"Leave her alone," Toxique said, to their surprise. "You don't get poison out of your system that easily, you know. Leaves you feeling pretty down, even if you are a physick." And getting up and taking his plate, he went over to sit beside Vandra, talking to her in a low voice until eventually Danny could see her responding.

"Do you think Vandra's still going on the mission?" Dixie asked.

"I don't know," Danny confessed. But by the time they had finished breakfast, Vandra appeared to be talking normally to Toxique. And when Blackpitt announced class, she came over to them.

"Toxique was telling me about the poison—he's never seen anything like it before. He's trying to find out what it's made from."

"How are you feeling?" Dixie asked.

"Still not great, but I'm getting better. I keep getting . . . like waking nightmares, you know—feathers and flying and stuff . . ." Dixie squeezed her hand.

"You better pull your socks up for the mission," Les

198

said, "it's been brought forward!" And quickly they told Vandra what had happened.

"I'll . . . I'll be okay," Vandra said, but as she did so she covered her eyes with her hand and frowned. "Just don't tell Devoy about the nightmares."

As they were leaving Ravensdale, Toxique came up behind Danny. The calm presence who had comforted Vandra was gone. His eyes were red and he was muttering to himself. As he was passing Danny he spun around and grasped his shoulder. "Blood!" he muttered. "I see you and blood!" Just as suddenly he let go of Danny and stalked off. Danny looked after him. He was nervous enough about the mission as it was. It's just the way he is, he told himself. But part of him remembered Toxique in maths class, and his uncanny ability to predict what was about to happen. Danny shook himself and walked after the others. He had to stay focused.

That day was a blur of preparation. After breakfast the cadets crammed into the lift with Brunholm.

"Where are we going?" Danny asked as Brunholm pressed the lift button and waited for the ancient elevator to start.

"The Room of Identities on the first landing," Brunholm said shortly. "We need a private place to rehearse your new lives."

The cadets were quiet in the elevator. They were squashed, and Brunholm gave off an overwhelming odor of garlic and strong cologne. Danny was feeling quite ill by the time the lift stopped. They got out onto a sunlit landing, where Brunholm opened a small timber door.

They followed him into a high-ceilinged room with filing cabinets lining one wall and a screen and an old-fashioned projector on the other side. The room felt as if it had not been used in a very long time.

Brunholm took a sheet of paper from his pocket and consulted it.

"Now, Knutt, market trader," he muttered. He went to a drawer and pulled it open, producing several outfits, male and female, from which he selected one—a donkey jacket with a flat cap, breeches, and a leather purse on a belt for keeping money. He also took out a reel of film.

"You're to be a trader in Westwald market, Knutt. Try on the outfit, then watch the film. It'll tell you what you need to know. There's plenty of trash in the market, so you'll fit right in. Our little physick is to get a hospital job and a nice nurse's uniform, and Cole, you will be a domestic servant."

As the day wore on, Danny started to get bored and felt a little left out. His friends' new identities involved a lot of learning of market slang, hospital procedures and, in Dixie's case, simple domestic tasks at which she was hopeless. So Danny was pleased when Blackpitt announced that Cadet Caulfield's presence was required in the library of the third landing. He slipped out, leaving his three friends to study.

He paused in the corridor and, curious, peered out one of the tall windows. It looked down on an internal courtyard that seemed to belong in an old people's home. There were bath chairs and aluminum walkers and deck chairs scattered about. No one was in the courtyard, but just as he was about to go, he saw Gabriel enter. The elderly Messenger looked about very carefully, scrutinizing the windows around him. Danny ducked back. When Gabriel had satisfied himself that there was no one looking, he carefully unfolded his wings and, with tentative flaps, rose a few feet off the ground. He landed and folded the wings quickly, glancing around with an air of innocence. He did this a few more times, and then finally the wings beat powerfully and he shot high into the air. He landed quickly, looked guiltily around the courtyard, then walked quickly back into the building.

Does everyone in Wilsons have a secret? Danny thought.

Danny negotiated the staircase to Devoy's office carefully. Devoy was at his desk, going through papers, and did not look up immediately. When he did, he seemed distracted.

"Yes, Cadet Caulfield," he said, "Suzerrain Longford. I know from old that he will probe you, test you, even though we have sent enough information his way to hint that the fifth member of the Ring has been discovered. He will be bending his will toward finding you, and that is where he is vulnerable. He is desperate to complete the Ring, so, in the depths of his heart, he wants to believe you! Remember that."

"Is he . . . dangerous?" Danny asked.

"Of course. He would kill you without a thought. Or rather, Rufus Ness would do it for him. But you have a quality . . . I can feel it . . . that he will recognize, and will want to believe in, because he recognizes it in himself. The quality most valued by the true spy."

"What quality?" Danny had a feeling he wasn't going to like the answer.

"Faithlessness."

"Sorry?"

"The ability to be treacherous, to betray a friend. As Longford betrayed me."

Danny's fists clenched. "I will not betray my friends, ever."

Devoy's tone did not change. His face gave away nothing. Yet even through his own anger, Danny could feel Devoy's pain. "Just because you were betrayed doesn't mean that I will let my friends down."

"You will need this." Devoy handed him a leather purse. Danny looked inside. It was full of banknotes and silver and gold coins. Then Devoy waved his hand in dismissal.

"That's all for now. I cannot teach all the secrets of spying in a few days or weeks. All I can hope for is that you get an understanding here"—he struck his chest with his hand—"of what it means to be a spy."

AN UNWELCOME VISITOR

Danny met Les, Vandra and Dixie on their way to Ravensdale. They were carrying massive folders containing details of their new identities. They had to learn whole new lives—new parents, new upbringings and new jobs.

As they took seats in the Consiglio dei Dieci, Exspectre glared at them from the far side of the table.

"How's Smyck?" Les asked.

"Sitting up, fighting off the venom. He'll be out and about tomorrow."

"He'd be all right if it wasn't for the poison that vampire pal of yours put into his body," Exspectre spat out. Vandra froze.

"What?" Danny exclaimed, outraged. Les jumped to his feet.

"Everybody's saying it," Exspectre went on. "He had a dodgy stomach for a minute, but she couldn't wait to get her fangs into him."

"She saved his life!" Dixie was almost as pale as Vandra.

"And nearly did herself in and all," Les said. Toxique was staring at Exspectre, muttering under his breath. Danny caught the words "liar" and "vengeance." Vandra put her hand on Toxique's arm.

"No," she said, "no revenge. They can say what they like. It doesn't hurt. At least, nothing could hurt like last night. Let it go."

Les glared at Exspectre. Danny was afraid his friend was going to jump over the table and attack.

"Sit down, Les," Dixie said. "Devoy didn't pick that lot to go on a mission, did he?"

"And why do you think he picked you three?" Exspectre looked from face to face, a hint of color in his cheeks. "We all know why."

"Why's that, then?" Les kept his voice low.

"Because he can afford to lose you three. That's why. Wilsons would be better off without you, and that's a fact," Frieda said, her reedy voice full of malice.

"And you can go boil your head in a pot," Dixie put in, "if you can find a pointy pot."

"Cadets Caulfield, Vaunt, Knutt and Cole to Mrs. Spitfire's room immediately!" There was an urgent note to Blackpitt's interjection, as if he knew that trouble was brewing in Ravensdale. The four cadets filed out, Dixie

204

eyeing Frieda thoughtfully, as though she was seriously thinking about boiling Frieda's head.

When they got to Spitfire's room, they found the live-wire teacher in full mission mode. She was wearing some kind of uniform with a tin helmet, and had turned the lights down, leaving a single spotlight on the map of the city of Westwald.

"Quickly, ' Spitfire said, "gather round. As you know, the living map is a Chart of Near Likeness. It copies the features and the weather conditions of its subject—in this case, Westwald. Westwald is usually covered in cloud and smog. I've been waiting for a break, and here it is, so hurry, before the weather closes in again."

They gazed in wonder at the miniature Westwald. They had never seen the city so clearly. It was full of tall buildings that had once been elegant but were now down-at-heel, their fine stone carvings blacked and eaten away with toxic smoke. There were large department stores, but no lights burned in them. Other places looked closed as well: A building that might be a hospital. Tall hotels, their giant neon signs now dark. Only the market to the east of the city center seemed to be full of lights.

"Pay attention, now," Spitfire said. She pointed at a large dark building just off the main square. "This is the fortress of Grist, the headquarters of the Ring of Five and command center of the Cherb forces. It is said that those who are brought to the fortress of Grist as prisoners never emerge."

Danny shivered, looking down at the vast complex with its towering walls and many courtyards.

"You can feel . . . evil from it," Les said. Danny didn't comment. Yes, you could feel evil coming from the gloomy fortress, but you could also feel power: the fortress dominated everything around it.

"Over here is the market of Bree, where you will be based, Knutt." Spitfire was talking quickly now. Large clouds were moving in from the north of the map.

"The main hospital is closed. Vaunt, you will be operating out of a clinic to the west of the ghetto, just here. . . ." Spitfire pointed to a spot beside a large area of close-packed houses and tenements. The air looked smoky. Danny leaned forward over the ghetto. He could actually smell the poverty and despair.

The cloud was closing fast, already wreathing the top stories of Grist.

"This is the main post office." Spitfire pointed to a once-magnificent building on one of the main thoroughfares, now run-down and shabby. "With luck Les will be doing deliveries to Grist, and you'll be able to stay in contact with Danny."

The cloud was sweeping across Westwald now, hiding the docklands, the old factories to the west belching smoke, the brooding bulk of Grist, the uncared-for boulevards and fancy stores and the strange cluster of poverty-stricken houses in the center. Finally the city was completely obscured.

Leaving Spitfire's classroom, Danny was surprised to see that it was early evening. He walked along behind the others, sunk in thought. Spitfire's map had brought home to him that the chances of succeeding in their mission were next to zero. How could they pit themselves against the Ring, the cruel masters of Grist, and hope to win?

The others headed off to tea, chattering excitedly about the mission. Danny didn't have the heart to eat. Slipping his coat over his shoulders, he ducked out the front door. It was dusk outside, and drizzling. He knew that he should be careful, that there might be another attempt on his life, but somehow he didn't care. *It doesn't really matter,* he told himself; *the mission to Westwald is suicide anyway.*

In this gloomy frame of mind he wandered along the edge of the shrubbery. The rain grew a little heavier, and dark was falling fast. He realized that he had reached the woods and had just turned to head back when he heard the first noise, a scuffling from the direction of the forest. The scuffling turned to running feet and heavy breathing as something forced its way through the undergrowth. Danny, his heart pounding, measured the distance to the main building, now barely visible. He cursed himself for coming so far. If he crossed the lawn he would be completely in the open. Better to move along the perimeter. He broke into a run, but whatever it was seemed to be shadowing him, just out of view, crashing through the branches. Danny ran until his lungs were burning, his breath coming in great racking gasps, but still he could not draw ahead. His pursuer was gaining on him, and he realized too late that the intention was to cut him off. Before he could act, a shape crashed through the shrubs onto the grass in front of him and advanced on him menacingly.

Danny's hands went to his coat pockets. The derringer was in there somewhere, and the Knife of Implacable Intention, but in his confusion he couldn't remember which pocket he had put them in. His hand closed on the lockpicks, then the false mustache. It was too late. His pursuer was on him. A man, wild-eyed, his hair matted and tangled, his clothing torn and stained. He was drawing breath in ragged gulps. Yet despite the unshaven face and bloodshot, desperate eyes, Danny recognized him.

"Sranzer," he gasped. It was the border guard he had met on the first night traveling to Wilsons, the man who had disappeared and the mention of whose name had so upset Valant. But he was far from the arrogant, sneering official he had then been. The man looked to be at the end of his strength, hunted and desperate. He swayed, and without thinking, Danny put out a hand to steady him. Sranzer flinched as if he had been struck.

"It's all right," Danny said, "you're safe." Sranzer gave a harsh laugh.

"You think so? You're the Cherb boy, aren't you? Caulfield?"

"Well, yesss . . . ," Danny said cautiously, thinking that there was no way Sranzer could be the person who was trying to kill him.

"Been trying to get you on your own for days," Sranzer said. "Can't trust nobody in this place."

"What do you want with me?" Danny was mystified.

"Got something for you. Open it in a safe place." Sranzer took a battered and stained envelope out from under his jacket and thrust it into Danny's hands. Danny took it. As he did so, he saw something strange in the border guard's eyes. Just for a moment it appeared that Sranzer pitied Danny. But why? Danny decided he must be mistaken. And then suddenly Danny noticed that Sranzer was awkwardly carrying his right arm, as if it was injured.

"Listen, we need to get you indoors. You need food, and that arm needs to be looked at."

"You're not getting me in there." Sranzer's voice rose to a pitch and he backed away from Danny. "Not that place!"

"Wait!" Danny cried out. "Where are you going?"

"I don't know," Sranzer said, "just away from here." He looked as if he was about to bolt back into the shrubbery.

"Hold on," Danny said, fumbling in his pockets. Sranzer watched him suspiciously. Eventually Danny found what he was looking for—the leather purse. He pulled out several notes and handed them to Sranzer.

"Here, take this." Sranzer looked at the bills for a moment, then snatched them from Danny's hand.

"That'll help. For a day or two, anyhow," he said ungraciously. He looked around at the building again.

"I better go. I spent too long here already."

"I could get you some food."

"No." Sranzer said. "Anyway, you mightn't be feeling so generous once you see what's in that there envelope."

With that, he dashed back into the shrubbery. Danny waited until the sound of the man crashing through the brush was gone; then he turned to the envelope. It was thin—there couldn't be very much in it. Sranzer had said to open it in a safe place . . . the Roosts. There would be no one there at this time of night.

Walking quickly, Danny made his way back to the Roosts. He took the steps two at a time. The boys' Roosts were empty, the stove gleaming softly. There was a smell of warm timber, mingling with a faint but not particularly annoying odor of socks. It was the first time he had been in the Roosts on his own, and he thought how homey a place it was. The last homey place, he thought, that he might see for a long time.

He sat down on his bed, and angled the lamp above it toward him. He opened the envelope slowly. It smelt of sweat, and there were stains on it that looked suspiciously like dried blood. He felt inside the envelope. There was a single sheet of newspaper in it. He took it out and unfolded it. It was the *Times*, dated several weeks earlier—dated in fact three days after he had left home. His eyes ran down the page. In an instant, the world changed. It was as if someone had put a great weight on him, pressing him down into the bed. The cozy surroundings of the barracks became sinister and threatening, and the gentle crackle of the fire and the sigh of the wind outside became sounds of mockery. The paper fell from his trembling hand and

lay on the bed, the headline stark and terrible. Beneath the
headline ·

LOCAL COUPLE SLAIN

was a photograph of his mother and father, both smiling
a little shyly at the camera—a photograph he recognized,
for it had been on the mantelpiece at home.

Beneath that was his own photograph, taken in his
school uniform only the year before, yet seeming now to
belong to a long-ago time of innocence.

SON MISSING.

He forced himself to pick up the paper and read. In
some recess of his heart a voice said that it could not be
true, that they were not dead, that they were still waiting
for him in the big house. And at the same time the cold
hard voice of reality said: this is true.

The words streamed past his eyes without his
understanding them. "Brutal killing." "Discovered by
neighbors." He thought he had read every word on the
page, and then realized that there was another section below the fold. He looked at it, not wanting to take in any
more, but unable to stop reading.

SUSPECT SEEN FLEEING SCENE.

Police want to interview a man wearing dark clothing seen fleeing the scene. He is described as being of
medium build and having a distinctive mustache.

Beneath this was an identikit photograph, wrong in some details, but accurate in the most important ones. An unmistakable face, for Danny had spent most of the day with its owner. The face that looked out of the paper at him was that of Marcus Brunholm.

Danny did not know how or when he had started running, or when the storm had begun. He only knew that he was running through the forest, branches whipping at his face, his clothes soaked with rain. All he wanted was to put as much distance between himself and Wilsons as he could, never to see it again. But no matter how fast and how far he ran, Brunholm's face in the identikit photograph danced mockingly in his mind.

At last he could run no longer. As he staggered and stumbled, his foot was caught by a briar and he fell facedown in the sodden leaf mold. Around him the wind and rain lashed at the leafless branches. He twisted his body until he could see the sky, a full moon appearing in the gaps between fast-moving storm clouds. His hip ached where he had banged into a tree. His face was caked in dirt and dried blood from where the branches had whipped it. Wearily he pulled himself upright. He was in the middle of the forest, and lost. He could not—would not—go back to Wilsons. There was nothing to take him back to the Upper World anymore. Barely knowing what he was doing, he pushed his way through the undergrowth, repeatedly stumbling and falling, until at last a clearing opened in front of him. And in the clearing stood a familiar building.

He barely made it to the door of the summerhouse, where he and Les had talked and lazed in the sunshine. He struggled to close the door against the storm, stumbled across the room and threw himself down on the window seat. A length of threadbare curtain lay on the window-sill. He pulled it over himself and fell into a deep, troubled sleep.

21

NURSE FLANAGAN

"Wakey wakey, sleepyhead. Rise and shine, lie-abed. Get up, get up, before . . . you're . . . *dead!*"

Danny opened his eyes and froze. A shining blade hovered an inch from his face. He struggled to focus his eyes against the watery early-morning sun, then recognized the face looking down at him.

"Vicky?" he said.

"How do you know my name?" the siren said.

"We let you out of the cell. In Wilsons. You remember?"

"Oh yes, suppose you did." She sniffed. The knife wavered, and then withdrew.

"I nearly slit you," she said, looking a little disappointed. "Easier when someone's asleep. Obvious, really."

"I'm glad you didn't," Danny said, sitting up. Then it hit him again. His parents.

"What's wrong?" Vicky asked.

"I . . . I . . . My parents are dead."

"Oh. Did you kill them?"

"No! Of course not."

"Can't blame me for asking. Since you're on the run and all. There's an awful fuss going on up at Wilsons."

"Don't mention that place to me!"

"Touchy, touchy." Vicky's eyes narrowed and she ran her thumb along the blade of the knife thoughtfully. "No point in shouting at me, you know."

"Sorry. It's not your fault."

"That's right," she said, brightening. "It isn't. The whole place is in an uproar looking for someone, probably you."

"I don't want them to find me."

"Then you'd better get out of here."

"I don't know how."

Vicky paused and put her head on one side, listening.

"What is it?" Danny asked anxiously. Then he heard it, carried in on the wind, faint and distant: the sound of barking.

"What's that?"

"Bloodhounds," Vicky replied.

"Bloodhounds?"

"On your trail, I'd say. They belong to Brunholm." An image came into Danny's head: Brunholm standing over his parents' bodies. His fists clenched. Then the tone of the barking changed. The dogs were howling now.

215

"They've picked up your scent," Vicky remarked.

"Can you get me out of here?" Danny asked.

"Why would I do that?"

"You owe me one. We got you out of jail."

"By my reckoning, that slate is wiped clean."

"How?" Danny demanded.

"I could have cut your throat when you were asleep, but I didn't." Her voice was firm, and Danny knew there was no point in arguing.

"I can give you money," he said.

"Naw. Got plenty of money hidden away. Besides, there's nowhere for the likes of me to spend it." She picked her nails with the tip of the knife. The howling was getting louder and nearer.

"Is there anything else I can give you?" he said desperately.

"Well . . . I don't suppose you've got a new dress, or a bit of makeup—anything like that. You get tired of the same old look all the time," Vicky said, moodily, staring at her reflection in a dusty old mirror that hung from a nail on the wall.

"No," Danny said, deflated. He thought for a moment. "Hang on." He fished in the pockets of his coat. "What about this?"

He produced the limp ginger wig he had been given in the Stores. Vicky looked at it with interest, then took it from his hand. She fitted it over her head and looked at herself in the mirror, flicking it back with her hand. Danny thought it looked ridiculous, but Vicky seemed quite taken with it, turning first to one side and then to the other.

"Well?" Danny asked, trying to quell the desperation in his voice.

"I think it suits me," she said, "what do you think?"

"It's really you," he said. "Honestly, really sets off your . . . your eyes."

"You think so? You're not just saying that?"

"You're a new woman—siren, I mean." Vicky laughed coquettishly and did a twirl.

"Is it a deal?" Danny said. The cries of the bloodhounds were even louder.

"Okay," she said. "There's an old path leads down the back here to the main road. Walk backward for the first hundred yards and then it's easy."

Danny opened the door. The baying of the bloodhounds came from the trees on his left. He could hear voices as well.

"That way." Vicky pointed toward a barely visible path running through a reed bank. Danny took off at a run, just remembering to turn and run backward, as best he could, as he reached the start of the path. Panting and stumbling, he forced his way through the reeds, which had started to overgrow the gravel. Before the summerhouse disappeared from view, he saw Vicky skip onto the roof and run lightly along a branch of an overhanging tree.

When he judged he had gone one hundred yards backward, he turned again, running full tilt through the reeds. Behind him the baying of the bloodhounds reached a crescendo. They had discovered the fresh scent. Danny ran faster, gasping for breath. He realized that he hadn't eaten or drunk anything since the previous day, and weakness was seeping into his limbs. The howling dogs were gaining on him. He ran across a small bridge, and was faced with an iron gate in a stone wall. Shaking with the effort, he clambered over the gate and dropped down on the other side. With a start he recognized the road outside the Wilsons grounds. He looked left and looked right. The road was empty in either direction. A high stone wall overhung by trees on the other side meant that there was no escape that way. And behind him he could hear the dogs panting as they strained against their leads. He was trapped.

He felt in his pockets for the Knife of Implacable Intention. Brunholm would be with the dogs. Danny could at least get some revenge for his parents. Then he heard something. A buzzing noise in the distance, rising to a low, thrilling hum. He looked up. In the distance he could see a dot in the road, with a trail of dust rising behind it. The hum rose to a growl. It was a car, traveling fast. As it neared, Danny saw an immensely long red hood with chrome exhausts and a low-slung body, the paintwork gleaming in the weak morning sun.

The car slowed and came to a halt beside him, the throb of the powerful engine almost drowning out the slavering bloodhounds. The passenger window slid down, and Danny found himself looking at the woman he had glimpsed from the bus on the way to Tarnstone. Her black hair was piled on top of her head, held with a diamond clip. She wore a fur coat. Her lipstick was the deepest red he had ever seen. In one hand she held an unlit cigarette in a long holder.

"Do get in," she said, in a husky voice. "Really. When

one is being pursued, one shouldn't stand gawping. It looks so very loutish."

Above the engine noise and the bloodhounds Danny could hear Brunholm calling out.

"Cadet Caulfield! Caulfield!"

That decided it. Danny grabbed the door handle. In seconds he was ensconced in a luxuriant leather seat. He slammed the door and was thrown back against the seat as the car accelerated away.

"That's much better," the woman said. "I don't know who was after you, but it's so tiresome when one is being chased. My name is Nurse Flanagan. Cigarette?"

Danny looked down at the gold cigarette case that had suddenly appeared under his nose.

"No . . . no thank you," he stammered. He felt light-headed from the smell of leather mixed with musky perfume filling the interior of the car. Nurse Flanagan looked him up and down.

"Obviously spent the night sleeping rough. Always a bit of a tricky one."

Danny couldn't imagine the beautifully dressed Nurse Flanagan ever sleeping rough, and he found himself wishing she would look at the road instead of at him, considering the fact that they were traveling extremely quickly indeed.

"Food!" Nurse Flanagan cried. "Of course! That's what the boy needs. Open the glove compartment there."

Danny did as he was told. He took out a large tortoise-shell box and opened it. Inside he found, perfectly wrapped in crisp foil, a large portion of salmon sandwiches and a monogrammed flask, which turned out to contain hot sweet tea. He didn't have to be told twice to tuck in, glad that Nurse Flanagan had now switched her attention back to the road.

"Bad manners to ask someone why they're running. Mum's the word. But if you're trying to get away from someone, and you have some money, then my recommendation would be to try the Painted Wall. Although," she said, wrinkling her nose, "if I were you, I'd stay away from the Scrawnings. Foul stuff."

Danny nearly choked on his sandwich. A plan had been starting to form in his head, the starting point of which was the Painted Wall—and now here was Nurse Flanagan suggesting it to him!

"That—that would be great," he spluttered through a mouthful of sandwich, spraying the dashboard with crumbs, which drew a severe look from her. "Sorry," he muttered. She took a little silver atomizer from her pocket and sprayed perfume into the air, adding to the already heady atmosphere.

"That's the problem when one sleeps in one's clothes," she murmured. "They become a little . . . ripe."

Danny looked out the window. To his surprise they were on the outskirts of Tarnstone already. The car negotiated the traffic with ease, Nurse Flanagan handling the wheel expertly. They tore through the little square surrounded by restaurants, and found themselves on much narrower streets, although Nurse Flanagan didn't slow down all that much.

"None of my business, dear," she said, "but you are

trying to get away from someone?" Danny nodded. "There's something more, isn't there?" Danny turned away. His parents. He was trying not to think about them, but they were there all the time. He could see his father pottering about in his study, making models. He saw his mother in the garden wearing a shapeless hat. Tears started to his eyes as he looked out the window.

"Oh, my dear!" Nurse Flanagan exclaimed, and a tiny lace handkerchief drenched in French perfume fluttered into his lap.

"I'm okay," Danny said, gingerly handing the handkerchief back. She examined him curiously as the car screeched around a corner, narrowly missing a group of evil-looking sailors.

"Do you know, I hadn't noticed—I'm as blind as a bat," she said, "but you do look rather like a Cherb."

"I'm *not* a Cherb!" Danny said hotly.

"Oh good gracious, I know that now. I mean, whoever heard of a Cherb weeping?"

"Er, Nurse Flanagan?" Danny said as the car hurtled toward a blank wall. But with an expert spin of the wheel, Nurse Flanagan took a sharp left into an alley. With only inches to spare, the car careered at top speed down the narrow passage. Danny remembered what she had said about her eyesight and shut his own eyes.

Abruptly the car screeched to a halt, and the engine was switched off. Cautiously Danny opened one eye and then the other. They were right outside the Painted Wall.

"I am," Nurse Flanagan pronounced, "most dreadfully thirsty. I think I shall join you, if you have no objection?"

221

Danny couldn't imagine how anyone could object to anything Nurse Flanagan might want to do, so he merely nodded dumbly, and scrambled after her as she got out of the car and made her way toward the hidden entrance. When she got to the painted cloth door, she stood to one side. Danny hurried to hold the cloth back for her.

"Thank you," she said graciously, and swept past him. Danny hesitated. Nurse Flanagan wasn't in his plan. Then he looked at the deserted street, and he thought about Brunholm and the baying bloodhounds. The Painted Wall was his only chance. He took a deep breath and plunged after her.

By the time he caught up, Nurse Flanagan had reached the bar. There were only a few people at the bar itself, although Danny knew there might be more in various alcoves. The barman obviously knew her. He raised an eyebrow.

"Don't be tiresome, Raymond," she said, "you know the vintage."

With an apologetic bow, the barman swept a bottle of champagne onto the counter.

Obviously not everyone in the bar knew her. An oily-looking sailor in suspenders and a filthy blue tunic edged up to her.

"How about a taste of that there champagne, miss? Maybe me and you could—"

No one got to hear what the sailor might propose. Nurse Flanagan lifted a knife used for slicing lemons. The knife flashed in the direction of the sailor's belly. The sailor looked down in horror, thinking he had been stabbed, then, with comic panic, seized his trousers. She had sliced his suspenders, and the trousers were in danger of ending up around his ankles.

"By that uniform you're off the ship *Arcane*," she said. "Tell Captain Jonas I was asking for him."

The sailor sprang to attention.

"You—you know Captain Jonas?" he spluttered, and tried to salute with the hand that was holding up the trousers, which slid down, revealing a pair of grubby boxers, to the great amusement of the rest of the bar.

"Creates quite a distraction, doesn't she?" Danny jumped as someone spoke beside him. He spun around. It was the gray-eyed man he had met when he was disguised as the ugly little dwarf. The eyes narrowed as they met Danny's gaze.

"Do I know you? I have a feeling we've met."

"I've never been here before," Danny said, hurriedly. Starling took him by the elbow and steered him toward a dim corner. At the bar Nurse Flanagan laughed gaily as the cork popped from the champagne bottle.

"I'm curious," Starling said.

"Curious about what?"

"First of all, Brunholm's agents in town are instructed to find a boy who looks like a Cherb. And then that boy walks into the Painted Wall, along with the notorious Nurse Flanagan, who proceeds to make a scene at the bar to distract attention from her companion."

Danny stared at Nurse Flanagan. Was that what she was doing? And were Brunholm's agents scouring the town for him already? He looked around the bar nervously.

"What kind of nurse is she, anyway?"

"You don't want to know," Starling said. "She was struck off years ago. So tell me. Why did you come to the Painted Wall?"

"I need to get out of Tarnstone."

"Do you indeed? You know that by treaty there is no access to the Upper World. If you want to get out, the only place you can go is the Lower World."

"I know."

"And it costs money."

"I've got money."

"And," Starling went on, "if you are captured by the Cherbs, they'll bring you to the Ring of Five. Do you know that?"

"I do." Danny took a deep breath. "I know that. That's where I want to go."

"Indeed?" Starling's eyes betrayed no expression. Danny waited. He felt as if time had stopped.

"Well," he burst out, "can you help me? You said . . . I mean, I heard you were an importer and exporter. Can you get me to the Lower World?"

"I can try. The question is, do I want to? I could end up involved in something I don't want to be involved in. Brunholm is not a good man to have as an enemy. Not to mention the Ring."

Danny took the wallet Devoy had given him from his pocket, opened it and showed the contents to Starling. Starling rubbed his chin thoughtfully, then reached in and removed a sheaf of notes, which promptly disappeared into a pocket.

"All right," he said, "come on. There's not a moment to lose. Brunholm's men will be watching the ports, but they might not all be in place yet. Let's go."

"What about Nurse Flanagan? I should say something to her."

"Don't be a fool. If you go up to her at the bar, every eye in the place will be on you. Wilsons agents will be all over this place. Forget Nurse Flanagan."

Danny followed Starling, but glanced back from the exit. Nurse Flanagan was sitting at the bar, glass of champagne in one hand, cigarette holder in the other. Her great liquid eyes swept over him, but did not stop. He remembered what she had said about her eyesight, and wondered if she hadn't been able to see him across the room.

"Hurry," Starling hissed, "do you want to get caught?" Danny hurried after Starling.

Behind him Nurse Flanagan replaced her glass on the counter thoughtfully. She motioned to the bartender.

"Phone," she said. The bartender placed it on the counter. She lifted the receiver and began to dial with one finely manicured finger. She waited, then spoke.

"Thank you for the tip, Marcus. All has gone smoothly. Yes, yes, of course I will bear your . . . cooperation in mind."

Nurse Flanagan replaced the receiver. She smiled thinly and just for a moment looked much older, her face gaunt, her eyes a nest of wrinkles.

ESCAPE FROM TARNSTONE

Starling led him through a maze of small alleys and squares, the houses getting poorer and shabbier. They saw no one, although mangy dogs growled at them from rubbish-strewn backyards. Danny tried to question Starling about where they were going, but he wouldn't answer. Danny noticed the way that Starling moved— light-footed and furtive, making no sudden movements, each step flowing into each other.

Eventually the alleys began to open up, and Danny could smell the sea. There were people on the street, and cooking aromas. The people looked Chinese to Danny, but the language they spoke did not sound Eastern. The men wore caps with tall peaks and earflaps. After a while he and Starling rounded a corner and emerged on a busy shopping street.

"Wait here," Starling said. He was back within minutes with one of the peaked caps.

"Put that on and keep your head down so that no one sees your eyes. They're not too fond of Cherbs around here."

"Who are these people?"

"Skreens, they're called. They're allowed to trade between Tarnstone and Westwald, which makes them useful. Unfortunately, it means they're watched as well."

Starling's head moved continuously from side to side. Sometimes he stopped Danny and ushered him into an alley while someone passed.

"Not sure about him," he would mutter, or, "Definitely one of Brunholm's."

"Does Master Devoy have any spies in Tarnstone?" Danny asked.

"He does," Starling replied, shooting Danny a look, "and so does the Ring."

He pushed Danny through a door with a sign that read C. D. NAGLE, LICENSED DEALER. They went up a long dark staircase. At the top there was a shabby wooden door. Starling knocked and went in without waiting for an answer. Danny followed.

The room behind the door was tiny and almost filled by a large desk and an enormous leather chair. The desk was covered with bills, receipts, dockets, invoices, statements, bills of lading, checkbooks and every other conceivable form of paper that people used to do business. Behind the desk, on the enormous leather chair, was a tiny man with shrewd black eyes. His head was entirely hairless, covered in wrinkled brown skin. He wore an immaculate black pinstripe suit and a miniature bow tie.

"Afternoon," he said tonelessly.

"Afternoon," Starling said, and then without any more formalities, "Cargo."

"Cargo?" Nagle—for Danny assumed it was his name on the sign—replied, with a slightly raised eyebrow.

"To Westwald."

"Westwald. Alive or dead?"

"Alive." Danny wasn't sure he liked the way the conversation was going. He guessed he was the cargo, and he didn't like the "alive or dead" question. Nevertheless, the two men continued the conversation as if he wasn't in the room.

"How much?" Nagle asked. Starling took out the bundle of notes he had taken from Danny, peeled off about half, and handed them to Nagle. Nagle held the money in his outstretched hand, not moving. Starling peeled off two more notes. Evidently satisfied, Nagle folded the money carefully and placed it in a large wallet that he took from an inside pocket. Then, for the first time, he looked at Danny.

"Many people looking for you," he said, "pay good money as well. But Mr. Starling is friend, so I give him discount." Nagle laughed wheezily, then got to his feet. "Come." He beckoned. There was a door behind the chair. Nagle waited by it as Danny and Starling made their way around the desk, then flung the door open.

The contrast with the quiet little office couldn't have

been more startling. The door opened onto a vast warehouse, piled to the roof with all sorts of goods, from carpets and fridges to oil drums and wine crates. Forklifts whizzed from stack to stack, and burly stevedores bellowed instructions to each other across pulleys and conveyor belts.

Paying no attention to the cacophony, Nagle led them down a steel staircase and across the floor.

"Keep your head down," Starling shouted above the noise. "They're all Nagle's people—but still . . ."

Danny did as he was told, following Nagle's feet, which were encased in shiny black patent shoes and moved very quickly, almost twinkling as the little man bustled along.

Gradually the noise subsided. Danny felt a breeze on his face and risked a look up. They were emerging from the warehouse onto a quay. The far end was busy, but here it was much quieter. A flotilla of boats with sails like those of Chinese junks were moored together, and Danny could see that there were whole families complete with babies and dogs on board. Beyond the wooden boats was a rusty battered tramp steamer with two salt-encrusted funnels. Nagle hurried up the gangplank. The captain was standing on the battered bridge—he was a hard-looking man with a scar on his cheek, and a limp. Nagle spoke to him quickly in their language—Skreenese, Danny called it to himself—then came back to them.

"Captain Strank will take you over. You must hide when customs check ship. Ship will drop you in Westwald. After that . . ." Nagle shrugged, as if to say it

229

was none of his business if Danny wanted to throw his life away.

"Thanks," Danny said.

"No thanks," Nagle said, "business. Finished now." With a brisk nod to Starling he sped down the gangplank and across the wharf, then disappeared into the warehouse. Danny looked at Starling in confusion.

"Yes," Starling said, "I'm coming too. I've got business in Westwald and I knew Nagle would give me a better deal on two."

Danny didn't say anything. He was glad Starling would be with him. He leaned over the rail and saw families having lunch together on the boats in the water below. A wave of loneliness swept over him. In the nearest boat a mother dandled a little boy on her knee. The child saw Danny looking down and clapped his hands and laughed. Danny covered his face with his hands. He was alone and hunted in a strange land, destined for more danger. He felt a brisk clap on his shoulder.

"When was the last time you ate?" Starling asked.

"This morning."

"I'll buy some food off the captain," Starling said, looking at Danny expectantly.

"Oh yes. Here." Danny handed him some coins. Starling went off and came back with a kind of chicken stew and fresh white bread. The stew was heavily spiced, but Danny wolfed it down.

"We have to wait until nightfall," Starling said, and promptly sat back against one of the funnels, closed his eyes and went to sleep.

It was a long day. The captain and crew ignored Danny and set about loading a cargo of oil drums. The whole afternoon was filled with the clang of drums and the shouts of the crew. Danny was tired, but he could not sleep. Images of his parents drifted into his mind. He pushed them away, closed them off. His mind felt cold and clear. He knew what had to be done. He did not know whether everything he had heard at Wilsons was true. But he did know that Brunholm had killed his parents. He scanned the quayside watchfully, but all he could see were Skreens. He had the feeling he was in a Skreen stronghold, and that everyone around him was loyal to Nagle before anyone else.

When the hold of the ship was almost full, the captain suddenly appeared agitated. Various items were gathered up off the deck and shoved into cubbyholes and hidden openings that appeared on the deck. Starling opened one eye just as the captain approached them. He ushered them quickly to the forward funnel and grabbed a piece of tubing attached to the side of it, and to Danny's surprise, a door appeared—it was a false funnel!

Starling and Danny stepped inside, and the captain slammed the door behind them. It was dark and musty, but light got in between the rusty steel-plate walls. There were objects all around them, mysterious boxes and bales—things that the ship was smuggling, Danny thought.

"Hope we're not in here for the whole journey," Danny said. Starling, who was peering through a crack in the funnel, put his finger to his lips. Danny found another crack. When he saw what Starling was looking at, he felt rage well up inside him. Brunholm! The Wilsons instructor stood on deck with a team of men in uniform with white peaked caps.

"Customs inspectors," Starling whispered. But Danny's attention was focused on Brunholm, who was arguing with Captain Strank. With a sweep of his hand, Brunholm ordered the two customs inspectors into action. They began throwing aside tarpaulins, turning water butts on their sides, poking inside lifeboats. Brunholm seemed to be insisting that the hold with the oil drums be searched. When the captain threw up his hands, Brunholm produced a revolver and shot a hole in the side of one of the drums. Heavy dark oil spilled onto the deck. Captain Strank turned pale. He motioned to the inspectors to descend to the hold. Brunholm grinned, showing his white teeth.

Danny realized that Starling was looking at him with curiosity, as if Danny's hatred was visible in his tightly clenched jaw and his fixed stare. Danny ignored him. It was all he could do to stop himself flinging open the door and racing across the deck to tackle Brunholm before the man could bring the revolver to bear. He felt Starling lay a warning hand on his shoulder. Reluctantly he tore his eyes away from Brunholm. Starling's gray eyes fixed on Danny's and held them. Although Starling did not speak, Danny felt as if words passed between them, words that warned him against hatred. A small voice inside him stirred and said that he was still Danny Caulfield, no matter what had happened to his parents, that he was still their son and nothing could take that away from him. But he hardened himself against the voice.

He put his eye back to the crack in the steel. Brunholm was still there, but the urge to attack him was gone. Danny's revenge would take time, but it would be thorough. It was not enough to kill Brunholm. The man had to be caught in a web of intrigue first. The revenge had to be savored.

The search took over an hour. It was dark before an angry Brunholm and the customs men left the ship, taking with them some small items of contraband. By the time they were clear a cold wet fog had drifted in over the dock. The captain cast off. Danny stood on his own in the bow as the ship eased away from the wharfside. Harbor lights glowed a dull yellow behind the fog. Dark shapes loomed from the quay. A mournful hoot from the pierhead foghorn was answered by a blast from the ship's own horn, which was swallowed by the wreathing vapors. Oily water lapped softly against the barely moving hull.

And then Danny realized that they were alongside the pier, almost close enough to touch it, so that he leaned out for one moment as if to brush his fingers against the pier wall. But it was too late. The pier dissolved into the fog, and they were on the open sea. Seconds later a breeze parted the fog, and Danny saw in the distance the lights of Westwald. In the dark and damp, all plans seemed futile. Danny had left everything behind. Only the Ring of Five awaited.

WESTWALD

The crossing was to be longer than Danny had supposed. There were strong currents in the strip of sea, and the steamer had to sail up against the current, then allow the force of it to carry her down. The engines labored, and gouts of black smoke from the rear funnel trailed the ship.

"It will take three to four hours," Starling said. "You might as well get some sleep."

Danny didn't think he would, but he had barely slept the night before in the summerhouse. There was a rough bed in the fake funnel. He thought he would just lie down for a minute to rest. He pulled a filthy blanket over himself with a grimace, and within seconds he was fast asleep.

On through the night the little ship sailed, rising and falling on the choppy swell. As they neared the far shore Starling stood and looked down at Danny for a moment.

Then he went out and stood in the bow. By the time the first glimmer of dawn appeared in the east, the ship was sailing down the coastline toward Westwald. Starling could not see the shore yet, but he could hear surf growling on the hard shingle beach. After a while he saw a light ahead. He waved to the captain of the steamer and it slowed in the water. A fishing boat came into view, manned by people with hoods pulled over their heads, their faces hidden. Tossing badly in the swell, the boat pulled alongside the steamer. Without a backward glance, Starling slipped lightly over the rail and stepped onto the rolling deck. In minutes the fishing boat had disappeared into the predawn darkness.

The blast of the ship's siren woke Danny. He leapt up in a panic, and raced out on the deck. The ship was on a wide waterway with docks and warehouses to either side. The water was teeming with boats of all sizes trying to make their way up or down the crowded shipping lane. A few hundred meters away, a sinister black patrol boat moved menacingly among the other vessels. The air smelt smoky, and a fine pall of smog hung over the buildings to either side.

Danny tried to remember Spitfire's geography class, which seemed so long ago now. The main harbor should be near. He felt a prickling in the back of his neck. He turned. Just behind him, keeping pace with the boat, was the sinister black craft he had seen moments earlier. The windows were smoked, so he couldn't see inside, but on the top of the wheelhouse two soldiers manned a gun. Danny felt a thrill of fear run down his spine. Cherbs!

They wore black uniforms with silver markings, and polished black leather boots. Their faces had the same pixie shape as his own, and he imagined, the same eyes—one brown and one blue. But there the resemblance ended, or at least Danny hoped it did. For the two Cherbs wore expressions of mingled brutality and cunning. Danny had seen Rufus Ness, of course, but that had been in the relatively tame surroundings of the Painted Wall. Here they seemed much more threatening.

The black boat inched closer. The two Cherbs examined him with open curiosity. Danny smiled weakly and waved at them. They stared for another moment; then the engine of the boat roared, her stern dug in and the boat sped off. Danny breathed a sigh of relief.

"What do you think you're doing?" Captain Strank barked angrily. "They could have boarded us."

"I'm—I'm sorry," Danny stammered.

"You never do see Cherbs until too late," Strank grumbled.

"Where's Starling?"

"Gone. Went over the side at dawn onto a fishing boat." Danny stared at Strank, feeling a wave of panic. He hadn't entirely trusted Starling, but he had been glad to have him there. He quelled his fear by summoning an image of Brunholm. In an instant his mind was ice-cold. He turned his back on Strank and stared straight ahead. He didn't need Starling.

Much of the geography lesson about Westwald was hazy, but there was one thing he did not forget. As the steamer forged up the river, a shape began to resolve itself, dominating the town, massive and grim, so that Danny felt at once repelled, and, on another level, attracted. Even though you could barely see it through the smog, every soul in Westwald knew it was there every moment of every day, though they muttered and turned aside and averted their gaze. It was always there, and for many it was their final destination: the fortress of Grist. Headquarters of the Cherbs, home of the Ring.

The ship began to slow and Danny could see a busy dock up ahead. There was a redbrick railway station on the quay. As they got nearer Danny could see that the windows were begrimed and the steel pillars were rusted. On the roof there was a gun emplacement manned by uniformed Cherbs. The quayside was in a state of chaos. A crane had dropped several sacks, and golden grain spilled from them across one of the railway lines. Armed Cherbs stood on a dirty-looking locomotive, shouting at the crane operator.

The Cherbs yelled at a group of men who were unloading another boat, and the men scurried to clean up the mess. The men were thin and poorly dressed against the damp, cold early-morning air. Danny could see that they were nervous. They didn't seem to be fearful of the Cherbs on the train, but kept glancing upward. He followed their gaze. There were birds circling high above the city. No, not birds . . . great winged shapes wheeling in the dirty air.

"What are they?" Danny asked Strank.

"Seraphim," the man muttered, and a shadow of fear crossed his face. Danny looked back at the men clearing the railway track. A gout of oily smoke from the locomotive drifted across them, and one of the men, under cover of the smoke, scooped some of the grain into his pocket.

It took only a few minutes to clear the track. Danny was sorry to see the grain swept up. The golden corn had looked like a pool of sunshine against the dreary background of the dockside. The locomotive got up steam and, billowing black smoke, hid the wheeling Seraphim from view.

As the ship made fast to the quay, Strank called Danny over.

"My job is done now. You get off my ship."

"Don't worry," Danny said, "I'm going."

"You got papers?" Strank asked, suddenly looking worried.

"Why? You afraid you'll get into trouble? Don't worry. You might even get a medal or something for taking me to Westwald."

Strank looked puzzled. Danny went down to the lower deck, where two of the Skreen deckhands had put a gangway to the quayside in place. The minute the gangway touched the quay, two Cherb soldiers were in place at the end. Danny studied them for a while. They looked down at passing people from under the shiny peaks of their caps, and he could see that in their turn, the shabbily dressed passersby gave them a wide berth. The soldiers stood with their thumbs hooked into the belts of their black uniforms, guns slung over their shoulders, obviously seeing themselves as far superior to anyone else on the dock. That might work to my advantage, Danny thought. Once they see my eyes, they'll think I'm one of them. They'll be eating out of my hand.

Without another thought he strode confidently down the gangplank to the Cherbs, who watched without expression.

"Hi," he said. The nearest Cherb looked him up and down without saying a word. He was tall for a Cherb, with a mole in the center of his forehead just above his two slanting eyes, which gave him the odd appearance of having three eyes. The other Cherb seemed to be pretending that Danny wasn't there.

"Er, hello," Danny said.

"What do we have here, Sergeant?" the first Cherb said.

"I don't know, Lieutenant." The second one turned and pretended to notice Danny for the first time. This one had shiny dark brown skin stretched tight on his face, which made him look like a snake.

"I think what we have here," went on Three Eyes, as Danny was starting to think of him, "is a deserter."

"A deserter, sir? You mean one of our lads who has gone on the run?"

"I'm afraid so, Sergeant."

"No, no," Danny said, "I'm here to see Rufus Ness." The two Cherbs smiled, revealing rows of sharp little teeth.

"Are you now, sonny," Snake said. "And why do you have to see Mr. Ness?"

"I need him to bring me to Suzerrain Longford." The two soldiers looked at each other in mock amazement.

239

"Suzerrain Longford, is it?" Snake said. "Why, certainly. I'll bring you myself."

"Will you?" Danny said eagerly.

"Of course not, you horrible little toerag!" Snake bellowed. "Where are your papers?"

"I haven't got any," Danny said faintly.

"It ain't got any, sir," Snake reported to Three Eyes.

"Are you stupid or insane, or both?" Three Eyes inquired. "You come walking off a ship demanding to meet those whose names your filthy little mouth shouldn't even know how to form, and want to be taken to them. What unit did you desert from? Answer me now!"

"I really have to see Suzerrain Longford," Danny said desperately. "I . . . I know he'll want to see me. . . ."

The two soldiers roared with laughter. Danny could see passing workers giving him a pitying look, which should have made him stop, but he couldn't help himself.

"Stop laughing!" he shouted. "Take me to see someone from the Ring of Five!"

The laughter stopped. The two Cherbs were looking at him with hard expressions on their faces. Danny felt a cold shadow fall over him. He looked up in time to see a great wing sweep overhead, then dip behind one of the ship's funnels.

"He wants to see the Ring, does he," Three Eyes murmured. "This Cherb might see them sooner than he thinks."

"I'm not a—" Danny was going to say "a Cherb," but he stopped himself in time. "Are you going to take me?"

"There's only one place you're being took," Snake

240

said softly; then, quicker than the eye could see, his hand shot out. Danny's head blazed with pain. He fell to the ground.

He came to in a railway carriage. He was sitting between two Cherbs he had never seen before. The carriage was shabby and dirty. Some of the overhead lights were broken, and the windows were so filthy, it felt like night. The rest of the carriage was crammed with people, but despite that, the seats around Danny and the Cherbs were empty, and people averted their eyes when Danny looked up. The men wore cheap suits and looked pale and ill-fed. The women wore shapeless dresses, patched here and there, although sometimes one had tried to enliven the outfit with a colorful brooch or a ribbon, or a slash of brightly colored lipstick. No one spoke. Their faces were sad and careworn.

Danny felt his head. There was a large bump just above his ear. What a fool he had been! Thinking he could just waltz in and get to talk to the most important man in the city.

"Take your hand away from your head," one of his captors growled.

"Where are we going?" Danny groaned.

"Where do you think you're going? Punishment battalion is where. Harden up them soft hands of yours."

"What's the punishment battalion?"

"That's enough talk out of you. Shut up." Danny opened his mouth, but the Cherb lifted his hand. Danny closed his mouth. His head was sore enough already.

The train stopped at several overground stations.

241

The platforms were grimy and unkempt, although Danny could see ornate tilework and wrought metal underneath the layers of dirt. The stations after that were underground. Eerie, silent places with dim lights and passengers scuttling about in the gloom. At each stop more of the passengers got off, until in the end there were only Danny and his two guards in the carriage. The train sped up. Danny had the feeling that they were going deeper and deeper into the earth. The carriage started to get warmer.

"Where are we—" he started to ask, but a booted foot crashed into his shin and cut off his question.

"You'll find out soon enough," one of the guards growled.

There were no lights in the tunnel outside now. On and on the train sped. Danny thought he saw deserted stations through the window; unlit platforms rushed past, and he felt that they were traveling through an underground ghost city. Despite the pain in his hand and his leg, he started to doze fitfully, each time waking with a start and looking wildly around at the jolting, rushing carriage before realizing with despair that he was a captive.

He didn't know how long it took—time meant nothing in the empty tunnels—but in the end, the train began to slow. Danny felt his heart lift a little. Nothing could be worse than the long descent into darkness. One of the Cherbs must have sensed what Danny was thinking, for he grinned an unpleasant grin.

"The fun ain't even started yet," he said.

Up ahead Danny could see lights, and he strained to see through the filthy windows. The track widened and another train appeared going the other way, its freight carriages loaded with rocks and soil. The brakes of Danny's train squealed as without warning, the tunnel widened into a large cavern hewn out of the earth. Everywhere there were people working, digging, wheeling barrows, breaking rocks, filling wagons. And everywhere there were black-clad Cherbs with whips and clubs, standing guard over the workers. As the train halted, Danny saw a skinny Messenger who looked like Les pushing an overloaded barrow. He fell to the ground and was beaten until he got to to his feet.

The guards hauled Danny up and pushed him through the open door. Danny saw dozens of workers hauling earth from a great opening in the ground. The shouts and curses of their guards and the whimpers of the beaten echoed in the great chamber. Sweat and dirt mingled on the faces of the workers, doing little to disguise their weariness and despair. One of his captors flung him forward so that he fell on his knees on the platform.

"Welcome to the tunnel," the Cherb growled.

24

THE SERAPHIM

Danny lost all sense of time. There was no day or night on the punishment battalion, just relentless grinding work. They were building a tunnel, but to what end, Danny did not know, and before long he stopped wondering. They worked in semidarkness, stooped over painfully in damp hot shafts, and slept where they fell—when they were allowed. Meals were a thin soup and hard black bread, and they drank water from the puddles that formed at the edge of the tunnel. There was no slacking—a Cherb guard was always nearby—and no talking either, although Danny had no one to talk to anyway. The ordinary people and Messengers would not talk to him, thinking that he was a Cherb, and Danny had no desire to talk to the hard-bitten Cherbs who had found their way onto the punishment battalion.

Apart from the Cherbs, his fellow toilers were the same cross-section of people he had seen on the streets of Westwald, although thinner and more harried-looking. There were women and children as well. As the days wore on he saw that the guards, though brutal, sometimes looked the other way—bribed, he thought, although how the money to bribe them was brought in, he didn't know. Once he looked down a dark shaft and saw light at the end of it, and children sitting in rows in front of a blackboard. One of the Messengers saw him looking and aimed a piece of timber at his head. Danny only just got out of the way. And once he saw a child perched on a rock, engrossed in a brightly colored book.

At the start, when he tried to speak to the other workers, they glared at him and moved away. Suspecting some kind of trap, he thought. As his imprisonment wore on, he thought that he could see some compassionate looks. The Cherbs were harder on him than they were on the others, as though in some obscure way he had let their side down by ending up on a punishment battalion. He was mocked relentlessly, and beaten even when he had done nothing. They often stole his food and he went hungry for days. Once, when he was on the point of collapse from hunger, he looked up to see a piece of gray bread sitting on a rock beside him. He seized it and crammed it into his mouth. When he had finished he looked warily around. The thin Messenger who reminded him of Les was watching from the shadows. He nodded brusquely at Danny and turned away.

Danny stumbled on in a fog of weariness. When it all

became too much for him he summoned a picture of his parents—a day at the seaside with them, or a birthday party—until even these bright images began to fade, and he could call on only one picture to drive his weary limbs onward: Brunholm. That was the reason he was there. That was the reason he had sought the Ring of Five.

Many miles away Master Devoy stood on the balcony of the fourth landing of Wilsons. It was a Balcony of Distant Perception, known only to the masters of Wilsons, from which you could see great distances. But he could not penetrate the gloom over Westwald.

"What have we done, Marcus?" he said softly to himself. He went down the main staircase, his feet leading him to the Gallery of Whispers. He hesitated, then mounted the narrow stairs that brought him up to the walkway under the great dome. He tried to frame a question in his mind. He knew that the gallery would answer his question truthfully, but in a puzzle.

"Has Danny found the Ring of Five?" he asked, and waited. The question moved around the gallery as if it was passed from voice to voice in whispers, the sound of his own voice repeated many times echoing in the dome above his head. It faded as it reached the far side, then grew louder again, until, in his own voice, he heard the whispered reply:

"They have found him."

Devoy considered the answer. It told him something and it told him nothing. The web had been spun—his web, with Danny at the center of it. The others were in place. All he could do now was wait.

Danny did not know how many days had passed. He was sleeping, and in his dreams a Messenger swooped from the skies and deposited a parcel in his hands.

"Fish and chips," the Messenger announced, but when Danny opened it, it contained feather-conditioning powder, which he threw away in disgust. He heard voices and tried to ignore them. Then a rough hand shook him by the shoulder, and a boot kicked him in the ribs. He cried out in pain and turned to see two Cherbs standing over him.

"Get up," they commanded. "We're taking you with us."

Danny knew better than to argue. He clambered stiffly to his feet, blinking. His joints felt like those of an old man, and the skin on his hands and knees was cut and broken from clambering through tunnels. One of the Cherbs appeared to be an officer. He was taller than most of the small-statured Cherbs, perhaps six inches bigger than Danny, and there was an air of authority about him. He carried leather gloves in one hand and slapped them lightly and impatiently against the palm of the other as Danny straightened; then he set off through the tunnel, walking quickly so that workers had to jump out of his way.

The tunnel was busy—as one shift slept, another worked—and Danny could see other captives watching him with a look of dread mingled with relief at not being the one singled out. Danny thought about bolting away and running into the darkness, but it wouldn't do him any good. There was nowhere to go.

At the end of the tunnel there was a bank of steel-cage elevators. Danny was shoved inside one. The tall Cherb pulled a lever and the elevator juddered to life, building speed as it rose upward. The two Cherbs stood in silence, Danny dry-mouthed between them.

After what seemed an eternity, the lift stopped with a metallic clang. Danny breathed in—fresh air! Pushed from the cage, he could see the night sky, the smog gone for once, and the stars glittering against a black backdrop. It was cold, but he didn't mind. It was good to feel the crisp air in his lungs.

He was pushed across an open space toward an office, its windows covered in wire mesh. There was a dim light on inside.

"Wouldn't be in your shoes, mate," the smaller Cherb muttered.

"Quiet!" the tall one barked, his voice like a pistol shot in the cold night air. They reached the office. Danny could feel the fear from the Cherb beside him. What could be so frightening?

"Push him through the door first," the tall Cherb said.

I don't like this, Danny thought. I don't like this one bit.

The two Cherbs stood to either side. One of them

opened the door. The other pushed Danny in. As he pitched forward onto his knees, the door slammed behind him.

He lifted his head slowly. His eyes, used to the darkness of the tunnel, found even the dim light harsh. In front of him was an old desk, and behind that a filing cabinet. Beside the filing cabinet was a tall coat stand, with brown coats hanging from it.

No. Not a coat stand.

The brown folds stirred. Danny, his knees weak with fear, realized that what he had taken for coats were enormous wings, folded round a tall thin body. And above the wings was a face. A long dark face, the color of burnished mahogany, with slanted yellow eyes and jet-black pupils. Lank strands of black hair hung to the creature's shoulders. Danny lifted his eyes to meet the yellow orbs, and he fell back, such was the force of the proud cruel stare that met his. From the folds of the wings a long skeletal arm appeared, the finger crooked, beckoning him near. Without getting off his knees, Danny shuffled forward. As he neared he could hear the creature's rasping breath. There was an odor that was musty and ancient, as of some unwholesome thing lain forgotten in a crypt.

"What . . . Who are you?" Danny whispered. The creature put its head on one side, and Danny could feel its eyes move over his body, like dead things crawling on him.

"I am Conal," the creature said, its voice like that of some proud and cruel old lord. "I am Seraphim."

The burning yellow eyes examined him. There was something familiar about them, something that Danny had seen before. . . . The Messengers!

"You're . . . you're a Messenger," he croaked.

"Messenger?" There was cold amusement in the tone. "Perhaps. Once. But now I am Seraphim. Stand up."

Danny stood up, as though invisible strings lifted him. He sensed something strange from the Seraphim. At first Danny had felt like a worm; such was the way that the Seraphim looked down on him. But now there was something else in the Seraphim's eyes—almost respect. Don't let it see you are afraid, he thought.

"What are you looking at me like that?" Danny kept the fear out of his voice.

"You are as they described you," the Seraphim replied.

"What's that supposed to mean?" Danny's voice sounded shrill in his own ears, but the Seraphim regarded him gravely.

"You are clever," he said, "and you feel the power of the Five. And there is anger too, and bitterness. But all of those things would be of no avail if you did not have the Mark of the Fifth."

"What's that?" Danny tried to sound as if he was indifferent.

"Your eyes and your face. The Fifth was half human and half Cherb. His descendant was always one of the Ring of Five. The line was lost. It may now be found." There was harsh excitement in Conal's voice.

"If I am this . . . this Fifth"—Danny made his voice

harsh and cold—"why did you put me down a hole to dig filth with rabble?"

"We did not know. One of the Seraphim told us that someone had been asking for Rufus Ness and the Ring. It was only when I heard your description. If it is true . . ."

"Longford," Danny said, in a voice that did not seem to be his own. "Take me to Longford."

For a moment he thought he had gone too far. The creature's wings shot high in the air. The Seraphim loomed over him like a giant winged insect. He was en-folded by the wings and the scent of decay as Conal brought his face close to Danny's. Danny allowed every-thing that he felt about Brunholm to show in his face, even as the Seraphim's hissing breath filled his ears. He couldn't bear the weight of Conal's searching gaze. Then suddenly the Seraphim rose to his full height and Danny heard him call the Cherbs.

"Bring me food and something to drink," Danny said in his new hard voice.

"Be quick," the Seraphim hissed. "The Ring awaits."

25

THE FORTRESS OF GRIST

The Cherbs brought water and sandwiches containing a pink meat. Danny didn't dare ask what it was, but he wolfed them down, along with the fresh water, some of which he saved to wash his face. There was a small mirror in the office and he looked at himself in it. His face was thinner and harder—he looked more like a real Cherb than ever. He was amazed to see that his overcoat was clean. He had refused to take it off despite the heat of the tunnel, and now felt reassured that he had it, along with all the gear in the pockets—the Cherbs had searched him, but, true to its nature, the Marburg coat had appeared empty.

He tried to take his time, aware of the waiting Seraphim, the golden eyes following him impatiently, the hissing breath filling the room. But at last he stood up.

"Time to go," he said, as if the Seraphim had been holding him up.

"More than time," Conal said, throwing the door open. Outside, the waiting Cherbs shrank away from them.

"Put your arms around my waist from behind," the Seraphim said. Danny hesitated, then did as he'd been told, finding his face pressed into the Seraphim's feathered back, the odor almost unbearable.

"Don't let go," Conal warned. With a dozen powerful strokes of the wings, Danny found himself aloft, clinging grimly to the Seraphim's bony sides as the ground fell away. He was flying from danger into even deadlier peril, but he shut his eyes, and for a moment remembered the time he had clung to Les's back and glided from the Roosts to the ground, and the way they had laughed. And he grinned to himself, remembering how Vicky the siren had charmed the old Messenger into flying. How long ago had that been? A week? A month? He no longer knew. The Seraphim gave a harsh cry as he flew over cold sleeping Westwald, and Danny awoke from his thoughts of friendship and remembered that he was clinging to an evil beast, flying through the frozen skies of a hostile city, on his way to meet a spy ring of terrible power.

The flight did not last long. He was aware of the slumbering city under him. They flew by two great factory chimneys belching sulfurous yellow smoke. Then, without warning, they were above the grim bulk of the fortress of Grist. There were towers around the perimeter, hard and cold. The high walls were topped with spikes. Inside

253

the walls there were armories, parade grounds, barracks, cookhouses, firing ranges, factories and, interspersed with the others, windowless stone buildings, their walls stained with age. All the buildings were roofed with the same gray slate. All had metal doors and gun slits cut into the walls. The fortress, Danny thought, must have spread across the top of the small hill over hundreds of years. He felt a shiver run down his spine, a dark thrill. He was so close to the Ring.

There was a green square at the center of the fortress, and it was this that Conal was aiming for. They were gliding downward, across the tops of ancient beech and chestnut trees, toward the square, with its well-cut lawns and redbrick buildings. Swooping through low branches, the Seraphim landed gently on his feet. With huge relief Danny slid to the ground. He did not see the figure watching them from a mullioned window at the far end of the square, a coffee cup in his hand.

"Where are we?" Danny asked.

"Suzerrain Longford's residence," Conal replied. "Follow me."

The building was not what he had expected as part of the fortress of Grist. He followed Conal through a low stone doorway, emerging into a hallway that was homely in a shabby way. There were oil paintings of smiling men and women on the walls, and a worn carpet over polished floorboards. A narrow staircase led off the hall, and Conal mounted it. In the shadows, with his wings folded around him, he looked like some kind of sinister statue.

They went up to the second floor and paused in front

of a wooden door. Danny could feel his heart hammering in his chest.

Before they had a chance to knock, the door swung open. Suzerrain Longford stood before them—but instead of the proud and shrewd man from the portrait in Wilsons, here was a smiling, boyish-looking man with warm blue eyes and a flap of hair that fell over his eyes so he had to push it back with his hand.

"Danny!" Longford cried, seizing his hand and wringing it warmly. "I'm so glad to meet you. Sorry about that awful old tunnel. Between you and me, I can't say I approve of the Cherbs' methods, but we're stuck with them for the time being. Come in, come in!"

He threw out his arms to welcome Danny into the room, knocking over a vase, which Danny caught and replaced without Longford's seeming to notice.

"Thank you, Conal, thank you," Longford said distractedly. The Seraphim loomed in the doorway, then disappeared.

"Sit down." Longford waved to a comfortable-looking armchair beside a glowing fire. The small room was decorated with flower-patterned wallpaper, and there were drawings of country scenes on the wall and golf trophies on the mantelpiece.

Longford poured a cup of coffee for Danny and pushed a plate of hot buttered muffins toward him.

"You're looking at me a little strangely," Longford said. "Ah, yes—you've seen the portrait in the library at Wilsons. Not really me at all—the painter tried to jazz me up a bit. How's Master Devoy getting on? We fell out,

255

I'm afraid. We both want the best for people, and we both know we have to use not-very-nice types sometimes. I have the Seraphim, and Devoy has Brunholm."

"He killed my parents," Danny blurted out.

"What?" Longford got to his feet.

"Brunholm. He killed my mum and dad. That's why I'm here."

"Oh, my dear boy!" Longford looked distraught. "My poor young man. I had no idea."

"That's why I want to join the Ring."

"Is it? Is it indeed." Longford leaned forward. The kindly manner dropped away. The eyes that examined Danny were deep-set and shrewd.

"You say that to yourself." Longford's voice was low. "But in your heart you know that is not the real reason. You feel the power of the Ring, the dark attraction. No. Do not deny it or be ashamed. I felt the same attraction, and when I entered Westwald I realized that the darkness is a tool—a tool that can be used to set the world and worlds to rights. Devoy is a good man, but a fool. You saw how weak Wilsons is. If it were not for me, the Cherbs would have torn through the Upper World like a knife through butter."

"But they didn't. You are waiting for something." Danny felt hypnotized by Longford's words.

"Ah, strategic understanding in one so young. I was waiting for you! For the Fifth, and for the Ring to be intact."

That word again. The "Fifth"!

"But first, tell me about how you got to Wilsons."

Danny started talking, and the words tumbled out: About Fairman and his taxi. All about Wilsons and the attempts to kill him. About the teachers. About Devoy. And, of course, about Brunholm. He left Les, Dixie and Vandra out of it. After all, they were not to blame for what had happened. Longford was sympathetic. He was interested in everything, and laughed uproariously when Danny told him about Vicky the siren and the Messengers. But his questions guided Danny skillfully, searching for any indication that Danny was deceiving him.

"So you trusted Devoy and Brunholm at first?"

"Yes," Danny said truthfully, "but then . . ."

"Your parents. Of course. A shocking thing. Brunholm was always like that. Leave no witnesses behind. I am sure that Devoy—how do I put this delicately?—he would have acted for the greatest good for the greatest number. And if your parents had to be sacrificed, then so be it. You are safer with us. Some of our members are no better than they should be, but at least you can see that with your own eyes.

"Of course, we must meet with the others. Conal knew that you were the Fifth the minute he set eyes on you. And the others will as well. Can you imagine what it would be like, Danny? To march at the head of an army of Cherbs. A disciplined army. A tool to a greater end. To put an end to war and famine in the Upper World!"

Danny could see it. Who would call him Danny the Pixie then? His parents would be so proud of him. And then it came over him in a great wave: they would not be there. They would not be there, and it was because of Brunholm.

"When do we meet?" The harshness had crept back into Danny's voice.

"Tomorrow," Longford said. "But first you have to rest. You've had a bad time. We have a room all ready for you. Come with me."

Longford led Danny out of the room and down a crooked little corridor. Danny stifled a yawn. He couldn't remember the last time he had had a proper night's sleep.

"Er, by the way, did anyone help you escape?" Longford queried. "I mean, you didn't get to Westwald on your own."

"No, of course not. There was a man called Starling. He got me to the ship."

"You don't recall the name of the ship, by any chance?"

"No," Danny said truthfully. "I was upset. . . ."

"Yes, of course. And this Starling?"

The lie was out of Danny's mouth before he knew it.

"He brought me to the ship and then disappeared with the money. He didn't get on board I never saw him after that."

"I see. Ah well."

Why had he protected Starling? The words that Starling had used came into his head: "I import hope."

Longford opened a door. Behind the door was a small room with a red coverlet on the bed. There was fresh hot chocolate on a side table, and a girl in a white uniform and cap was tending to a bright fire. Longford gave the bed an approving pat.

"Nice and cozy," he said. The girl stood up and turned around. Danny saw her face and stifled a gasp.

Dixie!

Digging his nails into his palms to stop himself from crying out, Danny stared at the girl. She gave him a wink.

"That's the fire done, sir," she said.

"Good girl. You can go to bed now, and I'll fetch our young guest here some fresh muffins for supper. I have to say there's nothing like a muffin toasted on an open fire."

Dixie carried her bucket of coal to the door and went out. Longford followed her, rubbing his hands together and humming. Danny heard the door close, but when he turned back to the fire, Dixie was standing there.

He jumped. "What are you doing here?"

"We're on a mission to find you and bring you back." Dixie kept her voice low. "Les is working at the market in town, and Vandra's here in Grist. She's a nurse in the Cherb hospital. She doesn't like it very much. Having to suck the blood of Cherbs with athlete's foot and the like."

"If you get caught . . . I mean, if Conal caught you . . ."

"I saw him. Smelly big thing, isn't he? It's kind of fun being on a mission, though. So how do we go about getting you out? You shouldn't have run away like that, you know."

"Out?" Danny said. "I don't want out. I want to be here."

259

"How could you want to be here?" Dixie looked puzzled.

"I'm . . . I'm joining the Ring," Danny said.

"Don't be silly."

"I'm not being silly. I'm doing it. I'm the Fifth."

"You're a twit is what you are. Never mind. Devoy said you'd be like this."

"Like what? Joining the Ring because Brunholm . . ." There was a noise at the door. Dixie disappeared and reappeared behind the door. It swung open and Longford came in. With another wink at Danny, she was gone. Longford put a fresh plate of muffins on the table.

"There. That should do for supper. Now. It is very late. We will talk in the morning. And Danny?"

"Yes?"

"Welcome aboard." With a broad grin, Longford swept out the door, knocking over a lamp and two plaster dogs on a low table as he did so.

Danny waited until he had gone, then tried the door. It was locked. There would be no more contact with Dixie that night. He sat down at the fire, bone-tired, and tucked into the hot chocolate and muffins. A torrent of thoughts ran through his mind. The other cadets' mission had obviously changed—they had been told to rescue him. Was it a plot by Brunholm and Devoy to use his friends to deliver him back into their hands? He wondered too about all that Longford had known about him—even his name. How had he found out? There must have been spies in Wilsons despite the shadows. I bet it was Smyck, he thought.

He rubbed his hand across his eyes. He was too tired to think. It was all he could do to drag himself to the bed, pull off his clothes and tumble in between the clean linen sheets. In seconds, he was asleep.

Conal was waiting for Longford in his study.

"What do you think?" Conal's yellow eyes burned with a strange fire.

"It's him," Longford said briskly. "Not just the eyes and the shape of the face, but you can feel the hunger for power."

"And the ability to betray."

"Yes," Longford said thoughtfully, "it is the great art of our profession as spies, the ability to betray, and I think Danny will be good at it. After all, he has already turned on Wilsons with barely a backward glance. But there will have to be a test. Betrayal is a skill to be learned like any other."

"I have an idea. We picked up a spy. One of Wilsons, we believe. He was caught stealing. The Cherbs gave him a hard time, but he wouldn't admit his guilt."

"Does Danny know this boy?"

"There aren't that many pupils—he must. The boy would make a fine first subject for Danny's lesson in betrayal."

"What is the boy's name?"

"He is called Knutt. Les Knutt."

26

THE RING OF FIVE

Late the next morning Danny sat up in bed and looked around. Someone had been in during the night, though he had heard nothing. There was orange juice and fresh bread and jam on the table, and, lying on the end of the bed, a black uniform. He picked it up. It was like the ones that the Cherbs wore, but not the same. A black tunic with a belt around the waist, trousers, a peaked cap and a pair of black leather boots, supple and close-fitting. He hesitated, then quickly put the tunic on, cinching the belt around his waist. It fit perfectly. He put on the cap and the boots, then went into the bathroom and stood in front of the full-length mirror. He saw a different person looking back at him. The Danny in the mirror was an officer, full of pride and danger. No one was ever going to call him a pixie. The cap made him look older, and brought

262

out the triangular shape of his face. His eyes made him look dangerous, rather than like something to be made fun of in the schoolyard. Even the boots made him move differently—he strutted rather than walked. There was a silver badge on the collar of the tunic that he hadn't noticed before. He fingered it gently. It was a sharp-toothed skull, cold to the touch, the eye sockets slanted in an unmistakable way. He glanced at his Marburg coat, which lay crumpled on the floor.

There was a knock at the door. Danny started.

"Hello, anyone home?" Longford said.

Danny looked down at the uniform and felt himself blush, but when he went out Longford stepped back, as if in amazement.

"I am awestruck, my dear boy. The uniform is wonderful, as if it was made for you."

"Who was it made for?"

"It was made for the Fifth. It has remained unworn for many years."

"I . . . I don't understand."

"The Fifth has been lost for a long time, Danny. We believe he is found again. We knew you were at Wilsons, but we didn't expect you to leave it the way you did and come to Westwald. Those idiot Cherbs at the quay sent you to the tunnel. It took us a little time to find out where you were."

"You keep saying 'the Fifth.' I mean, I know the Fifth is the fifth member of the Ring, but who . . ."

"Yes, indeed, that is the question, Danny, who is the Fifth? I spent many nights in the libraries of Wilsons, reading through old books of secrets, many of them full of lies and half-truths."

"How did you know about me at Wilsons?"

"Ah. You will find out about that later. For the moment, we have to show you off."

They went out into the corridor and walked down the stairs. Halfway down he saw Dixie—she was polishing a mirror—or pretending to polish it, as it was still covered in streaks. As they drew level with her, she looked Danny up and down, shock in her eyes at his new appearance. Danny did not notice that she was pale, and that her normally dreamy face was tense and strained. She subtly mouthed words, but he couldn't figure out what she was trying to say. He gave a little shrug—there was nothing he could do. As they reached the hallway, he glanced back and saw her looking anxiously after him.

Outside, a little sunshine had penetrated the normal smog of Westwald, and it was pleasant under the trees. They crossed the square and went through another doorway, this one of dark wrought metal. Danny found himself standing in an enormous room with a high ceiling, pillars reaching off into the gloom. Now and then a shabby figure hurried through. Otherwise, it was quiet.

"Welcome to the fortress of Grist," Longford said quietly.

Afterward, Danny would struggle to recall details of the fortress. It was vast, with long, snaking corridors, dimly lit, leading to endless rooms. There were restaurants, classrooms, vast canteens, whole floors dedicated to the production of weapons. There weren't many Cherbs around.

"They're in the field preparing for an . . . event. I can't tell you much about it," Longford said, and tapped the side of his nose with a smile

There were offices where civilian clerks toiled over clattering typewriters, and hospital wings full of empty beds, as if they expected many casualties soon. Danny looked for Vandra, but there was no sign of her.

"What's that over there?" Danny asked as they crossed a parade ground between buildings. He pointed to a long, low black building with barred windows.

"That is the prison," Longford said, a note of sorrow in his tone. "It is an unfortunate necessity for any society. It is of course appointed to the highest specification."

Danny eyed the long building uncomfortably. There were watchtowers at each corner, and guns poked from each one. Longford led him into another building. This one was different. There was ornate plasterwork on the walls, and glass chandeliers hung from the ceiling.

"I have arranged a small reception in your honor," Longford said. He threw open a set of double doors. In front of the doors, a grand staircase swept down into a ballroom, thronged with men in dinner jackets and military uniforms, cruel-faced generals and fat businessmen accompanied by beautiful women in gowns. Everyone in the room turned to see Danny at the top of the stairs, and they stood to applaud. Dazzled by the applause, and by the sumptuous room, Danny moved uncertainly down the stairs.

"The Fifth!" he heard murmured through the crowd. "It's him. It's really him!" A glass was pressed into his hand, and an admiring crowd surrounded him. Danny felt his head reeling. Did the Fifth mean so much in Westwald?

"Such a handsome boy," breathed a sharp-faced woman in a gown studded with diamonds.

"Looks like the man to me," wheezed a fat red-faced man who looked as if he was about to burst out of his tuxedo. "About time we got rid of Wilsons and opened the Upper World to business—our kind of business!"

Longford steered Danny through the crowd by the elbow, greeting people as he went. Then Danny got a shock. They were heading toward an elegant woman in a long red dress. She had a cigarette holder in one hand with an unlit cigarette in it—Nurse Flanagan! He realized that he hadn't mentioned her part in his escape to Westwald, but she was sure to recognize him. However, when Longford introduced him, Nurse Flanagan merely lifted a gloved and perfumed hand to be kissed.

"A pleasure, I'm sure," she purred. Danny remembered that she was shortsighted, but he was sure no one was that shortsighted. Was she playing some kind of double game against Longford?

Danny turned, confused, but she had already raised her hand in a greeting to another guest. He turned back and got another shock. Dixie was standing right in front of him, a tray in her hand. Her face was fixed and pale, and he started as if a ghost had appeared in front of him, but then composed himself.

"A drink, sir," she said, and then in a whisper, "They've got—"

But before she had a chance to finish her sentence, Longford had whisked Danny away.

"No time to stand around chatting to waitresses," he said. "A piece of business has arisen that requires our attention. Do you know the girl?"

"She's just a servant," Danny said, an edge to his voice. "I get the idea she's a bit flaky."

Dixie stared after him as he stalked off.

Longford led Danny through another room, where men were playing cards on green felt tables. One of the players seemed to be winning more than anyone; great piles of poker chips stood at his elbow. He was an immensely fat man with at least four chins, and he was sweating profusely, wiping his brow every so often with a large handkerchief.

Danny lagged behind, his eyes on the play but his mind feverishly trying to work out what Dixie had been trying to tell him. The game was poker—Texas hold 'em, the same game he had learned at Wilsons. Longford joined him, looking amused.

"That's Cranbull, our head of prison. A great poker player." As they watched, a man in a tuxedo threw down his cards in despair, burying his head in his hands.

"I'm ruined," he sobbed. Cranbull grinned and wiped his face again.

"A rather brutal man," Longford said. "Now, Danny, we have a little unpleasant business to attend to."

They left the room and entered a long corridor—if "corridor" was the right word for it, for it was more like a gallery or a museum, high-ceilinged and ornate, the walls hung with gilt-framed oil paintings depicting Seraphim and Cherbs. The marble underneath echoed their footfalls.

"You have met three of the four members of the Ring of Five," Longford said. Danny looked at him, startled.

"Have I?"

"You haven't realized yet?"

Danny thought about it.

"You are one?"

"Of course."

"And Conal?"

"Very good. The Seraphim have to be represented." Longford smiled. "Now you can meet the Third."

As they reached the end of the grand corridor, they came to a towering marble gallery. In the middle of the gallery was a broad desk, and at the desk sat a squat powerful figure.

"This is the third member of the Ring of Five. Rufus Ness, commander of the Cherbs."

Rufus Ness. For a moment Danny panicked, thinking Ness might recognize him from the Painted Door. Then he realized that he had been in disguise when he had seen Brunholm meet with Ness.

The Cherb stood up. He was taller than Danny, and his body underneath the Cherb uniform was hard and muscular. His forehead was higher than that of most Cherbs, and his gaze was shrewder, more penetrating.

Without warning, he reached out and grabbed Danny's chin between two steely fingers, then turned Danny's head as if he was examining a fruit in the market. Danny felt that Ness could snap his neck like a twig if he found a flaw. Instead, he grunted and released Danny.

"Looks like the Fifth, all right. Smells of treachery and all. We'll see for sure in the next while, won't we?"

Nice to meet you too, Danny thought.

"We will, won't we?" Longford said.

"What are you talking about?" Danny asked.

To Danny's amazement, the wall in front of them began to part. Danny found himself looking on a great room with pillars of black marble. The floor was black, as were all the velvet hangings that adorned the walls. The darkness was broken only by tall ice-white lamps, their light glistening off the polished black surfaces. At the center of the room was a round table with five chairs around it. And running round the edge of the table, a thick golden ring, the light playing off it as if a fire burned within. There were two cloaked figures sitting at the table. Danny heard hissing breath: Conal. Longford and Ness stepped forward and sat at the table.

"Do you summon the Fifth?" Ness said.

"I do. I summon the Fifth," Longford replied. "Step forward, Danny, and take your place at the table."

As if in a dream, Danny walked into the room, hearing the wall slide to behind him. He looked around the table. Longford and Ness were there, of course, as was Conal. The fourth figure was hooded and still, but Danny could smell a rich perfume.

"Nurse Flanagan!" he said. The woman threw her hood back and smiled a wicked smile.

"Rather a big moment, don't you think, the Ring of Five becoming complete?" she said.

"Each of the four has met Danny. Each is satisfied that he is the Fifth," Longford said. "Therefore, let us bring our minds together. Place your hands on the Ring!"

One by one they put their hands on the Ring. Danny, shaking, put first one hand, then the other on the golden ring on the table. For a moment nothing happened. Then it started. Danny could feel dark power flowing through him. He could feel the thrill and the tug of it, the desire to command, to rule. And then the sensation changed so that he could feel the lust to manipulate and conspire. Delicious plots and schemes tumbled through his mind until he could almost taste intrigue on his tongue.

A whispering began in his mind, a sense of female wiles, of situations manipulated, almost like a heady perfume that clouded his thoughts. . . . He was inside Nurse Flanagan's mind! The perfume cleared, making way for thoughts of old intrigues, creaking and dark, like wandering through an ancient castle reeking of pride and treachery. Conal! Then he was in the mind of Rufus Ness, and this time it felt like being part of a street gang, all thuggery and cunning. And lastly, he entered Longford's mind, which was like being in a palace of mirrors where you could not tell what was real and what was not, only that danger lurked everywhere.

He knew that just as he was in their minds, they were in his—he could feel them prowling in every corner, wanting to know his secrets. Unbidden, the photograph of his parents came to mind, and the picture in the newspaper of Brunholm as the man seen running away. He knew that the rest of the Ring of Five knew what he was thinking. He could feel their satisfaction. They knew that he wanted revenge against Brunholm.

And finally, with a great rush, their minds came together, and Danny knew that no force could match the Ring of Five for cunning and guile. His hand slipped off the gold ring. A dark thrill coursed through his body. He was not a pupil anymore. He was a master of spying. Longford was smiling at him.

"Now you are truly the Fifth," he said. "Bring the prisoner!"

Danny looked around the table. The members of the Ring had been in his mind. If he had been only pretending to go along with the Ring, they would have known. A thought took form, then was driven away as if it had never been. Two Cherbs dragged in a crumpled figure and threw him on the floor, where he lay barely moving, blood oozing from a cut on his face, his wings ragged, the feathers bent and broken.

It was Les.

"The prisoner stands accused of spying for Wilsons," Conal said. "He has refused to identify himself. Can any member of the Ring name him?"

Danny looked down at Les. The power of the Ring was still coursing through his veins.

"Think, Danny," Longford whispered. "Think of the Ring. Think of what you will be!"

Light gleamed on the death's-head badge on his uniform. What had Brunholm called Les? A thief and a liar. Danny knew this was a test. If he passed it, then what good he could do back in his own world! He could end war and famine. People would come to him and he would dispense judgment and forgiveness. Except, of course, for Brunholm. Les moaned and stirred.

"Well, Danny," Nurse Flanagan said, looking bored, "do you know him?"

He is your friend, a voice inside his head said, *your friend!* Danny wavered. And then he felt it flow through him; a dark, overwhelming lust, burning and irresistible—the urge to betray, to break faith with those who trusted him.

"I know him." His voice felt as if it was coming from very far away. "His name is Les Knutt. He is a cadet at Wilsons."

"Take the prisoner away," Longford said, satisfaction in his voice. Danny stared at Les as the Cherbs started to drag him away, transfixed with horror at what he had just done, and yet with a feeling of having satisfied a terrible longing. It was then that the thought that had been trying to form in his mind broke through. With a mixture of wonder and dismay he saw it all—the web of deceit woven by Devoy and Brunholm with Danny at the center. He could see it laid out, suddenly as clear as day. A plot of cruel genius designed to get him to the heart of the Ring of Five. He groaned and put his face in his hands. He had been meant to betray Les.

A JUICY BAIT

Danny could feel the eyes of the rest of the Ring on him. He had to pull himself together! Longford put a hand on his shoulder.

"The first great betrayal is always difficult. To turn your back on a friend . . ."

"But isn't that the most fun?" Nurse Flanagan said brightly. "To do the dirty on a real friend? After all, when you get to our stage, you don't have any real friends."

"Perhaps," Conal said, "when he is older he will learn how to relish betraying someone, to go over it in his mind and savor it."

"Can't see the big deal," Rufus Ness complained. "A piece of Messenger trash. No great loss."

"I remember my first husband," Nurse Flanagan said

with a fond smile. "The look on his face when he realized that I'd double-crossed him . . ."

"You'll be fine in a while," Longford said reassuringly. "Now we've done betrayal, let's move our young friend here on to revenge, shall we? Equally satisfying in its own way."

"Should we?" Conal nodded toward Danny. "After all, he has only just joined the Ring. . . ."

"He is the Fifth," Longford said. "He has a right to know. Besides, the attack is to take place almost immediately. Within forty-eight hours Wilsons will be ours."

Forty-eight hours! Danny tried to force himself to concentrate, but his thoughts were in turmoil. Devoy and Brunholm had created a plot of such complexity that his head reeled.

Focus, he told himself; you're no use to anyone like this. As he struggled to hide his thoughts, the center of the table started to turn misty in front of his eyes. What was happening now? The mist turned to smoke. Longford leaned forward and blew gently on it, and it disappeared completely. Danny found himself looking down on a living map of Wilsons Island. The sea heaved gently; smoke hung in the air over Westwald. On the other side he could see tiny car headlights moving on the roads around Tarnstone. There was nothing moving around Wilsons, though. It appeared to be asleep, unaware of looming danger.

"The tunneling is almost complete," Longford said. "The workers have been withdrawn."

"The tunnel?" Danny's voice still sounded strange in his own ears.

"Ah yes." Longford chuckled, pushing back the flap of hair. "I forgot you were a guest worker on the tunnel! It goes from under this railway building here"—he pointed to a huge metal-roofed shed—"and it comes out . . . here!"

He was pointing to the parade ground at Wilsons!

"We'll take Wilsons first and then roll down into Tarnstone," Rufus Ness growled.

"The Seraphim will fly ten minutes before the tunnel mouth is opened to make sure that there is no resistance," Conal said.

"I am so looking forward to seeing Wilsons again." Nurse Flanagan's eyes glittered. "I was also a pupil there. I cannot wait to see it, and I ache to see it burned to the ground."

"What do you think, Danny?" Longford said.

"I can't wait to see Wilsons taught a lesson," Danny lied. He was thinking frantically. Devoy and Brunholm had taken a terrible risk with their plan—but when he thought about it, there was nothing else that they could have done. Sranzer's appearance with the newspaper detailing his parents' death must have been a setup, the paper a fake. He had been meant to flee to Westwald and join the Ring to seek revenge against Brunholm. His parents had not been killed—he was sure of that now. He was horrified at how he had been used, but a part of him could only admire the fiendishly complex plan. He'd had to be utterly convincing when he joined the Ring, so Brunholm and Devoy had fooled him into thinking that his parents were dead!

Rufus Ness and Longford were talking about supplies. Nurse Flanagan was examining her highly polished nails. Conal sat without moving, his face looking as if it had been carved from wood.

At last the discussion about troop movements finished. The living map was hidden again. Longford got to his feet.

"The Ring is whole once more, for the first time in many years. You are part of us now, Danny. There is no force that can stand against the Five!"

Danny looked around the table, each face seeming crueler and more cunning than the next. He knew that he held the fate of the Two Worlds in his hands. He had to get back to Wilsons and warn them—but how?

"What will happen to the Messenger?" Danny asked, trying to stay casual.

"You're not still worrying about that, are you?" Nurse Flanagan snorted.

"Execution," Longford said. He saw the look on Danny's face. "Oh, it's not as bad as that—no hanging or anything of that sort. A physick does it. Kind of like an injection that sends you to sleep. You hardly feel a thing."

Danny gritted his teeth. What had he done? He felt something inside him harden. He was not leaving Grist without Les.

*   *   *

Far away, in the library of the third landing, Devoy stared at Brunholm.

"Even for you, Marcus, that was a terrible thing."

"You said yourself, Devoy: we had to send the boy to the Ring the way we did. If we had not, they would surely have seen that he was trying to fool them when they entered his head. It had to be like that."

"But the young Messenger, Knutt."

"It was a sacrifice, but I know the way the Ring works. They needed Danny to make a choice, to betray his friend as a test, to prove that he was really part of the Ring. Knutt was the obvious choice, and a juicy bait to leave in their path. It was a simple and, I think, elegant plan. Need I remind you we must find out what the Ring are planning. I have sent many agents in and none have come back."

"But when Danny realizes that he has wronged his friend . . ."

"He will also realize that it was necessary."

"No, he won't. You think everybody is as ruthless as you, Marcus. Danny will try to rescue Knutt—and if he gets caught, then all is lost. You may have jeopardized everything."

When the Five left the gallery Danny found that the reception to celebrate the completion of the Ring was in full swing. A small orchestra was playing with abandon, and the dance floor was filled. People were eager to meet Danny, and his hand was shaken so much that it became sore. He scanned the crowd for Dixie, but he didn't see her. A plan to rescue Les was forming in his head, but it was risky, and time was running short.

The band got louder and the atmosphere more hectic. Longford was dancing with Nurse Flanagan. Rufus Ness stood at the bar with a group of Cherb officers in uniform, drinking from large tankards of beer. Conal led a female Seraphim onto the dance floor. She wore a long silver chainmail dress and black lipstick, and her dry dead-looking hair was piled high on her head. Danny shuddered.

At last he saw Dixie at the other side of the room and caught her eye. He circled the room until he found a small deserted scullery and ducked in. Just as the door swung shut, Dixie appeared beside him. Danny jumped.

"What—" Dixie began.

"Listen," Danny said, "we don't have much time. What happened when I left Wilsons?"

"Brunholm told everyone that you were a Cherb all along, and that you had betrayed us. They sent bloodhounds after you. Then Devoy called me and Les and Vandra in. He told us to go ahead and take up our positions in Westwald. He sent us across on a ship."

"I need to tell you what Devoy and Brunholm did. They arranged for me to find out that Brunholm killed my parents—it was a lie, but it made me hate them. I wanted to join the Ring to get revenge."

"But why?"

"They had to do it that way. They had to make me really hate them. If I had only been pretending to want to join the Ring, Longford would have found out—they go inside your head." Dixie shook her head, her face white in the gloom of the scullery.

"It's cruel. Poor you, Danny."

"I got what Devoy and Brunholm wanted. I know what the invasion plan is."

"Danny, I've been trying to tell you—they arrested Les."

"I know."

"You know?"

Danny hesitated; then, taking a deep breath, he told Dixie about the Ring of Five, and how Les had been brought in front of them.

"I named him, Dixie. I was . . . I was so angry. . . ."

Danny couldn't bring himself to tell the truth, that some dark part of him had wanted to see what it felt like to betray a friend. Danny waited for Dixie to tell him off, shout at him, anything. But she said nothing. Instead, he could see tears glisten on her cheeks.

"I'm going to get him out. I've got a plan," he said desperately. "I'm not going without him. . . ."

"When . . . when the Cherbs killed my mum and dad," Dixie said slowly, "I wanted to hurt somebody. Anybody. Just to make the pain go away."

"Thanks, Dixie."

"I didn't say I forgive you," she said fiercely. "Not until we get him back!"

"We will. I promise." Danny bowed his head, glad that Dixie couldn't see his burning cheeks. She sniffed.

"Okay," she said, "what's the plan? What do you want me to do?"

"Listen," Danny said.

Forty minutes later, Danny was in the card room watching the game of Texas hold 'em. The noise from the reception next door was beginning to die down. The fat jailer Cranbull dispatched opponent after opponent. Only a razor-thin man wearing a pinstripe suit remained in the game.

"Is there nobody else out there who'll give me a game?" Cranbull grumbled, stuffing his mouth with an enormous handful of peanuts.

"I'll give it a go," Danny said.

"Ah." Cranbull's grin spread through the fat on his face. "The Fifth himself! An honor, I'm sure. By all means, sit down. Bring us new cards. It will be a pleasure to take on one of the Ring. Conal and Longford don't play, and even I wouldn't dare play with Nurse Flanagan in case she got vexed and put a bullet in my delicate little heart."

Danny pulled up a chair. He flexed his fingers. His throat was dry. He was about to play for Les's life, and he was pinning all on something he had seen as he had watched Cranbull play earlier. As he reached into his pocket for the bag of money Devoy had given him; he prayed that he wasn't wrong.

Cranbull dealt. The first few hands were cagey, Cranbull and Danny trying to figure out the way the other played. The thin man was skillful as well. Danny was trying to lose, but not too much—he wanted Cranbull confident. At one point he almost lost everything to the thin man. If not for a king in the last hand dealt, he would have been out of the game. He could feel sweat trickle down the back of his tunic, but he fought to keep his face still. He remembered the little maths teacher at Wilsons. "You have to play the cards," Docterow had said, "but you also have to play the man. Don't give anything away."

The minutes ticked away. Danny was winning more. The pots were growing bigger and bigger. Eventually the thin man threw down his hand.

"This is getting too rich for me," he said. There was only Danny and Cranbull left. It was time to put his idea into practice.

Danny could not know that high above them, in a darkened gallery, Conal and Longford were watching.

"He plays well," Longford said.

"But what is he playing for?" Conal replied.

"We'll see."

Danny started to raise the stakes, and soon there was a massive pile of cash and chips in the middle of the table. He was holding his own, but only just. It felt like only minutes had gone by, but the room outside had gone silent. They were on their own.

Danny had noticed that Cranbull wiped his sweating face with his spotted handkerchief at the end of every hand, but suspected that when he was bluffing and wanted his opponent to believe he had a really good hand when he didn't, he unconsciously flicked the handkerchief before he put it back into his pocket. Danny tried out his theory. He had a poor hand next time out. Cranbull looked at him through his little piggy eyes and shoved a pile of money into the middle of the table, He took out his handkerchief and wiped his forehead. Flick. Danny matched the pot and showed his hand. Two kings. Cranbull's eyes narrowed—he put his cards facedown on the table. Danny scooped up the money.

They played on, heedless of the passing hours. For Danny there was only the green felt table under a single light, and his opponent. Although Cranbull's expression gave nothing away, Danny could feel the man's anger building, his cold little eyes unblinking in the dim light. All the spectators had long ago drifted away, but high in the gallery, Longford and Conal watched.

"It's the handkerchief," Longford said. "He flicks it when he's bluffing. Danny spotted it. A worthy Fifth, I think, Conal."

"We'll see," the Seraphim said coldly.

Cranbull's losses were huge, as was the pile of money in front of Danny. As Danny put another huge bet on the table, Cranbull hesitated.

"What's wrong?" Danny jeered. "Running out of money?"

"I can't match your bet," Cranbull said. Danny leaned across the table. Cranbull's face glistened with sweat.

"I'll do you a deal," Danny said. "You have something I want. You can bet with that."

"What?" Cranbull's voice quavered.

"The Messenger. Knutt."

In the dark gallery, Longford and Conal exchanged glances.

"I can't turn over a prisoner to you! Conal would skin me alive."

"I don't want to take the boy," Danny's voice was cold. "I want him dead, and I want to see him die."

"I can't . . ."

"He is nothing to you."

"Why . . . why do you want him dead?"

"What do you think? He comes from Wilsons, and Wilsons killed my parents. Well, are you playing?"

Cranbull licked his lips. His eyes ran greedily over the money on the table.

"The execution has to be done lawfully. By a physick."

"I've arranged it."

He took out his handkerchief to wipe his face. This was it, Danny realized. He had to go on this hand. Cranbull took out his handkerchief. He wiped his brow with it, and went to put it back in his pocket. Then disaster struck—the handkerchief snagged on the edge of the table and dropped to the floor. Cranbull did not bend for it. Danny had no way of knowing whether the man was bluffing or not! He stared hard at the backs of Cranbull's cards as though they might reveal his hand. Concentrate! he urged himself. As he did he looked up sharply, knowing straightaway that Longford was above him in the darkness, and knowing, as clearly as if Longford had spoken, that the spymaster could see Cranbull's cards and that he was bluffing. The dark and deceitful joy that was the connection to the Ring coursed once more through his veins.

Danny shoved his pile of money into the center of the table.

"All the money against the boy. On this last hand."

"All the money?" Cranbull croaked. "All right."

Danny turned his cards up. Cranbull groaned. Danny had won. In the gallery above, Conal turned to Longford.

"Well?"

"We'll let him kill Knutt, if that's what he wants. It ties him to us all the more."

There was a knock at the card-room door. Danny opened it. Vandra was standing there, her head bowed.

"You asked for me, sir?" she said.

"Yes," Danny said coldly. "I need a physick."

"You're serious about this," Cranbull said. He stood up, all his chins trembling. He looked as if he was about to burst into tears as his eyes kept returning to the money on the table.

"Of course I'm serious about it. Let's go." Danny scooped the money on the table into one of his Marburg coat pockets, which was able to take it all without so much as a bulge on the outside. Out of the corner of his eye he glimpsed Dixie, who had slipped through the door and concealed herself behind a statue of an ugly Cherb.

Cranbull took a key from his pocket and unlocked a small door, wood-paneled like the wall around it. Danny and Vandra followed him into a dark corridor. In contrast to the rooms outside, the corridor was stone, caked with old filth and cobwebs. Cranbull produced a small torch from his pocket and turned it on, then closed the door. Danny was afraid that they had left Dixie behind, but he glimpsed her white face in the gloom behind them.

"Did Dixie tell you the plan?" Danny whispered. Vandra nodded. She looked nervous.

"Can you do it?"

"I think so. I've got the right drug in my teeth. I . . . I hope so, anyway."

Without looking around, Cranbull set off at a great pace for such a big man, and they struggled to keep up as he led them through a labyrinth of corridors, each one murkier and filthier than the last, piled with ancient debris. There were rats too, rustling in the strewn rubbish, and once Danny jumped as a bat brushed his hair and disappeared into the dark. He kept looking back, making sure Dixie was still with them. In front of them the fat man scuttled along, the torchlight bobbing as he moved.

When they had lost track of time, weary and dirty, the corridor started to wind upward again. They were climbing up a cracked and broken staircase. Vandra fell and skinned her knees. By the time Danny had her on her feet, Cranbull had almost disappeared. They caught him just as he was opening a large, brass-bound door.

"Quickly, quickly," Cranbull said, his face slick with

sweat. Danny held back a little to allow Dixie time to catch up. For a moment he thought he caught a flicker as she passed him, and then the door was slammed shut.

"This is the deepest, oldest part of the prison," Cranbull said, his voice rasping in the stillness. The torchlight gleamed off damp stone walls with strange mosses and lichens growing on them. The air in the corridors had not been good, but the air here was utterly foul, as though old things had rotted away in the dark. Vandra shivered, and Danny was surprised when she grasped his hand. He caught sight of Dixie hidden behind a buttress. She made a face and grasped her throat as if the dank odors were choking her.

They were in a long prison corridor with rusting iron doors spaced six feet apart. At the end of the corridor two Cherb guards sat at a table littered with foul scraps. Both were deathly pale, as if they had spent all their lives in that place. One had a pasty face covered with large boils. The other had a growth on his forehead like a giant wart. Lump and Bump, Danny christened them. They rose to their feet as Cranbull approached, darting glances at Danny. Obviously news of the Fifth had reached here.

"The Messenger!" Cranbull barked. Bump took a bunch of keys from his pocket and opened one of the cells. Danny was aware of Dixie in the shadows halfway down the corridor.

Les was lying on a wretched pallet of straw, pale and ill, his breathing uneven. He did not stir when they entered. There was no light in the cell, but Cranbull's lantern cast grotesque shadows on the wall. With pity and guilt Danny saw the Messenger's twisted and filthy wings. Behind him he heard a sudden intake of breath from Vandra.

"Well?" Cranbull said. "Finish him off quickly. I take it you don't want a chaplain!" He laughed mirthlessly. The two guards backed away from Vandra.

"Physick," Danny said, "do your work." Vandra walked slowly forward. She knelt beside Les.

"I don't know . . . he's very weak," she said with a pleading look at Danny.

"Weak!" Cranbull laughed. "In a few minutes he'll be dead. Don't worry about weak."

"Do it!" Danny ordered. Les would die anyway if they left him here. She held Danny's eyes for a long time; then she bent over Les, casting a vampirish shadow in the flickering light. Danny heard a deep intake of breath from one of the Cherbs. There was a long silence; then Vandra raised her head. Danny saw, with a feeling of horror that he couldn't quite suppress, that there was a drop of blood on her chin. Vandra dabbed at it, then apologetically wiped it away. Cranbull stepped over to Les, lifted his wrist to take his pulse. Danny could see that his friend's chest was no longer rising and falling.

"Dead as a doornail. You've had your satisfaction, Fifth." He nodded to the two guards, who seized Les's feet and arms.

"Where are they taking him?" Danny asked, trying to hide his alarm. He hadn't expected this.

"Rue Morgue," Cranbull said shortly.

"Where's that?"

"The street of the dead." Danny stepped forward to stop the guards, but Vandra grasped his sleeve. With a sick feeling in his stomach he watched Les being carried out of the cell. Cranbull went out with them.

"Let them take him there," Vandra whispered. "I know where it is—it's the only way we can get him out."

"Is he all right?" Vandra's big brown eyes met Danny's. He could see the two sharp incisors on her lower lip.

"I don't know," she said. "I injected the anesthetic like you asked—he's in the deepest sleep possible. His heart is barely beating. But we need to get to him fast."

"If we don't . . . if we don't, Les is dead. And we killed him," Danny said.

28

RUE MORGUE

Danny insisted that Cranbull let them out of the prison on the perimeter of the fortress. The jailer led them to a tiny doorway in the fortress wall.

"A traitors' gate," he said with an unpleasant grin. "It's where we take in the prisoners we don't want anyone to see."

Danny shivered at the thought of it—the fear those people must feel with the walls of Grist towering above them.

Cranbull pushed them through the door and slammed it behind them with such haste that once again Danny was afraid Dixie might not make it through. But there she was, sucking at a cut on her hand.

"Nearly took the hand off me coming through the

door," she said. "Is that place grim or what? What about Les?"

"We have to get to him quickly," Danny said shortly, thinking how if it wasn't for him, Les wouldn't have been there in the first place.

"I don't like it here," Vandra said, and shivered. Danny looked around. They were isolated against the sheer wall of the fortress. Patches of damp mist floated through the air, but otherwise, they were completely exposed.

"Seraphim patrol the sky at night, the big hairy vultures," Dixie said. "Time to be gone."

"What direction is the Rue Morgue?" Danny asked urgently.

"Follow me," Vandra said.

Danny and Dixie set off after the physick. None of them noticed the shadowy figure that had been standing so close to the wall of the fortress that it seemed part of the stone. And none of them saw it detach from the wall and follow them.

They reached the first buildings of the town. Vandra led them downhill. It was very late. There was no one else about. The streets were dimly lit by yellow gaslights. The houses and shops felt hostile, barred and shuttered, offering no hiding place. Danny's feet sounded too loud on the wet cobbles. They kept looking up nervously for signs of patroling Seraphim. Dixie stayed close to Danny.

"You okay?" he whispered.

"I was afraid of being left behind in the dark," she

whispered back. He looked at her to see if she was joking, but he saw no smile.

The next street was filled with shops. Some had razors hanging above the door. Others had sharp-toothed saws above the door, or lengths of bloodstained bandages.

"What's this?" Danny asked.

"The Street of the Doctors," Vandra whispered. "Rue Morgue—the Street of the Dead—is next one down."

"Why am I not surprised?" Dixie said with distaste, staring at a display of suspiciously used-looking hatchets in one window.

"Shh!" Vandra hissed. A great birdlike shape wheeled in the sky ahead of them. For a moment they thought it was coming their way, and they shrank against the shuttered shops; then it turned, as if drawn by some other prey, and was gone.

"Come on!" Vandra led them out into the street again. At the top of the street was a statue.

Dixie whistled. "Look at that," she said. The statue was of a skeleton caught in the middle of a grotesque dance, a skull firmly grasped in each hand. On the statue's base was carved: RUE MORGUE.

Danny looked at Dixie. She shrugged.

"After you," she said. Vandra was already moving quickly ahead. They followed.

On Rue Morgue there were headstone dealers and wreath stores. The sickly scent of lilies filled the night air. There were dingy-looking coffin shops, and windows filled with cremation urns. There was a shop with embalming equipment in the corner. Danny didn't even want to think what the coils of rubber piping and brass tubing were used for. There was a whole display of mournful-looking death masks with rolls of black crepe underneath. There was a music shop called Mournful Moods.

At the bottom of the street there were rows and rows of shops with signs bearing the title UNDERTAKER or FUNERAL DIRECTOR. There was only one light on—in the dingiest, dustiest-looking window in the whole street. A flaking wooden plaque promised NIGHT BURIALS, EMBALMING SERVICES, and on the second line: BONE AGENT AND ORGAN BROKER BY APPOINTMENT.

"Organ broker? Does that mean . . . ," Danny began.

"Don't think about it," Vandra answered, grasping a frayed bell pull and yanking on it. Far in the distance a bell tolled. In response to Danny's look, Dixie grinned.

"Well, you didn't expect violins, did you?"

There was a long pause before they heard footsteps approaching. The door was opened by an ancient Cherb woman. She had apple cheeks, insofar as a Cherb could have apple cheeks, and a kindly smile on her wrinkled face. Her hair was piled high on her head in a bun. Dixie nudged Danny and nodded to the pin that held her hair in place. It was a bone. Could it be human?

"Good evening, my dears," she said in a sweet, trembling voice. "What sad event brings you here so late? Perhaps your parents have succumbed to a plague and left you as dear little orphans? Or a youthful friend has just drowned in a tragic swimming accident? I like to see a young corpse come through the door. Young people do so brighten a place up, don't you think? I'm Granny Grimley."

"We were looking for a friend of ours—Les Knutt. A young Messenger . . ."

"Oh yes, one was dumped here just an hour ago. They do that, you know, leave bodies on the doorstep. Most thoughtless. They try to save on funeral costs, then what does Granny Grimley have to do? Sell the body parts, I'm afraid. One doesn't want to, but costs have to be defrayed. There's usually a little left over to bury, which is nice."

"You haven't, I mean . . . started yet . . . ?" Danny looked at her in horror.

"No, the doorbell interrupted, but if you want him, you'll have to pay. . . ."

"I've got money," Danny said. Granny Grimley raised an eyebrow: then she took in the black uniform he wore, and her expression softened. "Lots of it," Danny said. "But if he's damaged . . ."

"Not even the smallest incision," Granny Grimley said, "but I mustn't keep you here chatting. The fog's coming in. You'll catch your death."

It was true. Behind them a heavy bank of fog was rolling down the street toward them. Granny Grimley grabbed Danny by the arm and hauled him into the hallway. Vandra and Dixie followed.

There was old linoleum on the floor, and faded flocked wallpaper, which Danny noticed was encrusted here and there with bits of things he didn't want to look at too closely. Granny Grimley took them through a small living room, shuffling ahead of them in slippers. There was a bright fire burning, and there were pictures of kittens on the walls. The room would have been cozy except for the fact that every surface was covered in jars with gruesome objects floating in them.

"Is that a real hand?" Dixie said. "Wow!"

"Please . . ." Danny looked away and found himself staring at a jar of eyeballs. Granny Grimley threw open a set of doors that looked as if they'd come from an operating room. The room they entered was in complete contrast to the rest of the house. Stainless-steel shelves lined the white-tiled walls, and on the shelves was an array of every kind of surgical instrument you could think of. There was a gleaming sink; everything was bathed in powerful lights hanging from the ceiling. In the center of the room there was a large stainless-steel table and, in the middle of that, looking very small and bedraggled, was Les.

All three made to move toward Les.

"Excuse me," Granny Grimley said pleasantly. She didn't say anything else, but she was standing beside a shelf of very large meat cleavers.

"Yes, of course," Danny said quickly. He went over to her and pulled wads of notes from his pocket. Granny Grimley's pleasant smile returned. She scooped the cash into a pocket of her apron.

"And what will you want to do with the young man? I can of course provide a coffin. A little expensive, perhaps—the Messengers are so difficult to fit in—the wings you see. Of course, they can always be removed. . . ." Granny Grimley pointed to a large circular saw.

"That won't be necessary," Vandra said quietly. She bent over Les. Danny looked away. Granny Grimley's eyes narrowed. Vandra straightened. There was a long silence. Les didn't move.

"A little more antidote . . . ," Vandra said, leaning over him again. But once again, the Messenger boy did not move. Minutes passed.

"I only have a little left," Vandra said, looking worried. She tried again. "That's it," she said despairingly.

"He's not moving." Dixie reached out and touched Les's cold hand.

"You can't cheat Death," Granny Grimley said. "Death will have his way."

"Wait," Danny said. He reached into his coat pocket and brought out the signal mirror he had been given by the Storeman. He held it over his friend's cold lips. A little mist formed on it—Les was alive!

"Rub his arms and legs, get the circulation going!" Vandra cried. Together they worked on Les. Some little color returned to his cheeks. He moaned and stirred. His eyes opened. Granny Grimley's mouth pursed.

"He's supposed to be dead," she said. "Where would we be if everyone who was supposed to be dead started waking up again?"

"Where . . . am I? . . . I thought . . . ," Les said, opening his eyes and looking wildly around.

"You're okay, Les," Dixie said, "you've just been for a sleep, is all."

They got Les into an upright position.

"He needs rest," Vandra said.

"We haven't got time." Danny looked anxious. "We have to get him back to Wilsons."

"I can walk," Les said, tottering to his feet.

"About as well as you can fly." Dixie fingered his tattered wings.

"We need to make our way to the docks, see if we can find a ship. We'll have to help him. Put your arm around my shoulders." Les draped one arm over Danny's shoulders. Vandra took the other.

"I've never seen the like in all my born days," Granny Grimley declared. "What would the Society of Morticians say? I'd be drummed out."

"You've been well paid," Vandra said, "and we'll take our leave of you now."

Grumbling, the elderly Cherb led the group to the door and opened it. Thick yellow fog billowed in.

"It's the kind of night that the living shouldn't be about," Granny Grimley warned.

"You're not scaring us, Granny," Dixie said.

"You may laugh, but there's many that laughed yesterday lying on a slab cold and dead today." Granny Grimley wagged her finger at Dixie as she closed the door.

"Am I glad to get out of there or what?" Dixie did a little skip of relief.

"The fog will help a bit," Danny said. "Keep the Seraphim off our backs. I hope we can find the docks, though."

"Easy—just keep going downhill until we get our toes wet," Dixie said brightly.

They started walking, slowly. Les turned his head painfully to Danny.

"I knew you wouldn't leave me there," he said, speaking with difficulty. Danny said nothing. He had condemned Les to the prison in the first place.

Down the hill they went, but not alone. A shape followed them in the fog, keeping just the right distance.

Granny Grimley took out the money and looked at it. It was far too much for a skinny Messenger. And where had the boy in black got it, never mind the fancy uniform? After thinking for a moment, she reached for her big black telephone, pausing only to pick off a few globs of greenish matter adhering to it, and began to dial.

29

THE FLYING WESTMAN

The damp fog clung to them, tendrils wreathing inside their clothes, plastering their hair to their foreheads. The yellow streetlights cast their own shadows on the fog, enormous and crabbed. Danny thought of an old picture he had seen of grave robbers. Sounds were muffled, so that once, when they heard the long and mournful blast of a ship's foghorn, they could not tell from which direction it had come.

They had walked for about ten minutes when they heard another noise cut through the fog, one that they had never heard in Westwald before, though they knew instantly what it meant. It was a siren, a high, piercing, urgent sound, rising and falling and making the hairs on the backs of their necks stand up. It rang out for only a few minutes, but panic began to set in, and they moved more quickly, dragging Les between them. Just as the siren halted and the hollow silence rolled back again, Danny felt a strong hand grasp his shoulder.

In an instant he wheeled around, the Knife of Implacable Intention in his hand.

"Don't move or I'll slit your throat," he said, a snarl in his voice that surprised even him.

"I heard you had become the Fifth. I wasn't sure whether to believe it," a familiar cool voice said.

"Starling!"

"What is it, Danny?" Vandra's voice coming through the fog was anxious.

"It's okay," Starling called out, "I'm a friend."

"Are you?" Danny asked. He met the gray eyes and for the first time they could not meet his. With sudden insight, he knew that Starling was carrying a great secret, and had been doing so for many years. He took the knife from the man's throat as the others joined them.

"They say that the Ring can see right into a man's mind," Starling said. "Is that true?"

"This is Starling," Danny said, without replying. "He helped me get across."

"The siren means an alert at Grist. They'll be scouring the city for you."

"Can you help us?" Vandra asked as Les swayed and almost fell.

"Why should I help the Fifth?"

Danny looked at Starling again and, in a flash of dark insight, knew his secret.

Danny leaned close to his ear.

"I know who you are."

Starling looked at him, uncertain.

"If you know who I am, then the Ring . . ."

"They don't know anything. I only just realized."

"Can you hide it if they enter your head again?"

"I don't know."

"Shh!" Starling suddenly crouched down.

"What is it?" Then Danny heard wings flapping close by. The flapping slowed, then halted.

"Seraphim," Starling whispered. "They can't hunt from the air in this fog, so they're landing. Keep down!"

Only twenty or so feet away, a shape loomed out of the mist, a Seraphim, its wings wrapped around it like those of a vulture stalking the night for carrion. The fog swirled and it was gone again.

"Follow me," Starling said. Danny didn't argue.

The next few hours were nightmarish. Every time they got near the port a Seraphim appeared in the fog, so that they had to turn and carry Les back up the hill. Even there they were not safe. It was Danny who shoved them into an alley, where they crouched, terrified, as a Seraphim passed close enough to the entrance for them to hear its hissing breath and the rustle of its feathers. A foul odor hung in the air behind it. When they could carry Les no longer, Starling forced open the door of an old warehouse and they crawled inside, exhausted.

"We'll have to wait until morning and try then," Starling said.

"We can't wait," Danny said.

300

"Why not?"

"They're using the tunnel they've dug to come out in the parade ground at Wilsons. We have to warn them."

Danny could see Starling thinking; then the man drove his fist into the palm of his hand.

"Fool! I knew there was something. The old pumping station north of Tarnstone—there was talk that it was working again and that Nurse Flanagan was seen there. The tunnel goes under the sea, so it needs to be pumped out continuously."

"What would happen," Danny said slowly, "if we turned the pumps back so that the water went back into the tunnel . . ."

"Yes," Starling said, "yes . . . it might just work . . . the water that was no longer being pumped from the tunnel and the water that was being pumped in—that would flood it, I think . . . but we have to get there."

"And we can't get near the docks," Vandra said gloomily.

"There is a way . . . ," Starling said slowly, "a last resort."

"Yes?" Danny looked at him.

"The Flying Westman."

"Sounds exciting." Dixie turned her big eyes on Starling. "What is it?"

"A train. I've been working on it. All it needs is a head of steam. I've been keeping it in case I need to get out of here in a hurry. And there's a station at Wilsons, behind the parade ground."

"I thought the railway bridge to Tarnstone was destroyed?" Danny said.

"The railway line is intact—just. The structure of the bridge is still there. It definitely wouldn't support the weight of a full train. It might take the Flying Westman, but there's no telling how weak it is. . . ."

"Until you take a train over it," Dixie said. "Absolutely too thrilling!"

"Do you ever take anything seriously?" Vandra said crossly.

"Don't argue," Danny said. "How long does it take to get up a head of steam?"

"About half an hour."

"And where is the train?"

"On a siding near here. We can take them by surprise, but we'd better hurry. It'll be dawn soon."

Dragging themselves with tiredness, they left the warehouse and made their way through another maze of side streets. The fog had lifted slightly, and above their heads was the first pale glimmer of dawn.

"The Seraphim will be up again soon," Starling said. "Hurry!"

At last they saw a tumbledown railway shed ahead of them, and a length of rusty track. Out of the remaining fog loomed old coaches and freight wagons.

"There she is—the Flying Westman," Starling said.

The Flying Westman didn't look like much. Most of her paintwork had gone, and her rusty metal was battered and dented. Her funnel was at an angle to her body, and her bell was held on by a piece of wire. The wheels were caked in old grease and oil. Vandra sniffed meaningfully, but Danny was thoughtful. Underneath the neglect, he could see her clean, low-slung lines. The Flying Westman wouldn't let them down for speed.

Starling clambered into the cab and lit the boiler. He helped them get Les up into the heat.

"Where am I?" Les moaned, his eyes barely open. "My wings . . . my wings hurt. . . ." His face contorted with pain. With a glance at Danny, Vandra leaned over him. In a moment he was asleep.

"We need to get him somewhere comfortable," Vandra said.

"Danny," Starling said, "get up on the tender and start throwing down wood."

For half an hour Danny threw down wood and Starling fed the firebox. Vandra held Les's head in her lap. Dixie found a bit of rag and set about polishing the bell.

It was not quite dawn by the time the fire was roaring, and steam was starting to wreathe around the wheels.

"I think she's ready," Starling said. Danny jumped down and Starling eased the engine into gear. Groaning and protesting, the train began to move forward.

Keeping up a fast walking pace, the train creaked through the predawn fog. Anyone who had seen it might have supposed it was a ghost train. Starling looked anxiously down the track. The light in the east was growing.

"I can see the bridge ahead," Danny said. The Flying Westman began to pick up speed.

*　　*　　*

At the heart of Grist fortress, a terrified Cranbull cringed in a corner of the Ring of Five gallery. Rufus Ness stood over him. Longford sat at the table. There was no sign of the amiable academic whom Danny had first met. Longford's eyes were cold and hard.

"You have told us everything?" he said coldly. Cranbull nodded, too petrified to speak. The door opened and Nurse Flanagan came in.

"They took the Messenger boy from Rue Morgue. He wasn't dead after all."

"They'll be heading for Wilsons," Longford said.

"The invasion . . ." Rufus Ness looked up from Cranbull.

"Must be launched immediately. Alert the tunnel and summon the Seraphim."

"So much for the Fifth," Nurse Flanagan said.

"It doesn't matter. He has joined the Ring. Sooner or later he will be ours—do you not understand? He betrayed his friend, and now he has betrayed us. Treachery will stalk him from now. His only home will be with us, the most treacherous of all. Whether he wants to believe it or not, the blood of the Fifth flows in his veins. He will come back. And as for you . . ." Longford transferred his gaze to Cranbull. The jailer's layers of fat shook like jelly. Longford gestured with his hand. A figure stepped out of the shadows.

"No . . . ," Cranbull said hoarsely. "No . . ." A physick neared him, one who did not have Vandra's liquid brown eyes and gentle, serious expression. Instead, her eyes were red-rimmed, her face a ghastly white. Her mouth stretched wide in a mirthless grin that showed two long yellowed fangs, and her long black cloak muffled Cranbull's screams as she bent over him.

A CROSSING

The Flying Westman picked up momentum on the slope down to the bridge. The sky to the east was bright. Starling eased the throttle open and the engine responded. They sped past the tall begrimed buildings that backed onto the track.

"We've got a clear run!" Vandra cried.

"Not quite." Dixie pointed ahead. A Seraphim stood on the track, great wings spread wide, hot yellow eyes glowing. Starling's hand did not leave the throttle. The train bore down on the Seraphim. Dixie hid her eyes. At the last moment the Seraphim sprang aside, its wings brushing the smokestack as it soared upward.

"Hold on!" Starling shouted. Ahead of them was what looked like a tangle of steel girders. Starling opened the throttle fully, and this time, even Dixie looked worried. At the last minute a gap appeared, just wide enough for the Flying Westman. With a great clang, the engine was on the bridge. Danny grabbed the side of the cab as the train swayed alarmingly. Behind them a massive girder crashed onto the track. Everywhere were signs of shelling—scorched sleepers and twisted metal. The track was bent and buckled in places. It held, but the train pitched each time it struck a twisted rail.

"She'll derail!" Danny shouted.

"I have to keep up speed!" Starling shouted back.

"Get down!" Dixie roared. They ducked as a protruding piece of metal from the bridge struck the side of the cab and gouged the metal where they had been standing. They raced across the bridge. In places there were only the rails left—or at least, that was the way it looked as they gazed down on the dark, angry sea below them.

"At least the fog is lifting," Vandra said. "We can see where we're going." And then she cringed as a shadow fell over her. They looked up. Keeping pace easily, but distanced from them by the twisted latticework of girders over their heads, was Conal, his yellow eyes fixed on Danny. Ahead, Danny could see the chimneys of Tarnstone nearer by the minute, the speeding train far outpacing the steamer he had come across in.

Then Danny felt a strange sensation steal over him: warmth seeping into his brain. He felt as though pleasurable things were being offered to him, or as though he was slipping into a hot bath filled with scented oils. He heard Dixie shouting at him.

"The gun! Give me the gun." Without thinking, he

reached into his pocket and handed her the little derringer. He understood the message—unknown delights
would be his if he just pulled that lever, the brake. . . .

There were two sharp reports by his ear and he
jumped, his dream broken. He looked over the side and
saw a long red speedboat with teak decks and polished
brasswork keeping pace with the train. At the helm was
Nurse Flanagan, and beside her was Longford, a long
knitted scarf flowing out behind him. Nurse Flanagan,
however, was examining with a scowl the neat hole in the
exact center of her crisp white yachting cap. Dixie
grinned and blew imaginary smoke from the barrel of the
derringer.

"Are you okay?" Vandra was looking at Danny anxiously.

"Yes," he said, "I'm okay now."

"Look out!" Starling shouted. The engine swayed so
violently that Danny was almost flung against the red-hot
firebox. Then the Flying Westman was out in the open as
she thundered onto a piece of track that was totally exposed to the sky above. Conal, seizing his opportunity,
swooped. Vandra cried out as his bony hand caught her
long hair. Danny, lying where he had fallen was too far
away to reach her. Frantically his hands searched the
pockets of his coat. He felt the outline of the tin of fingerprint powder. Vandra was lifted half out of the cab, Dixie
clinging to one of her feet. In desperation, Danny ripped
the lid from the tin and flung its contents at the Seraphim.
The cloud of fingerprint powder caught Conal in the

eyes. With a cry of pain Conal released Vandra and wheeled away, blinded. Still traveling at speed, the Seraphim struck the iron bridgework—so hard that Danny heard the clang—and dropped like a stone into the sea. With a scowl Nurse Flanagan slowed the speedboat and stopped beside the floating Conal.

"We're in the clear now," Dixie said. "Go, baby, go!" They could see the buildings of Tarnstone clearly in the cold morning light. But Starling looked worried.

"We're losing pressure, and the bridge is becoming unstable," he said. It was true. They could feel the bridge flexing below them, and at the same time, the engine slowing.

"Look!" Vandra said. There was a hole in one of the pipes leading from the firebox, and a jet of steam was escaping from it. Danny took the fake mustache from his pocket and jammed it in place with a piece of wood. There was a shudder as the whole bridge slipped sideways, and the Flying Westman's bell gave a mournful clang. The engine picked up speed again, the wheels struggling for grip on the tilted track. A tangle of iron girders fell off the bridge and landed with an enormous splash, sending freezing seawater over the cab.

"Hold on!" Starling shouted. The bridge lurched again and they were speeding through more spray, clinging on to anything they could find, and then the wheels bit and the engine shot forward. With an almighty crash the whole span of the bridge behind them collapsed into the sea. They were on dry land. They had made it.

* * *

Grim-faced, Starling worked the controls as the train sped through the outskirts of Tarnstone.

"We're running out of time," he said. It was daylight now. There was smoke coming from some of the chimneys in Tarnstone.

"We need to warn Wilsons first, then get to the pumping station," Danny shouted over the noise of the engine.

"I know what to do," Dixie said. She reached up and grabbed a cord. An earsplitting whistle rent the morning air. She pulled again and again. As they passed a group of trees, a sleepy surprised face appeared on one of the lower branches—Vicky the siren rubbed her eyes and looked again. Dixie gave her a cheery wave and blew the whistle once more.

Several miles away, Devoy was the first to wake. He went to his bedroom window, looked out and saw the smoke from the train funnel speeding toward the school.

"Mr. Blackpitt?" he said. There was some mumbling; then a sleepy voice replied.

"Whassit?"

"Mr. Blackpitt. This is Master Devoy. I want the whole school roused immediately."

"The whole . . . What . . . At this time . . . ?"

"Mr. Blackpitt!"

"Yes, yes, of course, Master Devoy . . ." This was followed by discontented muttering.

Devoy dressed quickly. He went out into the corridor, where he met Brunholm, who wore a dressing gown with a garish rose pattern on it.

"I do believe our young agent may be returning to us," he said.

"In a tearing hurry too," Brunholm observed.

"Attention. Attention. All cadets, Messengers and instructors to be in the main hall in five minutes. General alert. General alert," Blackpitt intoned.

The Flying Westman halted at the end of the Wilsons branch line in a cloud of steam. Danny and the others got Les to his feet and helped him down. Moving as fast as they could, they made their way through the trees, coming out on the edge of the parade ground.

"They haven't broken through yet," Vandra panted. Danny lay down and put his ear to the ground. He could hear rumbling, and what sounded like shovels, very close.

"They won't be long!" Half carrying and half dragging their friend, Danny, Vandra and Dixie ran across the lawns behind Starling. A knot of students had gathered around the front door. There was a stunned silence when they saw Danny.

"Where's Devoy?" Danny shouted.

"I'm here," a calm voice replied. Danny turned to see Devoy and Brunholm behind him.

"There's an invasion," Danny said, gasping for breath. "They're coming up under the parade ground. A tunnel."

"Options?" Devoy barked.

"The pumping station. We need to reverse the pumps."

"Good. We'll get all able-bodied personnel to the parade ground to hold them off. Marcus—you and I will take the pumping station!"

"We need to get the soldiers from the beach," Danny said. "They're no good down there now that the Cherbs are going to get in behind them."

"Yes," Brunholm said, "yes, of course. The soldiers. I'll deal with it directly."

Two miles away a red car sped along the road between Tarnstone and Wilsons. Nurse Flanagan was at the wheel, Longford in the passenger seat.

"We'll be just in time for the fun," Nurse Flanagan trilled gaily. A few hundred yards up the road, Vicky the siren, at her most alluring, lips parted, eyes modestly cast down, stood by the side of the road. She wanted a lift to Wilsons to see what was going on, and no motorist had ever been able to resist her.

Nurse Flanagan, however, was immune to her charms. As she drew level with Vicky, she swung the wheel violently, so that the bumper was heading straight for the siren. Vicky stared in disbelief, then launched herself into the air. The bumper swept through the space where she had been standing, and Vicky landed face-first in the bottom of a ditch filled with filthy water.

"I do find sirens rather irritating, don't you?" Nurse

312

Flanagan said to Longford. "It's always 'me, me, me' with them."

Vicky lifted her head from the ditch. Her hair and clothes were wet and muddy. She stared after the car, her fists clenched and her mouth set in a hard line.

Ten minutes later all the students and teachers were outside the Stores, and the Storeman was handing out pistols, sabers, cudgels, brass knuckles and canisters of tear gas. Vandra was making Les comfortable in the hallway. Mr. Jamshid came down in the lift and examined Les, shaking his head gravely. In the hallway Messengers milled around, some of the women still in dressing gowns and curlers. Vandra could hear complaints about being got out of bed so early, and demands to know what all the fuss was about.

"Why don't you lot do something?" she demanded crossly.

"Us?" An elderly Messenger who resembled a bird with a long pointy beak looked at her in astonishment.

"Everybody else has gone to fight the Cherbs and you're just here complaining. You could fly over them and drop things or something!"

"Don't be so vulgar," another Messenger said.

"Here. Help me," Jamshid said to Vandra, getting Les to his feet.

"What's going on?" Gabriel demanded, arriving in his dressing gown.

"This . . . this physick wants us to . . . to fly!" the birdlike Messenger said in a whiny voice.

313

Hot tears started in Vandra's eyes.

"Les was out trying to defend you lot, and look at him now!" She pointed to his broken and twisted wings. "At least you can fly. He'll never fly again!"

"How uncouth." The Messenger looked at the others for support. There was a murmur of agreement.

"I always said physicks were ill-bred," another Messenger said. Vandra kept her mouth shut tight. Gabriel stared at her with mournful eyes.

The pupils and teachers were gathered around the parade ground. The Storeman, armed with an ancient blunderbuss, perched on the roof of the Stores. Duddy, in disguise as a grenadier guardsman, crouched on the ground, clutching a rifle. Docterow had a baseball bat, while Exshaw swished a samurai sword through the air. Valant practiced a variety of martial-arts moves.

"Right," Devoy said, "the pumping station!"

"I think it's a bit late for that," came a man's voice. Devoy's face betrayed nothing. Longford and Nurse Flanagan appeared on the path to the pumping station.

"You can't stop us, Longford." Brunholm stepped forward.

"No," Longford replied, "but they can."

Behind Longford, rising into the air, appeared a deadly host of Seraphim. At their head was Conal, dried blood caked on his temple.

"We have reached the end, Devoy." Longford smiled.

"Perhaps."

Longford pointed to the middle of the parade ground. The earth started to shift; then part of it fell inward. A Cherb soldier started to clamber out of the hole. An object hurtled through the air and struck him on the head with a loud, hollow sound. As Spitfire's wooden-backed duster fell to the ground, the Cherb tumbled back into the hole.

Nurse Flanagan reached into her hair. In one easy movement she removed a long hairpin and flung it at Spitfire. The deadly pin flew straight for the teacher's heart. Danny grabbed the Knife of Implacable Intention and threw it, intercepting the pin.

"Ah, yes, Danny," said Longford, "you'll be coming back to Grist with us tonight."

"I won't be going anywhere with you."

"You're part of the Ring of Five. Treachery is working in your heart, and sooner or later you'll betray all that you hold dear. I don't know what they tell you in the Upper World, but you are the true-born Fifth."

Danny could hear their voices in his head telling him to walk across the parade ground and join them. He imagined the rush of forbidden pleasure as he turned back to the instructors and cadets and saw the betrayed look on their faces.

"Come on, Danny." He heard Nurse Flanagan's voice in his head, low and musical. Danny shut his eyes. What would happen to his friends if he crossed? An image of Les and his broken wings came into his head. He opened his eyes.

"I'm staying here," he said, barely able to get the words out of his mouth.

"Very well," Longford said grimly. "Attack!"

As one the Seraphim rose into the air and swooped on the defenders, the younger cadets shrieked with terror. Two Cherbs clambered out of the tunnel, followed by Rufus Ness.

"Steady now," Exshaw said, his samurai sword at the ready. "Steady!" And then the Seraphim were on them.

A mile away Vicky the siren walked up to a large building with wooden walls, talking to herself like a sulky child.

"It's not right, putting Vicky in a ditch like that. Her good dress ruined. And mud in her hair. And her shoes all wet."

Still complaining, Vicky leapt lightly up to a first-floor window and worked the latch loose.

"Thinks she's smart in her big red sports car. I was charming men off ships before Flanagan ever slapped lipstick on those two big lips of hers. I had frocks of finest satin from the trunks of poor drowned and departed ladies. . . ."

Vicky dropped lightly to the floor inside. The shed was dim and noisy. All along one wall, large machines moved great arms up and down. Vicky jumped onto the walkway running alongside the machines.

"The Ring think Vicky doesn't know what they're up to. They must think she's stupid or something. They think this little old siren doesn't see them sneaking up here and working at night."

Vicky stopped at the first machine and examined it.

There was a long lever on one side. She grasped the top of it and hauled until it pointed at the floor. The great arm on top stopped, then slowly began to move in the other direction. Vicky watched it with satisfaction. There was a whoosh and a loud gurgling noise from under her feet. She moved to the next machine and then the next. Soon all the pumps were moving in the opposite direction, and the whooshing and gurgling underfoot had increased. Vicky looked along the row of pumps with an air of satisfaction, skipped back up to the open window and was gone.

The sky darkened as the Seraphim fell upon the Wilsons defenders. The younger cadets shouted in terror at the sight of the lordly and stern faces. And the Seraphim sang a dread song as they descended. The instructors tried to rally the cadets. But the braver ones who stood their ground were felled by blows of the heavy maces that the Seraphim carried. Some cadets gathered round Duddy, who kept up a steady fire, while Exshaw drove off a group of Seraphim who had swept the Storeman off the roof of the Stores and were trying to finish him off. There was a loud scream from Smyck as he pointed to a forward party of Cherbs bursting from the tunnel mouth. Exspectre backed up against the wall of the Stores. To Danny's amazement Exspectre's body took on the colors of the wall, so that he faded completely into it.

"Now we know what his gift is!" Dixie said, and disappeared, to reappear in front of the leader of the Cherb platoon. She stuck out her foot, sending him tumbling and bringing down several of those following. Danny rushed into the fray. He felt in his pockets for a weapon, but the only thing he could find was the length of piano wire. He crept up behind a Seraphim who was trading sword blows with Exshaw, driving the instructor onto his knees. Quickly Danny looped one end of the piano wire around the tip of one of the Seraphim's wings and the other around a lamppost. The Seraphim drove Exshaw to his knees, arched its wings and rose into the air, intending to plunge the sword into Exshaw's heart. But instead, with a scream of surprise, the Seraphim flew in a tight circle and crashed straight into the side of the Stores.

Danny saw the Seraphim's sword on the ground and grabbed it. A Cherb ran straight for him then halted in confusion when he saw Danny's features and his uniform. Danny punched him.

"Master Devoy?" Devoy turned to see Toxique standing beside him.

"In three seconds' time a Cherb arrow will hit you in the heart if you don't move," Toxique said. Devoy took two quick steps backward. An arrow whistled through the place where he had been standing and buried itself in the ground.

"Fascinating," Devoy said thoughtfully. "You have a Gift of Anticipation."

Several more platoons of Cherbs emerged from the tunnel, their pinched and cunning faces eager for battle. Others were climbing from the hole in the ground. It's hopeless, Danny thought, looking around at the out-numbered defenders. But I have to try. He ran toward the Cherbs.

"Come on, you lot," he growled. "The woods are full of Wilsons men, get a move on!"

The Cherbs looked at each other uncertainly, but such was the tone of command in Danny's voice, allied to his Cherb features, that they set up a great cry and charged off in the direction of the woods. This gave him an idea. As Cherbs poured from the hole in the ground, he quickly formed them into platoons. One platoon he set to guarding the mouth of the tunnel.

"Don't let any more Cherbs through," he com-manded. "They are to be kept as reinforcements." To the others he shouted, "Follow me!"

As they did, he heard fighting start between the Cherbs still in the tunnel and those he had set to guard it.

He ran around the side of the building, followed by the Cherbs. He could almost feel their breath on the back of his neck. Finally he reached his destination: the Helix of Van Groening. The yew maze seemed very still and sinister after the turmoil of the battle.

"This place is full of armed cadets," he shouted. "Clear it out!"

With a howl the Cherbs charged into the maze. As they entered the Helix their voices became muffled. The howl died to a puzzled muttering, followed by thumps, rustlings and cries of pain. After a few minutes he could hear nothing at all.

"We won't be seeing them again," Danny thought with satisfaction.

When he rejoined the battle, things had turned decisively against the cadets. The Cherbs in the tunnel had fought their way out. The cadets were scattered in small groups, fighting desperately and bravely, but they were too few. Starling was isolated in the middle of the parade ground, battling two Seraphim. Dixie had run straight into one of the Seraphim, and its iron-hard flesh had dazed her, sending her reeling across the parade ground, appearing and disappearing at random. Duddy had been trussed up by some Cherbs and was being carried triumphantly back toward the tunnel.

"We'll get a good price for her on Rue Morgue," Danny heard one of them call out.

Vandra knelt over an unconscious Toxique. Devoy and the other instructors stood together, a press of Cherbs around them. Danny stopped dead. He could hear Longford in his head.

"It is you, Danny. You are the Fifth. You owe nothing to these people. You owe nothing to the man and woman who say they are your parents. Join us. Join us now."

Warmth flooded his mind, the offer of companionship. This time it was the voice of Rufus Ness, all the more seductive for being rough.

"The Ring, boy. Come to the Ring. We will show you fellowship. We will be joined as one."

Danny heard a sound and spun around. Smyck was standing behind him with a derringer in his hand. His eyes were wild and his voice was shaking.

"There's Cherbs attacking the building. I need help . . . I ran . . . I couldn't . . ."

Danny could see the shame in the boy's eyes, all of his sneering and bullying ways gone.

"You abandoned Wilsons to the Cherbs?" Danny said. His voice was low and menacing, and he enjoyed the effect it had on Smyck. The boy was trembling so hard he could barely stand.

"Give me the derringer," Danny said. With a shaking hand, Smyck handed it over. Danny placed the barrel of the gun against the trembling Smyck's forehead. He could feel the wave of approval from the other members of the Ring. Telling him there was a higher cause than mere mercy. Danny could feel his finger tighten on the trigger.

"No . . . ," Smyck whispered. But it was too late. Danny had passed over to the side of the Ring. He pulled the trigger. The hammer on the revolver descended on the chamber. And as it fell, Danny felt unnaturally aware of everything around him: of the trees swaying in the wind, of the scent of fear and blood, of each cry from the fighting defenders and Cherbs, each moan of despair. Aware of the worms in the earth beneath his feet and of the birds that wheeled in the air above the battle, the ravens . . . Danny braced himself for the recoil. . . .

It never came. The hammer clicked down on metal. The chamber was empty of bullets. The click dissolved the spell of the Ring, Danny realized with horror what he had tried to do. Smyck had fainted dead away in front of him.

A raven swooped and dashed the gun from Danny's hand. Danny sank to the ground, scarcely believing what had just happened.

He made to rise, then hesitated. He put his head back on the ground, his face intent. Under the earth there was a peculiar noise, a roaring, rushing sound. Danny sat up. There were no more Cherbs coming out of the tunnel mouth. Instead, there was an ominous rumbling. Everyone stopped fighting. A great gout of muddy water burst from the tunnel.

"They've flooded the tunnel!" Rufus Ness yelled.

The look of triumph on Longford's face was replaced by a snarl.

"Finish them off, Conal!"

The Seraphim and the Cherbs who had got out of the tunnel fell upon the cadets and instructors with renewed ferocity. Exshaw was unconscious. Blood streamed from a cut on Spitfire's head. Danny lay in a daze, not reacting even when a Seraphim placed a foot on his chest, squeezing the breath from his lungs. It put a sword against his throat. He tried to struggle, but it was useless. The Seraphim smiled mirthlessly. Pain surged through Danny's body. His lungs felt as if they were on fire. Then the pain disappeared and he was floating. This must be what it is like to die, he thought as the noise of wings filled the air. The weight vanished from his chest. He looked up and saw the Messenger Gabriel hovering directly above his head! The Seraphim pinning him down fell backward in surprise.

He raised himself up on one elbow. All the Wilsons

Messengers were in the air! A squadron of the elderly, some in support bandages and dressing gowns, wielding crutches and walking sticks, but flying expertly among the Seraphim, who were taken completely by surprise. Two Messengers seized a flying Seraphim by each wingtip. Unable to slow down or to turn, he flew straight into a tree trunk. Eluda Fanshawe used a crutch to pin a female Seraphim against the ground. A group of wizened Messengers entangled a haughty Seraphim's wings in a roll of bandage, sending him crashing to the ground. The cadets cheered and charged. The Cherbs, seeing the torrent of water pouring from the tunnel, and the sky above them full of decrepit but determined Messengers, turned tail and ran toward the woods. Rufus Ness ran after them, shouting, "Come back, you cowards!"

High above the parade ground, Danny saw a small dot. It got larger and larger as he watched it. It was a Messenger in a steep dive. As it closed in with blinding velocity, Danny saw who it was.

"Gabriel!" he cried out. The Messenger seemed certain to strike the ground at top speed, but at the last moment, in a breathtaking maneuver, he flipped sideways and headed straight for Conal. Gabriel skimmed Conal's right wing, stripping the lead feathers from it with his hand.

Gabriel halted above Conal and hovered. The Seraphim, barely able to stay in the air now, glared at Gabriel with hatred.

"You always did have slow reactions, Conal," Gabriel said with a smile.

Longford looked around him in disbelief and anger. Rufus Ness ran for Nurse Flanagan's car.

"Get in, Longford, or I'm going without you!" Nurse Flanagan shouted. Longford turned to Danny, his voice calm.

"You are of the Ring now. You are the Fifth, and one day the treachery in your heart will bring you back to us. I saw you, Danny. I saw you pull the trigger."

Longford smiled strangely and vaulted into the passenger seat of the car. The defenders watched in silence as the red car sped off.

"Retreat!" Conal shouted. The Seraphim gathered around him as he rose haltingly into the air. The Messengers cheered and crowed like schoolchildren as the proud Seraphim flew slowly away.

31

TREACHERY IS WHAT WE DO

There were many injuries among the cadets, some of them serious. Vandra and Mr. Jamshid worked long into the night. Some had been hit with poisoned weapons, and Toxique was called upon to help, identifying poisons from their effects and administering antidotes, a job that seemed to keep him calm.

It was after midnight before Dixie could persuade Danny to leave Les. The Messenger was sleeping soundly, his damaged wings disinfected and bandaged. Danny was beyond exhaustion, and didn't care about the other cadets and the way some of them looked at him. Smyck was busy spreading the story that Danny really was a Cherb, and that was the reason he had run away. Danny realized that Smyck had not mentioned what had happened on the parade ground—just as Danny had not mentioned the fact that Smyck had run away from the parade ground fight. Danny knew that Smyck would see this as a kind of twisted bargain where they protected each other.

There were darker rumors—that Danny had joined the Ring, and had tortured Les in the fortress of Grist. Danny didn't care. He was bone-weary. He dragged himself to bed without speaking to anyone, and fell instantly asleep.

The next morning he was woken by Blackpitt.

"Master Devoy wants your company, Cadet Caulfield." Blackpitt sounded disapproving. Did he suspect Danny as well?

Devoy was waiting for Danny in the library of the third landing. There were muffins and coffee in front of the fire, but Danny wasn't hungry.

"I owe you both an apology and an explanation," Devoy said, "but first I would like you to tell me about the encounter with the Ring."

Danny told him everything that had happened, from the first chance meeting with Nurse Flanagan ("She wasn't there by accident," Devoy said; "Brunholm tipped her off. Or rather, he tipped off Rufus Ness the day you saw him in the Painted Wall") to his joining of the Ring and the escape from Westwald. When he had finished, there was a long silence.

"I have an apology to make. You have worked out, of course, that your parents are fine"—My parents! Danny thought—"and that the newspaper report that you saw was a fake. And you have worked out that we had to drive you into the hands of the Ring. They would have seen through you immediately if you had tried to bluff. You had to truly want to join the Ring. It was cruel but necessary, and you have my most sincere apology. The betrayal of Knutt . . . Master Brunholm thought of that. I'm afraid he told the Ring that Les was in Westwald. It was a clever ploy—clever to the point of genius, but cruel to the point of insanity. Using Sranzer to deliver the paper to you was my idea. Sranzer isn't quite over it yet."

"But why didn't you tell me who the members of the Ring were?"

"For the same reason. You would not have acted naturally when you did meet them. You knew about Longford, of course, but then, he would have expected you to have that information."

"I don't understand, though. They really thought I was the Fifth."

"And that is the mystery," Brunholm said, stepping out from behind the statue. "You may in fact be the missing Fifth."

"No! I can't. I don't want to be. I'm Danny Caulfield!"

"I'm afraid he may be right, Danny," Devoy said. "By some strange accident of history, you may be the descendent of the original Fifth."

Danny felt his face grow hot.

"If I'm the Fifth," he said in anguish, "does that mean . . . that I'm evil?"

"No, of course not. Longford was not evil to start out

with. Nor was Conal. Even Nurse Flanagan was once known to be kind."

"But how do you know?" Danny demanded.

"I know because Longford and Nurse Flanagan were once my friends and fellow cadets at Wilsons."

"The whole operation was a triumph!" Brunholm broke in. "The Ring defeated. The invasion halted. A superb operation."

"Yes," Danny said slowly, "and we didn't even have to use the soldiers from the watchtowers."

"Yes, well . . . ," Brunholm said, uncomfortable. But Devoy was looking at Danny shrewdly.

"When did you know?"

"That there were no soldiers? It took a while. You disguised it well. All the talk of fighting at the front and casualties in the apothecary—by the way, when Vandra was in the apothecary we saw a casualty being brought in . . . ?"

"That was Duddy," Devoy said, "disguised as an injured soldier, of course."

"Then both of you were doing it?"

"Both?"

"You and Longford."

"What?" Brunholm exploded.

"He has a fake army of Cherbs as well. I realized it after he gave me a tour of the fortress of Grist. There were barracks and canteens and offices. But there were no Cherbs."

"There were supposed to be thousands and thousands of them," Brunholm groaned.

"I think those were most of his Cherb soldiers in the

tunnel. If he had thousands he would just have invaded across the sea."

"Spitfire's map. The Cherb positions . . ." Brunholm sat down suddenly.

"All fake. Longford was feeding you information and you were swallowing it, exactly as you were doing to him with your watchtowers and casualties. I wondered why the siren was so important. How many soldiers do you have?"

"Er, none," Brunholm said, looking at the ground.

"Which made our deception even more brilliant!" Devoy said. "Listen to me, Danny." Devoy put his hands on Danny's shoulders. "You are a member of the Ring. Nothing can change that."

"And who would want to?" Brunholm put in.

"But it does not make you evil like Longford. The seed of treachery has been woken in your heart, but it is up to you how to use it—either to become a great spy, who serves good . . ."

"Or become like Longford," Danny finished the sentence, "or even like Rufus Ness—if I am the Fifth then I am half Cherb!"

"Perhaps. But even the Cherbs have their role to play." Danny stayed silent, remembering what Longford had said—in the balance of good and evil, the Cherbs represented evil. But which of his parents was a Cherb? Neither of them looked like one.

"In the meantime, you will stay at Wilsons for the remainder of the term," Devoy said. "After that you can decide whether to return or not. You may leave us now,

329

Danny, and thank you. Your actions have saved Wilsons and your own world. Your mind has developed immensely. One day your name may be spoken of with awe as one of the great spies!"

"Yes, yes," Brunholm said, rubbing his hands together, "but how do we press home our advantage?"

He bustled over to Devoy, ignoring Danny.

Danny understood. He had served his purpose. The war against the Ring went on.

Les was sitting up in bed talking to Dixie. He was pale and thin, but his face lit up when he saw Danny.

"Hey, I hear you done brilliant. Apart from rescuing me and all. You took on the whole Ring and beat them, is what Dixie's been telling me."

"Not exactly the whole Ring. Even somebody as brilliant as me couldn't do that," Danny said sarcastically. Dixie gave him a look.

"Sorry," Danny said. "I was just with Brunholm and Devoy."

"That'd be enough to do anybody's head in," Les said. "So tell me about the whole thing."

Danny told him the whole story, leaving out the betrayal, aware of Dixie's eyes on him.

"I can't believe they done that to you, telling you your parents were dead," Les said indignantly.

"They had to," Danny said.

"Still, I think you were brilliant," Les said admiringly.

"But Longford says you're the Fifth," Dixie said.

330

"That's kind of cool and kind of scary at the same time."
Seeming to abandon the thought, she went on brightly.
"Are you going to stay at Wilsons?"

"I don't know," Danny said. "There's still somebody
trying to kill me, remember?"

Danny slipped away after a while. He couldn't take
the praise, or Dixie's accusing eyes.

He was walking moodily across the lawn when he
saw two people coming toward him. They were deep in
conversation, and didn't see him until the last moment.
One was the detective McGuinness. He was surprised to
see that the other person was Starling.

"I have some good news for you, Danny." It was
the first time Danny had seen McGuinness smile. "I have
found your assassin."

"You have! Who is it?"

"There were two mysteries to solve. One was the
statue, which fell from a place where no one could push it.
The other was the strange scratches on the door of the
Unknown Spy. It took me a while to work it out."

"Who is it?"

"Not who. What. What could have made the
scratches? What could have got to the statue? You would
have to be able to fly."

"Not one of the Messengers?"

"No. Not them. Other flying creatures inhabit
Wilsons." The penny began to drop for Danny.

"Not the ravens!"

"Exactly. Apparently they thought that you were in
fact a Cherb, and decided to get rid of you. The scratches

331

on the lock were beak marks. And a group of them was strong enough to push the statue down on top of you. Toxique finally synthesized the poison in the biscuit Smyck ate. It was made of foul scrapings from the bottom of ravens' nests."

Danny shuddered.

"So what do I do now? You can't tell a raven that you're not a Cherb."

"I believe Mr. Blackpitt has some influence with them. But I've never seen them take such a dislike before."

Danny looked up. A raven was watching him from the branches of an oak tree.

They don't hate me because they think I'm a Cherb, he thought. They hate me because they *know* that I'm the Fifth.

"There's something we have to talk about as well," Starling said.

"I know," Danny said.

"Have you told anyone?"

"No."

"You can speak in front of Mr. McGuinness."

"Are you sure?"

"Yes, of course." Starling's voice seemed more musical than usual, and the laugh he gave was light and warm. He clutched the detective's arm. "Mr. McGuinness is my husband. So tell me, Danny, how did you work out that I'm a woman? No one else has."

"It was the eyes. I remembered them from your photograph in Ravensdale. You're Cheryl Orr, aren't you? You're supposed to be dead."

"I've been in deep cover for years. I'll have to change now, of course. The Ring have seen me. It was clever of you to remember the photograph."

She had dropped the character of Starling completely—her face and way of moving changed so that it was impossible to think of her as a man. Danny watched McGuinness and Cheryl Orr walk off together, hand in hand.

Vandra looked serious when he told her about the ravens, and he caught her several times peering up into the rafters warily. Les was allowed back to the Roosts after a week. Smyck continued to spread rumors about Danny and the Ring. Vandra told them how Gabriel had knelt to examine Les, had held his broken wings, then told the other Messengers that he was going to fly, and fight, on his own, if necessary. Without a word the Messengers had followed him into battle against the Seraphim.

Danny found himself more and more on his own. He couldn't bear being with Les and seeing his broken wings. Every time he saw Dixie she looked at him reproachfully. Vandra stayed with Jamshid, looking after the wounded. A week went past, and then another. Classes resumed and the weather got colder. The end of term approached, and he knew he had to make a decision about coming back.

One evening, just before dusk, he made his way to the summerhouse. It was cold, but he found some old blankets there. Probably Vicky's, he thought, and wrapped himself in them while he stared moodily at the bare trees.

There was a sound at the door. He looked up to see Les.

"Mind if I come in?" Danny shook his head.

"Here," Les said, opening a tinfoil package. It was full of delicately cut chicken sandwiches. "The Messengers had them for a dance tonight. They won't miss a few. Funny, them old Messengers—any time anybody mentions them attacking the Seraphim, they ignore it or pretend it didn't happen. 'Nonsense, flying is for barbarians,' is what you get. Go on. Take a sandwich."

Danny reached out and took a sandwich. They munched in silence.

Then Les spoke. "I heard you," he said.

"What?"

"When you were with the Ring. I heard what you said."

"You heard me betray you?" Danny stared at Les.

"I was only pretending to be unconscious."

"And you . . . you didn't mind?"

"The way I figure it, you'd just been told your mum and dad were dead. Nobody acts that smart when you hear something like that. I know. You want to blame everybody."

"You're not mad?"

"I wouldn't be much of a mate if I was. Besides, I felt bad about the graveyard."

"The graveyard?"

"It was me and Vandra and Dixie faked it. We were working on making you feel guilty so that you'd stay."

"So the Knife of Implacable Intention . . ."

"It was me threw it at you. The knife was me dad's. You see, you're not the only one at the old treachery around here. We're spies, Danny. Treachery is what we do."

Danny reached into his pocket and took out the knife. "Here," he said, and held it out to Les.

"I want you to keep it," Les told him.

"Are you sure?"

"I've a feeling you're going to need it, mate. Tuck in."

They sat until dark, eating and discussing their time in Westwald. When they got back, Vandra and Dixie were sitting on the balcony in front of the Roosts. Dixie was delighted that they had spoken about the betrayal, and spent fifteen minutes disappearing and reappearing in unexpected places before she calmed down.

Danny lay awake until he was sure that everyone else was asleep; then he got up and put on his clothes quietly. He crossed the lawn under the cold moonlight. The silent bulk of Wilsons loomed in front of him. He slipped in through the side door and crept down the corridor past the ballroom. He was a spy now, he knew that. He could feel it in every bone and sinew as he moved, knowing that a watcher would see only a shadow flitting down the corridor.

He opened the curtain and stepped into Ravensdale. Frost glinted in the street. He looked up. The ravens were lined along the rooftops on either side, as if they had been awaiting him. They watched him, so still that they might have been taken for statues were it not for the glittering eyes that followed him. He walked further in, aware of the cruel beaks that would tear at his flesh if they chose to attack.

He stopped, drew his breath and asked the question that had been posed by the Gallery of Whispers.

"Who am I?"

His voice was loud, reverberating up and down the dark and still street. The echoes faded away. The ravens had not moved.

This is stupid, he thought. Ravens can't talk!

But as he watched, a small group of birds detached themselves from the rest and flew down. There was a whitewashed wall in front of him. They fluttered up against it, finding purchase, it seemed, in tiny cracks and fissures in the wall. First one, then all of the ravens gripped the wall and hung there unmoving. Their bodies and spread wings made a strange shape, a hieroglyph that Danny did not at first recognize, so strange did it appear. It was only when he took two steps backward that he realized what shape the ravens had made.

The number five.

Danny fled. Behind him the rustling of many wings sounded like soft laughter in his ears.

A LEAVE-TAKING

The remaining weeks flew past. Danny worked on improving his poker in maths class, and helped correct some parts of Spitfire's living map with his knowledge of Westwald. The Cherbs had stopped raiding. "Only a lull," Devoy called it. "The Ring will be plotting again." He gave Danny a knowing look when he said this.

One afternoon Danny was waiting outside maths class for Dixie and Les. He leaned on the windowsill overlooking the little square where he had seen Gabriel's secret flight. Once again he saw the Messenger walk out into the square, look around him quickly, then rise into the air. Danny heard voices. He looked up and saw Eluda Fanshawe and some other Messengers approaching. He thought about the look on their faces if they saw Gabriel, and how wounded Gabriel would be if his little secret became known. The warm urge to betray crept through him. He called out.

"Ladies, ladies! Come over here." The women approached him, looking suspicious. Why was he exposing Gabriel's secret? The Messenger had done nothing to him. But still, the urge to betray was there, the power of the Ring of Five reaching out to him even here.

"What is it, boy?" Eluda said, peering at him.

"It's . . . it's . . . nothing," Danny said, moving to block the window. There was sweat on his forehead. He felt sick with himself. Would he always have to struggle?

"Why don't you go back to where you came from?" Eluda said. "Your sort don't belong here."

Christmas was approaching. In the mornings there was frost on the windows. Danny was called to see Devoy one more time.

"Have you decided yet? Will you stay?"

Eluda's words rang in his ears. *You don't belong here.*

"I don't belong here," he said.

"Of course you belong, you're a spy," Devoy argued.

"I don't belong anywhere, but Wilsons gives me the best chance of finding out the truth. I don't belong here, but I must come back."

Devoy looked at Danny with new respect. Someday, he thought, Danny will outgrow us all. But whether that be for good or evil remains to be seen.

"But I want to see my parents. If they are my parents."

338

Danny longed for someone to take the burden of the Fifth from his shoulders, although he knew in his heart that they could not help him.

"There are many mysteries to unravel, Danny. Perhaps Brunholm's finding you was no accident. But we will see. I am glad you are returning. But before you leave I have one more thing for you." Devoy handed Danny something that looked like an old-fashioned transistor radio.

"What is it?"

"A Radio of Last Resort. We can use it to contact you, or vice versa, if the need is great. If you are, as we believe, the real Fifth, then the Ring may yet have plans for you. Brunholm has gone off to research the history of the Fifth to see if he can find out more. In the meantime, keep the radio close to you."

"How do I get back?"

"The same way you came. With Fairman. We do not yet know when he will come."

Devoy went to the window and looked out.

"Snow is on the way—in a few days, perhaps," he said almost to himself. "I like snow. You can move in it without being seen, with proper camouflage. You can hunt, or elude your hunter. You can lay false trails, or allow your tracks to be followed. Snow is a good medium for a spy. And you are a spy, Danny. It is in your blood. I can feel it."

It got colder still over the next days. Without telling anyone, Danny took some spare blankets from the Roosts and left them in the summerhouse for Vicky. That evening he went to Ravensdale as usual to eat, and then to the study hall. He eyed the ravens in the rafters. Their beady little eyes still made him nervous. Halfway through the study period, Blackpitt broke the silence.

"Cadet Caulfield to the front hall, and please don't spare the horses."

Danny left his books on the desk and went out. Valant was waiting for him.

"Fairman's on his way," Valant said urgently; "the snow is coming and he wants to get you out ahead of it. I've packed your case."

"I need to say goodbye. . . ."

"There is no time."

As they got to the hallway Danny heard a car skid to a halt outside the door. There was a loud banging on the door. Valant opened it. Fairman was standing there, his cap pulled down over his deep-set eyes, his mustache bristling.

"Time to go," he growled. "Snow's coming."

He stamped back to the car. Danny could see flakes of snow whirling through the night. Valant thrust his case into his hand.

"Have a good journey," he said.

"I can't go just like this!" he cried out. "My friends . . ."

"You must go," Valant said. "Fairman will not wait."

Then, just as Danny turned toward the door, he walked straight into someone.

"Oof! Dixie, where did you come from?"

"Here and there." She smiled. He heard running footsteps. Vandra and Les skidded around the corner.

"We saw your stuff gone," Vandra said, out of breath. Fairman tooted the horn.

"He only does that once," Valant warned. His friends followed him down the steps. Dixie planted a kiss on his cheek. Vandra looked as though she wanted to do likewise, but when she smiled and showed her long incisors, Danny put out his hand. She shook it.

"Take care, mate," Les said warmly. "Watch out for the Ring."

Fairman revved the engine. Valant held the cab door. It was all happening too quickly. Danny looked up. At the window of the third landing, Devoy watched him expressionlessly, then raised a hand in farewell. The snow was falling properly now, but through it he could hear the sound of an old-fashioned waltz drifting from the ballroom. The Messengers were dancing. Valant pushed Danny into the car and slammed the door. The taxi jolted to life. The last thing Danny saw was his friends waving to him, and then they, and the turrets of Wilsons school for spies, disappeared in the whirling snow.

He could see even less on the journey home than he had on the way to Wilsons. The snow gathered thickly on the side windows and on the windscreen, the wipers barely able to clear it. He tried asking Fairman where they were, but no answer came. The cab drove at the same reckless pace. Danny could feel the wheels fighting for grip, and once or twice the cab went into a long slide. But Fairman did not slow down, and there were no checkpoints this time. Hour after hour, the darkness rushed past. What was out there, what road was capable of crossing between two worlds?

It was cold in the cab, and Danny huddled in a corner trying to keep warm. He must have fallen asleep, for he was woken by being thrown forward. Stiff with cold, he picked himself up and looked out the window. The cab stood outside his house, silent and looming in the fresh-fallen snow. A light glowed in the hallway and in one of the upstairs bedrooms.

"You're here," Fairman grunted, getting out. He opened the door, seized Danny's case and threw it out onto the snow. Danny clambered out after it.

"I'll see you soon," he said. Fairman didn't answer. He jumped back into the driver's seat. The engine growled as the cab roared off down the drive. Danny watched the red taillights until they were gone. He stood alone in the snow and silence. Wilsons felt like a dream now. He would open the front door and step back into his old life. There would be his room with all his things in it. There would be dinner in the oven. But the two people he lived with seemed like strangers now, not parents. He thought about his bed in the Roosts. Les would probably be sleeping by now, and Dixie and Vandra. A light would be burning in the library of the third landing as Devoy and Brunholm plotted long into the night.

He sighed and trudged up to the front door, his feet crunching in the snow. He pushed the door. It was open. He stepped into the hallway. A fire burned in the grate, and the polished floor gleamed. He heard footsteps.

The woman who called herself his mother came into the hall, reading something. She looked up in surprise.

"Oh, there you are—I didn't expect you until the morning, with the snow."

She kissed him in the way she kissed her friends and acquaintances, her lips meeting the air over his cheek so that she wouldn't spoil her lipstick.

"How was school?" she asked, with the air of someone asking a polite question but not really caring about the answer.

"Good . . . ," he said. His face was red. The questions he longed to ask would not come out.

"Oh yes, we read all about it in your letters."

"Letters?"

"Yes. This one arrived yesterday. I only just got around to opening it." She showed him the letter in her hand. He skimmed it. Apparently while at school he had been on the basketball team, and had joined the photography and chess clubs. The handwriting was identical to his own. Brunholm, he thought. He must have forged the letters!

"I forgot to tell you about the cards," he said. Their conversation sounded like one between two strangers who had met each other on a railway platform.

"Cards?"

"Yes, I've got good at Texas hold 'em. Poker.'

"Really? How very interesting. Where did you get that dreadful old coat?"

"I kind of like it. Where's Dad?"

"Your father is away on another of his trips, and I'm afraid I have to go out now."

343

Danny abruptly noticed that his mother was wearing high heels and a long dress. Nothing had changed, then, since he had been away.

"There's supper in the kitchen. I am so glad you are enjoying school. I hope you're eating properly and that the big boys don't bully you or anything like that."

His mother prattled away, filling the air with talk, as if, Danny thought, she was afraid of the silence. She gathered up her coat and handbag and car keys and gave him another air kiss as she made her way toward the door.

"Mum?" he asked. She stopped in the doorway, silhouetted in the porch light. She looked very beautiful with her dress and golden hair, like someone from a film.

"Mum . . . ," he said hesitantly, "who am I?"

"You . . . why . . . you're Danny, of course."

"And what happened to my eyes?"

"You know it was caused by an operation when you were young. Don't ask silly questions, dear. Don't wait up for me."

She blew him a kiss and shut the door. He sat down on the stairs. He might have been mistaken, but when he had asked her who he was, a strange expression had flitted across her face. He heard her car start and pull off. Where was she going in the middle of the night? He sighed. Her perfume hung in the air. Danny frowned. He remembered smelling perfume in the Hall of Shadows, when he had taken his vow.

He ate his supper in the kitchen, then carried his suitcase upstairs to his room. He opened it and took out the Radio of Last Resort. He fiddled with the dials, but it remained silent. He put it on a shelf over the bed. All the struggles and triumphs of Wilsons seemed so far away. The Radio of Last Resort was only a battered old transistor. He had played his part, but now Wilsons had no need of him. He would probably never see Fairman's cab again.

He threw his coat over the back of a chair. Something fell from the collar. He bent to pick it up. It was a feather—and not just any feather, but a golden-tipped one. It must belong to Les. The young Messenger must have sneaked it under the collar when he was leaving! He ran his finger along it. No, he thought, his friends would not forget him. He put it under his pillow and climbed into bed. His mind raced. Every time he shut his eyes images of Cherbs and Messengers and stern Seraphim chased each other through his mind. Finally, exhausted, he fell asleep. Outside it began to snow again, the flakes falling gently on the trees and on the house, covering and hiding. If he had been awake he would have heard it, but he slept the sleep of the exhausted: close to dawn his door opened. The woman he knew as his mother walked softly to the bed and looked down on him. There was compassion and love on her tired face. She bent over him and kissed him gently on the forehead, then crept from the room again.

Above his head the dial on the Radio of Last Resort lit up for a second. The radio buzzed and crackled, as though a message was about to come through. But then the sound stopped, the light went out and the room was silent once again.

About the Author

EOIN MCNAMEE was born in County Down, Northern Ireland. He is the author of a trilogy for young readers: *The Navigator,* a *New York Times* bestseller; *City of Time;* and *The Frost Child.* He is critically acclaimed as a writer of novels for adults, the best known being *Resurrection Man,* which was made into a film. He was awarded the Macaulay Fellowship for Irish Literature, and has also written two adult thrillers under the name John Creed.